BLACK BEAUTY

broadview editions
series editor: Martin R. Boyne

BLACK BEAUTY:
HIS GROOMS AND COMPANIONS.
THE AUTOBIOGRAPHY OF A HORSE

Anna Sewell

edited by Kristen Guest

broadview editions

BROADVIEW PRESS – www.broadviewpress.com
Peterborough, Ontario, Canada

Founded in 1985, Broadview Press remains a wholly independent publishing house. Broadview's focus is on academic publishing; our titles are accessible to university and college students as well as scholars and general readers. With over 600 titles in print, Broadview has become a leading international publisher in the humanities, with world-wide distribution. Broadview is committed to environmentally responsible publishing and fair business practices.

Library and Archives Canada Cataloguing in Publication

Sewell, Anna, 1820-1878, author
    Black Beauty : his grooms and companions : the autobiography of a horse /
Anna Sewell ; edited by Kristen Guest.

(Broadview editions)
Includes bibliographical references.
ISBN 978-1-55481-288-2 (paperback)

    I. Guest, Kristen, 1967-, editor II. Title. III. Series: Broadview editions

PR5349.S48B53 2015   823'.8   C2015-906115-6

Broadview Editions
The Broadview Editions series is an effort to represent the ever-evolving canon of texts in the disciplines of literary studies, history, philosophy, and political theory. A distinguishing feature of the series is the inclusion of primary source documents contemporaneous with the work.

Advisory editor for this volume: Denis Johnston

Broadview Press handles its own distribution in North America
PO Box 1243, Peterborough, Ontario K9J 7H5, Canada
555 Riverwalk Parkway, Tonawanda, NY 14150, USA
Tel: (705) 743-8990; Fax: (705) 743-8353
email: customerservice@broadviewpress.com

Distribution is handled by Eurospan Group in the UK, Europe, Central Asia, Middle East, Africa, India, Southeast Asia, Central America, South America, and the Caribbean. Distribution is handled by Footprint Books in Australia and New Zealand.

Broadview Press acknowledges the financial support of the Government of Canada through the Canada Book Fund for our publishing activities.

Typesetting by Aldo Fierro
Cover design by Lisa Brawn

PRINTED IN CANADA

Contents

List of Illustrations • 7
Acknowledgements • 9
Introduction • 11
Anna Sewell: A Brief Chronology • 27
A Note on the Text • 29
Glossary of Carriages • 31

Black Beauty: His Grooms and Companions. The Autobiography of a Horse • 33

Appendix A: Biographical Context and Early Reception • 195
1. From Mary Bayly, *The Life and Letters of Mrs. Sewell* (1890) • 195
2. From George T. Angell, "Introductory Chapter" to the American Humane Education Society Edition of *Black Beauty* (1890) • 198
3. Review of *Black Beauty*, *The Nonconformist* (9 January 1878) • 199

Appendix B: Victorian Science: Questions of Animal Emotion • 201
1. From Charles Darwin, *The Expression of the Emotions in Man and Animals* (1872) • 201
2. From Thomas Huxley, "On the Hypothesis that Animals Are Automata, and Its History" (1874) • 204
3. From George Romanes, *Animal Intelligence* (1882) • 206
4. From George Romanes, *Mental Evolution in Animals* (1884) • 207

Appendix C: Victorian Industry: Horse and Machine • 211
1. From Fanny Kemble, *Record of a Girlhood* (1878) • 211
2. From Philip Hamerton, *Chapters on Animals* (1874) • 212
3. From W.J. Gordon, *The Horse World of London* (1893) • 213

Appendix D: Animal Cruelty and Animal Rights • 217

1. From Frances Power Cobbe, "The Rights of Man and the
   Claims of Brutes" (1865) • 217
2. From John Duke Coleridge, *The Lord Chief Justice of England*
   [*Baron Coleridge*] *on Vivisection* (1881) • 220
3. From Henry Salt, *Animal Rights Considered in Relation to Social
   Progress* (1892) • 222

Appendix E: Bits, Bearing Reins, and Equine Management • 227

1. From Henry Curling, *A Lashing for the Lashers: Being an
   Exposition of the Cruelties Practised upon the Cab and Omnibus
   Horses of London* (1851) • 227
2. From Sir Arthur Helps, *Some Talk about Animals and Their
   Masters* (1873) • 229
3. From Samuel Sidney, *The Book of the Horse* (1873) • 231
4. From Edward Fordham Flower, *Bits and Bearing Reins*
   (1875) • 233
5. From Samuel Smiles, *Duty* (1880) • 238

Works Cited and Select Bibliography • 241

List of Illustrations

1. Photo of a hansom cab, from *Street Life in London* (1876–77) • 32
2. Title page to original edition (1877) • 33
3. Frontispiece to original edition (1877) • 34
4. "Comfort," from Edward Fordham Flower, *Bits and Bearing Reins* (1875) • 234
5. "Discomfort," from Edward Fordham Flower, *Bits and Bearing Reins* (1875) • 235
6. "Torture," from Edward Fordham Flower, *Bits and Bearing Reins* (1875) • 236

Acknowledgements

I'd like to thank Don LePan, who first suggested I undertake this project and without whose support it would not be available in its current form, and Marjorie Mather, who helped steer it through the initial phases of development for Broadview Press. I would also like to thank the anonymous readers for Broadview whose suggestions enhanced the final product significantly, as did the editorial acumen of Martin Boyne and Denis Johnston. An earlier version of this project was published by Cambridge Scholars Press, and I am grateful for their permission to use much of that material here. Parts of the introduction first appeared as "*Black Beauty*, Masculinity, and the Market for Horse-Flesh" in the *Victorians Institute Journal* 38 (2010), and I thank *VIJ* for permission to reprint. My students at the University of Northern British Columbia contributed significantly to my thinking about *Black Beauty*, as did attendees of the 2009 "Victorian Markets and Marketing" conference in Vancouver who responded so generously to my earliest work on the novel.

I am lucky to be a horse owner when I am not busy being a scholar, and for encouraging both aspects of my life I thank my husband Dale. The wisdom and insight of Thomas and Shana Ritter have enriched both my interactions with my horses and my intellectual life. Their approach to training and their respect for horses truly model Sewell's ideal of kindness. Finally, the lived experience and histories of my own horses have been perhaps the greatest influence of all on my understanding of this novel. My efforts here are dedicated both to them and to horses everywhere who deserve lives shaped by human kindness.

Introduction

Continuously in print and translated into multiple languages since it was first published in 1877, Anna Sewell's *Black Beauty* is now considered a classic children's novel. Despite this association, however, *Black Beauty* was originally produced for a very specific adult readership. Writing to "induce kindness, sympathy and an understanding treatment of horses" among their routine handlers (Bayly 272), Sewell also offered a forceful critique of both the contemporary fashion for using bearing reins and harsh bits on harness horses and the ill-treatment of cab and dray horses. These aspects of the book were central for its earliest advocates, including Edward Fordham Flower (1805–83), a brewer and anti-cruelty activist well known in Victorian England for his opposition to the bearing rein, and George Angell (1823–1909), an American who acquired and distributed copies of *Black Beauty* as part of his work for the Massachusetts Society for the Prevention of Cruelty to Animals.[1] Though she died shortly after it was published, Sewell's book contributed significantly to late-nineteenth-century campaigns against the bearing rein and remains a seminal anti-cruelty text today. Coral Lansbury has suggested that Sewell's novel "is part of the social consciousness of the age" (76), while Lucy Bending connects it more broadly with anti-vivisection rhetoric (116).

The Life of Anna Sewell

Anna Sewell's life began 30 March 1820 in Great Yarmouth, England.[2] Her parents, Isaac and Mary, were Quakers whose lives registered the profound changes being wrought on traditional agrarian modes of life throughout the nineteenth century. Mary's early experience in a farming family was idyllic in many respects. Though never wealthy, the family maintained both a generational connection to local labourers and tightly-knit communal values that engendered a sense of stability and connection to the past.

---

1 See Gavin 193–94, 188–91.
2 The biographical information included here is indebted to biographies of Sewell by Gavin and Chitty.

For Mary's family, as for many others, this way of life was disrupted by rapid advances in technology and industrialism in the early years of the century. In 1809, when Mary was twelve, the country experienced an agricultural depression and her father gave up farming to enter the shipping business. When this endeavour foundered in 1817, Mary and her sisters found work as teachers and governesses to help contribute to the household. In 1819 she married businessman Isaac Sewell, a fellow Quaker. In 1820 Anna was born and the couple relocated to London where he established a draper's shop.[1] Two years later, following the birth of Anna's brother, Philip, Isaac Sewell's business failed and the family again relocated, establishing a pattern of economic instability and geographic displacement that continued through much of Anna's life. A sense of grounding came not through a sustained connection to place, therefore, but rather as a result of the values and emotional support provided by her mother. Like many middle-class Victorian women, Mary Sewell placed great emphasis on spiritual and moral matters. At home, Anna and Philip were raised to embrace an ethos of self-discipline and to eschew worldly pleasures. In the community, Mary was a tireless philanthropist who embraced such causes as temperance and education for the working classes, both themes that ultimately became central to Anna's novel, *Black Beauty*.

Unable to afford significant formal education for her daughter, Mary undertook some of this labour herself based on the system expounded by Richard and Maria Edgeworth in *Practical Education* (1798). Mary also began to write: her earliest book was *Walks with Mama*, a reader composed of one-syllable words, published anonymously in 1824. Later in life she became a successful author, producing a number of educational works in prose and verse that found audiences among children and the working classes. Though she and Anna left the Quaker faith in 1835 and were subsequently baptized into the Church of England, Mary's emphasis on spiritual values of hard work, moral character, and self-discipline influenced Anna's world view. In *Black Beauty* we thus find a character who perseveres, much like a Christian hero, despite significant trials. Anna's sympathy for animals was also shaped by her mother, whose interest in natural science was coloured by her belief in the divinity of all living

---

1 Gavin 13; a draper was a dealer in textiles and clothing accessories.

things. From an early age the Sewell children were taught to be kind to animals, and in later life when Anna witnessed animal cruelty it "roused her indignation almost to fury."[1] The process of writing *Black Beauty* unfolded over a significant period of time near the end of Sewell's life. An invalid spinster, Anna lived with her parents until her death at age 58. At 14, she suffered an injury to her ankle that limited her ability to move and throughout her life she experienced recurrent bouts of illness. Sewell's biographers suggest that her physical limitations contributed to her interest in horses, since riding and driving provided a sense of freedom and mobility.[2] Before being confined permanently to her home in 1871, Anna assisted her mother in establishing a Working Man's Club, as well as in temperance work and other charitable endeavours. Following her retirement from this aspect of public life, Anna began writing *Black Beauty*, her only novel. Prompted by strong feelings about the plight of animals, the work was informed, as early biographer and family friend Mary Bayly suggests, by Anna's conviction that "it was worth a great effort to *try*, at least, to bring the thoughts of men more in harmony with the purposes of God on this subject" (270). In November 1871 Anna recorded in her diary, "I am writing the life of a horse and getting dolls and boxes ready for Christmas" (Chitty 109). Work proceeded slowly, however. Anna was impeded by ill-health and at various points it seems that she dictated work to Mary, "writing or reading being equally impossible to her" (Chitty 164). In the winter of 1877, Sewell's health improved somewhat and she was finally able to complete her novel. It was sent to Mary's publisher, Jarrold and Sons, and was published in November 1877. Sewell died shortly thereafter, in April 1878, without living to see much of its exceptional success. In England, the book went through more than 35 printings in a decade, while in America, where it was marketed as "The *Uncle Tom's Cabin* of the Horse," more than one million copies were circulated by 1891. The novel was distributed widely to drivers and cabmen, as well as to schools, where *Black Beauty* began its career as a children's book.

---

1 Margaret Sewell (1852–1937), Anna's niece, quoted in Lopa Prusty, "Anna Sewell," *Dictionary of Literary Biography*, vol. 163 *British Children's Writers, 1800–1880* (Detroit: Gale, 1996), 260.
2 Chitty 109 and Gavin chapter 8.

Horses in Victorian England

As a didactic text, *Black Beauty* speaks directly to the working-class men who were primarily responsible for the care of horses during the Victorian era: the grooms, stablemen, ostlers, cabbies, deliverymen, and coachmen, as well as to boys whose working lives would ultimately involve horses. With this group in mind, Sewell highlights practical issues of animal care as well as broader questions about working-class morality and character. In many respects a primer of sound equine management, *Black Beauty* makes a case for proper stable arrangements, outlines humane practices for breaking colts to ride and drive, and documents good and bad methods of handling and caring for horses. Sewell's interest in animal welfare was prompted in large part by the widespread presence of horses in Victorian urban and rural society. Indeed, as Hannah Velten points out, far from being displaced by expanding technology and industrialization in the nineteenth century, horses became crucial links in the system that was required to transport the growing numbers of people and goods circulating in urban centres (54–55). At the same time, as *Black Beauty* makes clear, horses were also status symbols for the wealthy, who placed increased emphasis on the display of fine, highly bred horses throughout this era (Velten 49).

Black Beauty's experience takes in the full range of occupations for horses in late-Victorian England. Beginning life on a rural farm, as most nineteenth-century horses did, he is subsequently employed among the higher classes of society as a hack and carriage horse. Later, he descends through the social scale, becoming a hired job horse, a cab horse, and a delivery horse. In each case, Sewell documents realistically the working conditions and stresses characteristic of the work Black Beauty performs. As a carriage horse for an Earl, he is well fed but subject to the injurious fashion for a tight bearing rein used to raise and hold the head artificially high. Later, as an urban job-horse hired out by the hour, he is subject to poor stabling and bad drivers; then, as a cab horse, he first observes and then experiences first-hand the underfeeding, overwork, and physical stress characteristic of the trade.

Individualizing this experience, Sewell makes visible and tangible the experience of animals who were often treated as if they were machines and whose sheer numbers rendered ill-treatment an everyday sight for busy urbanites. Mechanistic views of horses came to prominence in the nineteenth century, underpinned both by the longstanding influence of Descartes's characterization of animals as automata (see Appendix B) and by new technologies associated with the industrial revolution (see Appendix C). As Clay McShane and Joel Tarr point out, the connection between horses and machines was informed by the emergence of new forms of power measured and quantified in relation to the pulling power of animals (2–3). Studies of the horse conceptualized him as a system of levers that generated force, and calculated his output in relation to the required energy supplied by feed (McShane and Tarr 4), while machines and engines were metaphorically named: "the locomotive was an iron horse, the spinning machine was a mule, the power of steam engines was expressed in horsepower" (Greene 15). Such views were further supported by businesses for whom horses were not regarded as living beings but rather as property intended to generate profit. By the last decades of the nineteenth century, Hannah Velten notes, there were an estimated 11,500 hansom cabs in London, while large-scale omnibus and cartage companies maintained fleets of horses each numbering in the thousands. Large companies often perceived the economic wisdom of maintaining their investments, offering good standards of routine care and implementing fixed hours of work for their horses. Among smaller establishments stretched to compete or larger ones employing horses that had already declined to their lowest value, however, the animals were often underfed and pushed beyond reasonable physical limits (Velten 50, 54). When a starved and overburdened Black Beauty collapses in the street near the end of the book, he plays out a scene that would have been all too familiar to Victorian readers.

If many Victorians regarded horses as machines rather than feeling beings, however, for others their plight fuelled a broader social interest in advocating against cruelty to animals. The earliest protective legislation, Martin's Act, was passed in 1822 to address the problem of cruelty to horses and livestock. Early enforcement of this law fell to the Society for the Prevention of Cruelty to Animals (SPCA), founded in 1824, which came under royal patronage in 1837. By the last third of the century, anti-cruelty activism began to address specific aspects of equine management, including the practice of whipping cab horses excessively, the provision of water troughs throughout the city for working horses, and the arrangement of relief for injured or ill horses via veterinary hospitals (Velten 68–71). Among these, protest against the use of the bearing rein figured prominently in the 1870s, in large part due to the efforts of Edward Fordham Flower, whose *Bits and Bearing Reins* (1875) went through seven printings in less than a decade (see Appendix E4). Such writing emphasized the moral duties of man to the creatures over which he exercised power, reflecting the religious background of many anti-cruelty activists whose tracts originated as sermons. From mid-century onwards, the emphasis of much anti-cruelty writing on personal responsibility and moral restraint also harmonized with views of the Victorian gentleman as a figure attuned to the feelings of others. Flower's writing on the subject is noteworthy insofar as it focuses attention not strictly on the working classes (who were often identified specifically in discussion about the mistreatment of cab, coach, and dray horses), but rather on the wealthy classes whose fashions influenced the behaviour of those further down the social scale. *Black Beauty* not only suggests how the upper-class fashion for the bearing rein was cruel and thoughtless in itself, then; it also demonstrates how the practice was assumed by those who aspired to genteel appearances. For Anna Sewell, the character of a gentleman was determined not by social position or economic status, but rather by compassionate dealings with others and informed by a fixed moral compass.

While concerns about the moral character of men comprised a significant thread in discussions about animal cruelty, this interest was complemented by changing attitudes toward animals that gained increased prominence over the course of the century. Horses, in particular, were understood to possess a notably moral character. As Kathryn Miele suggests, "the nineteenth century abounds with literature that specifically discusses the virtues and vices of horses," which were understood "in terms of making moral choices" (131). One result of this belief, Miele argues, is that discussions about the cruel treatment of horses asked readers to imaginatively place themselves in the horse's position in order to cultivate a sense of empathy on the one hand, and to suggest a shared lexicon of pains and pleasures on the other. Such perceptions of the continuities between humans and horses were heightened by training methods that aspired to shape the behaviour of horses without any visible effort on the part of the handler. The effect, Jennifer Mason notes, "produced animals that seemed to be not just self-regulating but even more malleable than humans to the forces of civilization" (19). The widespread popularization of pet-keeping also changed human attitudes toward animals, Mason points out, since strong affective bonds with animals meant that "it grew increasingly easy for people to believe that the animals they encountered through these practices possessed or had the capacity to develop some of the intellectual, emotional, and moral qualities previously held to be exclusively human" (19).

Animal Biography and Animal Emotion

Changing beliefs about the emotional and moral capabilities of animals in the Victorian era were connected not only to the emergence of cultural and social practices such as pet-keeping, in which domestic animals came to be regarded as family members with distinct, humanized subjectivities (Mangum 17), but also with the increased attention paid to questions about cruelty to animals in scientific contexts. The expanded use of live animal subjects for the purposes of scientific experimentation and demonstration over the course of the century culminated, in the 1870s, in the consolidation of a powerful anti-vivisection movement (see Appendix D). Beginning in the 1860s, the RSPCA focused actively on the issue, and in 1874 it undertook a high-profile prosecution against an experiment demonstrated at a meeting of the British Medical Association (Ritvo 159). In 1875 Frances Power Cobbe (1822–1904)—a long-time anti-vivisection activist—founded the Victoria Street Society (later renamed the National Anti-Vivisection Society), which listed many prominent citizens among its supporters. In the same year, a Royal Commission was struck to investigate the issue, and its conclusion, that the infliction of pain "is justly abhorrent to the moral sense of your Majesty's subjects,"[1] led to the passing in 1876 of the Act to Amend the Law Relating to Cruelty to Animals.

Intense public support for the anti-vivisection movement through the 1870s was inspired not only by the public's horror and disgust at common scientific practices, but also by the revelation that domestic animals were used as subjects. Dogs and cats

---

1 Quoted in Susan Hamilton's Introduction to *Animal Welfare and Anti-Vivisection, 1870–1910: Nineteenth-Century Women's Mission*, ed. Susan Hamilton (New York: Routledge, 2004), xxv.

were frequently employed in experiments, and anti-vivisection literature began to expound the evils of scientific practice both in argumentative prose and in fictionalized animal autobiography that included Frances Power Cobbe's *The Confessions of a Lost Dog* (1867), Ouida's *Puck* (1870),[1] and George Stables's *Sable and White* (1893). Such stories not only personalized animal experience, but they also—as Hilda Kean argues—"helped generate a sense of dogs as creatures with consciousness and almost with a sense of self" (98). Such texts were not original to the late-Victorian era; indeed, as Tess Cosslett points out, this subgenre first emerged in the eighteenth century where it was employed didactically to promote sympathy and kindness among children, and to comment satirically on the foibles of human society (63–64).

By the later years of the nineteenth century, the idea of animals speaking for themselves in autobiographical fiction addressed a problem often noted by anti-cruelty activists: that animals could not protest their treatment themselves. Sir Arthur Helps, for example, took up the question "why doesn't the horse protest" by suggesting the necessity of using "the aid of imagination, to enter, as it were, into its terrors" (58; see Appendix E2). His discussion about human/animal relations thus quotes in its entirety a letter to the editor of a newspaper in which the need for brakes on horse-drawn 'buses is explained from the perspective of a 'bus horse whose dropped aitches identify him as the animal equivalent of a working-class person. This imaginative fluidity is also evident in *Black Beauty*, Cosslett suggests, where the structure and form of the narrative "[allow] the reader to slide in and out of horse-consciousness, blurring the human/animal divide" (69). Such slippages between animal and human perspectives not only emphasized interspecies continuities, but also allowed parallel discourses of social reform to harness shared concerns. Thus, for example, in the absence of laws specific to child protection, reformers invoked laws related to animal welfare under the auspices of the RSPCA, while Salvation Army founder William Booth (1829–1912) actively connected the

---

1 Ouida was the pen name of Maria Louise Ramé (1839–1908); see also p. 223, n. 2.

experiences of working horses to those of working men.[1] In the 1870s, the reforming interest in expounding and imaginatively representing connections between humans and animals found an unlikely source of support in the later work of Charles Darwin (1809–82). Indeed, though Darwin personally supported (with some qualifications) pro-vivisection arguments—even testifying before the 1875 Commission—his *The Expression of the Emotions in Man and Animals* (1872) proposed that primary emotions were shared across diverse species (see Appendix B1). In making his case, which built on early observations recorded during his famous voyage on the *Beagle* in the 1830s, Darwin advanced an understanding of emotion as hereditary adaptation that was both universal (insofar as it posited continuities between common forms of expression across species), and understandable as a shared form of communication. Importantly, Darwin contended not only that emotions such as pleasure, pain, fear, or rage are manifest via a shared lexicon of responses adapted to the physiology of distinct species, but also that non-human animals possess a capacity for memory that is not merely instinctual. Darwin's work on animal emotion was subsequently taken up by George Romanes (1848–94), whose *Animal Intelligence* and *Mental Evolution in Animals* appeared in 1882 and 1883 respectively (see Appendices B3 and B4). Expanding on Darwin's view of animal emotion, Romanes posited not only that animals possess rudimentary emotions and memories, but also that they experience dream-states, are able to formulate mental images and personalized attachments, and possess the capacity to imagine. Although contested at the time and subsequently as anecdotal and excessively anthropomorphic,[2] the strand of late-nineteenth-century scientific research associated with Darwin and Romanes expresses more generalized beliefs about animals as feeling, conscious beings evident in the late-Victorian era.

---

1   On the relationship between animal welfare and child protection, see Monica Flegel, *Conceptualizing Cruelty to Children in Nineteenth-Century England* (Farnham, Surrey: Ashgate, 2009); in *In Darkest England and the Way Out*, William Booth made the connection between cab horses and working men (London: Funk and Wagnall, 1890), 33.

2   See Paul Ekman's Introduction to Charles Darwin, *The Expression of the Emotions in Man and Animals*, ed. Paul Ekman (London: HarperCollins, 1998), xxix.

Black Beauty, Autobiography, and the Politics of Sentiment

Given its publication in the 1870s, a decade in which scientific, legal, and popular engagements with animals as feeling, conscious beings were evident across a range of discursive fields, *Black Beauty* crystallizes questions about animal subjectivity by allowing the title character to speak for himself. Indeed, the novel, subtitled "Autobiography of a Horse," asserts Black Beauty's status as a conscious being who thinks and feels recognizably like a human being. He does so, moreover, in a way that prompts an emotional reaction among readers intended to act as a spur to social reform. It is thus a text that overleaps the specific concerns about animal welfare central to its initial conception to encompass diverse concerns with the effects of economic and technological modernity on human identity. As scholarly criticism of *Black Beauty* suggests, the plight of the central character may be understood variously as an analogue for slavery, as a mirroring of the experiences of servants and the working classes, or as an examination of women's oppression.[1] It is also, not incidentally, a text whose appeal to the emotions interrogates the contradictory views that structured human beliefs about animals in the Victorian era.

What ultimately connects readings that identify the hero's position with such a wide range of diverse—and even conflicting—experiences is Sewell's appeal to a sentimental world view. Though he experiences significant trials over the course of his life, Beauty remains a quintessential sentimental hero, bearing his suffering and maintaining a sense of good will toward his human owners, to whom he is unfalteringly obedient and kind. When he is finally restored to an idyllic rural environment at the end of the novel, Sewell seems to identify Beauty's good fortune as a reward for his good behaviour even as she affirms the potential for kindness in a world that seems hostile to feeling. In doing so, she makes a connection that Philip Davis has identified between the Victorian penchant for sentimentality and the pressures of modernization. "When people moved from the countryside to the towns and hardly knew where they were any more in that harsher and faster world," he suggests, "at least they still knew

---

1 See for example Dorré, Ferguson, Padel, and Stoneley.

the communal heart was in the right place" (23). In *Black Beauty*, Sewell uses the language of sentiment to distinguish the logic of what is "right" from the emphasis of human social hierarchy on economic systems. Beauty's suffering thus places him as a model figure, the "hero of good and noble heart" that Fred Kaplan identifies as central to the sentimental mode (19). If Beauty loses his connection to place when he leaves Birtwick Park and the countryside of his youth, then, his belief in the values associated with that place remain, and this belief is rewarded when he is returned to a lost Eden.

If it seems to offer sentimental reassurance about the enduring power of good feeling and the rewards of good behaviour, however, *Black Beauty* is a complex text that does not ultimately provide easy answers to the ills of modernity. As was the case for Anna herself, Black Beauty experiences the effects of massive social change associated with the advance of technology, industrialization, and an emergent global economy. Though Beauty's life at Birtwick Park affirms the values associated with idealizations of traditional agrarian hierarchy—it is a place where human and animal servants are treated kindly and valued as individuals— this mode of life proves to be fragile and is recursively disrupted by exigencies of ill-health and economic hardship. After Mrs. Gordon becomes ill and the family must go abroad, Beauty is purchased and sold a number of times, with each change of situation tending downward. The narrative shift from a rural to an urban setting that frames this trajectory emphasizes the increasing sense of alienation evident in Victorian social relationships. When he complains about being treated like a steam engine by his Cockney drivers, for instance, Beauty voices the experience of objectification in a labour market, an effect shared by animals and humans across a range of classes. If it draws our attention to the evils of economic individualism, moreover, this progression also suggests the extent to which the discourse of sentiment exists in tension with capitalist ideology in Sewell's text. Early in the novel, Duchess, Black Beauty's mother, offers words of wisdom that suggest the fragility of the individual's position in a world governed by economic considerations. Beauty relates, "She told me the better I behaved, the better I should be treated, and that it was always wisest to do my best to please my master." To this, however, she adds a significant caveat: "I hope you will fall into good hands; but a horse never knows who may buy him, or who may drive him; it is all chance for us, but I still say, do your best whatever it is, and keep up your good name" (p. 47). Though addressed specifically to the plight of the horse as an economic object, Duchess's description also suggests the extent to which human agency was determined and limited by economic chance throughout the Victorian era. Indeed, the prospect of financial ruin—through loss of employment due to shifting economic conditions, losses in the markets, or the collapse of banks—haunted Victorians across the social classes. This early passage thus intimates that despite the novel's subsequent affirmation of feeling as a fixed index of right and wrong, our experience is ultimately structured and determined by fluctuating economic conditions indifferent to considerations of good character.

The concern with chance evident in the novel might be dismissed as a matter of sentimental plotting intended to provoke an affective response. It is chance, after all, that delivers Black Beauty from certain death on the streets of London and leaves him happily situated in the novel's closing pages, just as it is chance that provides a benefactress for Jerry when illness threatens his ability to provide for his family. In context, however, the novel's representation of chance cuts deeper into core aspects of human and animal experience in the Victorian era. Though Beauty's mother advises that he keep up his good name, his cumulative experience suggests that a world governed by concern with economic utility offers no real place for recognition of one's moral fibre. Despite his repeated willingness to protect his masters at great personal cost, then, Beauty remains an economic object to be disposed of when he is no longer of use. Praised for saving the life of Lady Anne, Beauty is nonetheless liquidated from the Earl's stables after a reckless rider breaks his knees and he is permanently blemished. Though the Earl acknowledges feeling bad about ruining horses acquired from a friend "who thought they would have a good home with me," he concludes in favour of fashion: "I could not have knees like those in my stables" (p. 119). This pattern continues throughout the text, and when a starved and beaten Beauty collapses in the streets of London it is not sympathy that saves him from the knacker, but rather his owner's susceptibility to the economic argument that with rest and feed "you may get more than his skin is worth" (pp. 186–87). Even the aptly named Farmer Thoroughgood, who purchases Beauty at the urging of his grandson, does so with an eye to resale. When Beauty closes his story by assuring us that his newest owners "have promised that I shall never be sold, and so I have nothing to fear" (p. 193), sentiment makes us hope for his continued happiness, but experience reminds us of the fragility of such promises.

For Beauty, then, the tension between feeling and economic exigency cannot ultimately be resolved in the novel's sentimental ending. This conflict becomes even more central in the novel's other subplots, particularly when Sewell shifts her attention from studies of good character to questions about the role of environment in shaping "bad." The most noteworthy counterpoint to Black Beauty in the novel is Ginger, his stablemate and friend at Birtwick Park. Though Ginger's bad temper initially contrasts with Beauty's positive attitude toward others, her suspicion of humans seems justified when we learn how she has been treated by men. Unlike Beauty, who receives an exemplary education from Farmer Gray and thus has no cause to fear people, Ginger is tortured during her early training. As a result, she has little tolerance for ill-treatment and expresses decidedly political views about the subjection of animals to the whims of man—though her manner improves significantly when she is treated consistently and considerately. If Beauty's experience seems to validate sentimental ideas about the value of stoic suffering and the power of good character, then, Ginger complicates and unsettles this emphasis on individual agency by introducing questions about how character may be shaped by chance. Over the course of the novel, moreover, it becomes evident that possession of a good or bad attitude does not ultimately shape a horse's destiny. Though their training and manner are different, both Beauty and Ginger descend to the lowest ranks of the equine order, and both experience a level of suffering that lead them to wish for death. Though Beauty is ultimately saved, it is important to remember that this, too, is a matter of chance, while Ginger's death offers a more realistic account of the fate experienced by most working horses in the Victorian era.

Ginger's role in highlighting the negative effects of a system governed by economic concerns is further extended in the story of Seedy Sam. Just as Ginger and Beauty offer a counterpoint between good behaviour and bad, Sam and Jerry seem to be opposites. Jerry is a model cabman and one of the text's most notable "true gentlemen." Always kind to his horses and solicitous of their comfort, he refuses to work on Sunday, treats others the way he would be treated, and extols the values of temperance. By contrast, Seedy Sam is berated by the other cabmen for his shabby appearance and poor treatment of his horse. Rather than take up the matter as a question of individual failing, however, Sam responds by pointing out how a capitalist system practically excludes opportunities for kindness. Unlike Jerry, who owns his cab and horses, Sam must pay for the use of horse and cab at high rates; as a result, he points out, "if the horses don't work we must starve, and I and my children have known what that is before now." He continues, "'tis a mockery to tell a man he must not overwork his horse, for when a beast is downright tired, there's nothing but the whip that will keep his legs agoing—you can't help yourself—you must put your wife and children before the horse" (pp. 158–59). Sam's story frames a brief, if powerful, social critique that directs our attention to the limits of the text's moral vision as a panacea for the ills of modernity. As the chief cabman concedes, "You've beaten me Sam, for it's all true." His subsequent suggestion, "you might tell the poor beast that you were sorry to take it out of him that way" (p. 160), rings hollow in context insofar as it suggests the limited power of words to challenge or change overarching economic structures. Tellingly, Ginger and Seedy Sam die within pages of each other, and both characters offer a glimpse of the complex roles that economic and social environments play in determining one's circumstance.

For Sewell, who was not only emphatically religious but also passionately opposed to the effects of economic individualism, the maxim that everyone "take care of number one" (p. 89) is challenged repeatedly in *Black Beauty*. To raise the issue via the discourse of sentiment sets aside the public authority of sciences such as economics or biology, and prompts us—as Nicola Bown suggests—"to feel and act rightly as human beings and moral actors."[1] *Black Beauty* represents the complexities of a world caught between sentiment and economics, in effect challenging the distinction between private feeling and public conduct that these categories imply. If it unsettles the line between public and private spheres that anchored Victorian ideas about identity,

---

1 Nicola Bown, "Introduction: Crying over Little Nell," *19: Interdisciplinary Studies in the Long Nineteenth Century* 4 (2007): 4, www.19. bbk.ac.uk/article/view/ntn.453.

however, it also affirms the human capacity to act in a principled way toward others. Indeed, though individual agency is often overwritten by the social structures in which the characters are embedded, Sewell's text ultimately insists that our choices matter.

Though horses are no longer central to the economic function of contemporary society, such knowledge of choice continues to resonate as we contemplate the mistreatment of animals used for recreation, such as race and show horses, of animals used in scientific research, and of animals produced as part of industrialized agri-business. Indeed, our current cultural responses to issues of animal cruelty often veer between the sentimental and economic perspectives articulated in *Black Beauty*. Like the Victorians, we have a tendency either to focus on the sentimentalized, exceptional individual or to treat all members of a class as an economic aggregate—with the end result that overarching structures that support cruelty remain entrenched. As a novel with a specific purpose, *Black Beauty* had a tangible impact on abuses of the bearing rein. Yet one could also argue that Sewell's conservative commitments to an existing hierarchy are at odds with her text's more radical implications for systemic change. If we set aside binary assessments of the novel as either politically radical or conservative, however, we open ourselves to its real richness as a work that raises but does not resolve tensions between utility and feeling, self and other, the powerful and the powerless.

Anna Sewell: A Brief Chronology

1793 Isaac Sewell, Anna's father, born.

1797 Mary Sewell (nee Wright), Anna's mother, born.

1820 Anna born 30 March in Great Yarmouth, Norfolk; the Sewell family moves to London.

1822 Brother, Philip Sewell, born. Isaac's business fails, and the family moves to Dalston, outside London. Isaac begins work as a "commercial traveller," or travelling salesman.

1824 Mary Sewell writes her first book, *Walks with Mama*.

1835 Anna injures her ankle and becomes a semi-invalid.

1836 Family moves to Brighton so that Isaac Sewell can take a position as a bank manager. Anna and Mary leave the Society of Friends to join the Church of England.

1845 Family moves to Lancing, outside Brighton. Anna's health deteriorates.

1846 Anna journeys to Europe for treatment.

1858 Mary Sewell begins publishing her most popular works, including *Mother's Last Words* and *Homely Ballads*; the family moves to Blue Lodge, Wick, South Gloucestershire.

1867 Anna and her parents move to Old Catton, Norfolk, to support Philip, recently widowed with seven children.

1871 Anna confined for health reasons; begins work on *Black Beauty*.

1877 *Black Beauty* published by Jarrold and Sons of London.

1878 Anna Sewell dies, 25 April, Old Catton, Norfolk.

1890 *Black Beauty* published by the American Humane Education Society.

A Note on the Text

Anna Sewell sold copyright of her novel outright to Jarrold and Sons of London. The first edition was published as a complete novel by this publisher in 1877, with an American edition under the imprint of F.M. Lupton Publishing appearing the same year. Modern editions of *Black Beauty* have frequently used the 1915 Dent edition as copy text. The Dent version truncates the title, modernizes Victorian conventions related to punctuation, paragraphing, and dialogue, and eliminates front and end matter that identifies Sewell as the story's "translator" (including a short note at the end of the text directing the reader to further resources). In the interest of restoring these historical details, this Broadview Edition has adopted the original 1877 Jarrold and Sons edition as copy text. Typesetting errors have been silently corrected throughout.

Glossary of Carriages

break	a heavy four-wheeled carriage used to train and exercise horses, often in pairs.
brougham	a fashionable four-wheeled carriage with an enclosed sitting area for passengers and an open box seat for the driver; pulled by a single horse or a pair.
bus, 'bus	see omnibus.
cab	short for cabriolet: a light two-wheeled carriage drawn by one horse. It had seating room for a driver and passenger, with standing room behind for a groom. See also hansom.
cart	a two-wheeled farm or utility vehicle pulled by one horse.
chair, Park chair	a small, very light cart.
chaise	a light two- or four-wheeled carriage usually drawn by one horse.
dog-cart	a light informal two-wheeled carriage drawn by one horse.
dray	a low two- or four-wheeled wagon with no sides used to carry heavy loads.
fly	often a coach or wagon available for hire; also a term applied to light vehicles such as hansom cabs.
four-in-hand	a carriage pulled by four horses in which the reins are arranged so they can be handled by one driver.
gig	a light, fast, two-wheeled cart pulled by one horse.
hansom (cab)	a highly manoeuvrable two-wheeled vehicle designed by the English architect Joseph Hansom and patented in 1834. Combining speed with safety, with a low centre of gravity for safe cornering, it quickly supplanted the hackney coach as a common vehicle for hire, and soon became synonymous with that function. The driver sat above and behind the coach, which could be enclosed for the comfort of passengers (see Figure 1).
hearse	a heavy cart used for hauling large loads.
omnibus	a multi-passenger public conveyance, drawn by two or four horses; from the Latin word meaning "for all."

phaeton	an open, formal four-wheeled carriage.
spring cart	a light, two-wheeled vehicle drawn by one horse; intended for passengers, it had springs to make the ride more comfortable.
tandem	a carriage drawn by two horses, harnessed one in front of the other.
trap	a two- or four-wheeled carriage accommodating two to four people.

Fig. 1: Photo of a hansom cab, from *Street Life in London* (1876–77) by John Thomson and Adolphe Smith. Wikimedia Commons.

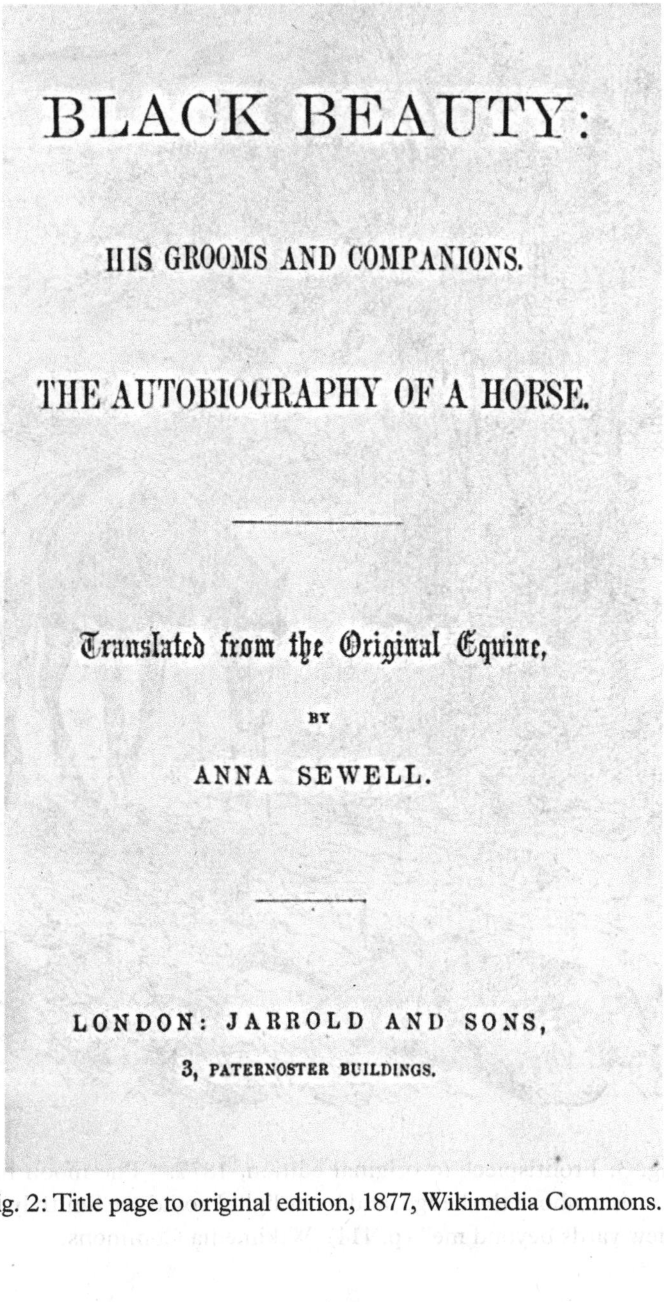

BLACK BEAUTY:

HIS GROOMS AND COMPANIONS.

THE AUTOBIOGRAPHY OF A HORSE.

Translated from the Original Equine,

BY

ANNA SEWELL.

LONDON: JARROLD AND SONS,

3, PATERNOSTER BUILDINGS.

Fig. 2: Title page to original edition, 1877, Wikimedia Commons.

Fig. 3: Frontispiece to original edition, 1877: "The moon had just risen above the hedge, and by its light I could see Smith lying a few yards beyond me" (p. 114). Wikimedia Commons.

TO
MY DEAR AND HONOURED
MOTHER,
WHOSE LIFE, NO LESS THAN HER PEN,
HAS BEEN DEVOTED TO THE
WELFARE OF OTHERS,
THIS LITTLE BOOK
IS AFFECTIONATELY
DEDICATED.

"He was a perfect horseman, and never lost his temper with his horse, talking to and reasoning with it if it shyed or bolted, as if it had been a rational being, knowing that from the fine organisation of the animal, a horse, like a child, will get confused by panic fear, which is only increased by punishment." From the *Life of Charles Kingsley*, Vol. II., page 9.

CONTENTS

PART 1.

1. MY EARLY HOME • 39
2. THE HUNT • 41
3. MY BREAKING IN • 44
4. BIRTWICK PARK • 48
5. A FAIR START • 51
6. LIBERTY • 54
7. GINGER • 56
8. GINGER'S STORY CONTINUED • 60
9. MERRYLEGS • 63
10. A TALK IN THE ORCHARD • 65
11. PLAIN SPEAKING • 70
12. A STORMY DAY • 73
13. THE DEVIL'S TRADE MARK • 76
14. JAMES HOWARD • 79
15. THE OLD OSTLER • 82
16. THE FIRE! • 85
17. JOHN MANLY'S TALK • 88
18. GOING FOR THE DOCTOR • 91
19. ONLY IGNORANCE • 94
20. JOE GREEN • 96
21. THE PARTING • 98

PART II.

22. EARLSHALL • 101
23. A STRIKE FOR LIBERTY • 104
24. THE LADY ANNE, OR A RUNAWAY HORSE • 107
25. REUBEN SMITH • 112
26. HOW IT ENDED • 115
27. RUINED, AND GOING DOWN-HILL • 118
28. A JOB HORSE, AND HIS DRIVERS • 120
29. COCKNEYS • 123
30. A THIEF! • 128
31. A HUMBUG! • 130

PART III.

32. THE HORSE FAIR • 133
33. A LONDON CAB HORSE • 136
34. AN OLD WAR HORSE • 139
35. JERRY BARKER • 143
36. THE SUNDAY CAB • 148
37. THE GOLDEN RULE • 152
38. DOLLY AND A REAL GENTLEMAN • 155
39. SEEDY SAM • 158
40. POOR GINGER • 161
41. THE BUTCHER • 163
42. THE ELECTION • 166
43. A FRIEND IN NEED • 168
44. OLD CAPTAIN AND HIS SUCCESSOR • 172
45. JERRY'S NEW YEAR • 176

PART IV.

46. JAKES AND THE LADY • 181
47. HARD TIMES • 184
48. FARMER THOROUGHGOOD AND HIS
    GRANDSON WILLIE • 188
49. MY LAST HOME • 191

PART I.

CHAPTER ONE
My Early Home

The first place that I can well remember, was a large pleasant meadow with a pond of clear water in it. Some shady trees leaned over it, and rushes and water-lilies grew at the deep end. Over the hedge on one side we looked into a ploughed field, and on the other we looked over a gate at our master's house, which stood by the roadside; at the top of the meadow was a plantation of fir trees, and at the bottom a running brook overhung by a steep bank.

Whilst I was young I lived upon my mother's milk, as I could not eat grass. In the day time I ran by her side, and at night I lay down close by her. When it was hot, we used to stand by the pond in the shade of the trees, and when it was cold, we had a nice warm shed near the plantation.

As soon as I was old enough to eat grass, my mother used to go out to work in the day time, and came back in the evening.

There were six young colts in the meadow beside me, they were all older than I was; some were nearly as large as grown-up horses. I used to run with them, and had great fun; we used to gallop all together round and round the field, as hard as we could go. Sometimes we had rather rough play, for they would frequently bite and kick as well as gallop.

One day, when there was a good deal of kicking, my mother whinnied to me to come to her, and then she said,

"I wish you to pay attention to what I am going to say to you. The colts who live here are very good colts; but they are cart-horse colts, and of course, they have not learned manners. You have been well bred and well born; your father has a great name in these parts, and your grandfather won the cup two years at the Newmarket races;[1] your grandmother had the sweetest temper of any horse I ever knew, and I think you have never seen me kick or bite. I hope you will grow up gentle and good, and never learn bad ways; do your work with a good

---

1 Established as the centre for British horse racing in 1605, Newmarket became host track for many prestigious races. It remains home to the Jockey Club.

will, lift your feet up well when you trot, and never bite or kick even in play."

I have never forgotten my mother's advice; I knew she was a wise old horse, and our master thought a great deal of her. Her name was Duchess, but he often called her Pet.

Our master was a good kind man. He gave us good food, good lodging, and kind words; he spoke as kindly to us as he did to his little children; we were all fond of him, and my mother loved him very much. When she saw him at the gate, she would neigh with joy and trot up to him. He would pat and stroke her and say, "Well, old Pet, and how is your little Darkie?" I was a dull black, so he called me Darkie; then he would give me a piece of bread, which was very good, and sometimes he brought a carrot for my mother. All the horses would come to him, but I think we were his favourites. My mother always took him to the town on a market day in a light gig.

There was a ploughboy, Dick, who sometimes came into our field to pluck blackberries from the hedge. When he had eaten all he wanted, he would have, what he called, fun with the colts, throwing stones and sticks at them to make them gallop. We did not much mind him, for we could gallop off; but sometimes a stone would hit and hurt us.

One day he was at this game, and did not know that the master was in the next field; but he was there, watching what was going on: over the hedge he jumped in a snap, and catching Dick by the arm, he gave him such a box on the ear as made him roar with the pain and surprise. As soon as we saw the master, we trotted up nearer to see what went on.

"Bad boy" he said, "bad boy! to chase the colts. This is not the first time, nor the second, but it shall be the last—there— take your money and go home, I shall not want you on my farm again." So we never saw Dick any more. Old Daniel, the man who looked after the horses, was just as gentle as our master, so we were well off.

CHAPTER TWO
THE HUNT

Before I was two years old, a circumstance happened, which I have never forgotten. It was early in the spring; there had been a little frost in the night and a light mist still hung over the plantations and meadows. I, and the other colts were feeding at the lower part of the field, when we heard, quite in the distance, what sounded like the cry of dogs. The oldest of the colts raised his head, pricked his ears, and said "There are the hounds!" and immediately cantered off, followed by the rest of us to the upper part of the field, where we could look over the hedge and see several fields beyond. My mother, and an old riding horse of our master's were also standing near, and seemed to know all about it.

"They have found a hare," said my mother, "and if they come this way, we shall see the hunt."

And soon the dogs were all tearing down the field of young wheat next to ours. I never heard such a noise as they made. They did not bark, nor howl, nor whine, but kept on a "yo! yo, o, o! yo! yo, o, o! yo! yo, o, o," at the top of their voices. After them came a number of men on horse-back, some of them in scarlet coats, all galloping as fast as they could. The old horse snorted and looked eagerly after them, and we young colts wanted to be galloping with them, but they were soon away into the fields lower down; here, it seemed as if they had come to a stand; the dogs left off barking, and ran about every way with their noses to the ground.

"They have lost the scent," said the old horse, "perhaps the hare will get off."

"What hare?" I said.

"Oh! I don't know what hare; likely enough it may be one of our own hares out of the plantation; any hare they can find will do for the dogs and men to run after;" and before long the dogs began their "yo! yo, o, o!" again, and back they came altogether at full speed, making straight for our meadow at the part where the high bank and hedge overhang the brook.

"Now we shall see the hare," said my mother; and just then a hare wild with fright rushed by, and made for the plantation. On came the dogs, they burst over the bank, leapt the stream, and came dashing across the field, followed by the huntsmen. Six or eight men leaped their horses clean over, close upon the dogs. The hare tried to get through the fence; it was too thick, and she turned sharp round to make for the road, but it was too late; the dogs were upon her with their wild cries; we heard one shriek, and that was the end of her. One of the huntsmen rode up and whipped off the dogs, who would soon have torn her to pieces. He held her up by the leg torn and bleeding, and all the gentlemen seemed well pleased.

As for me, I was so astonished that I did not at first see what was going on by the brook; but when I did look, there was a sad sight; two fine horses were down, one was struggling in the stream, and the other was groaning on the grass. One of the riders was getting out of the water covered with mud, the other lay quite still.

"His neck is broke," said my mother.

"And serve him right too," said one of the colts.

I thought the same, but my mother did not join with us.

"Well! no," she said, "you must not say that; but though I am an old horse, and have seen and heard a great deal, I never yet could make out why men are so fond of this sport; they often hurt themselves, often spoil good horses, and tear up the fields, and all for a hare or a fox, or a stag, that they could get more easily some other way; but we are only horses, and don't know."

Whilst my mother was saying this, we stood and looked on. Many of the riders had gone to the young man; but my master, who had been watching what was going on, was the first to raise him. His head fell back and his arms hung down, and everyone looked very serious. There was no noise now; even the dogs were quiet, and seemed to know that something was wrong: They carried him to our master's house. I heard afterwards that it was young George Gordon, the squire's only son, a fine tall young man, and the pride of his family.

There was now riding off in all directions to the doctor's, to the farrier's,[1] and no doubt to Squire Gordon's, to let him know about his son. When Mr. Bond the farrier, came to look at the black horse that lay groaning on the grass, he felt him all over, and shook his head; one of his legs was broken. Then someone ran to our master's house and came back with a gun; presently

---

1 A specialist in hoof care, including trimming and shoeing. In the Victorian era, farriers also undertook some aspects of veterinary care.

there was a loud bang and a dreadful shriek, and then all was still; the black horse moved no more.

My mother seemed much troubled; she said she had known that horse for years, and that his name was "Rob Roy;"[1] he was a good bold horse, and there was no vice in him. She never would go to that part of the field afterwards.

Not many days after, we heard the church bell tolling for a long time; and looking over the gate we saw a long strange black coach that was covered with black cloth and was drawn by black horses; after that came another and another and another, and all were black, while the bell kept tolling, tolling. They were carrying young Gordon to the churchyard to bury him. He would never ride again. What they did with Rob Roy I never knew; but 'twas all for one little hare.

---

1   Rob Roy Macgregor was an early eighteenth-century Scottish outlaw and folk hero, and the protagonist of Sir Walter Scott's 1817 novel *Rob Roy*.

CHAPTER THREE
My Breaking In

I was now beginning to grow handsome; my coat had grown fine and soft, and was bright black. I had one white foot, and a pretty white star on my fore-head: I was thought very handsome; my master would not sell me till I was four years old; he said lads ought not to work like men, and colts ought not to work like horses till they were quite grown up.

When I was four years old, Squire Gordon came to look at me. He examined my eyes, my mouth and my legs; he felt them all down; and then I had to walk and trot and gallop before him; he seemed to like me, and said "when he has been well broken in, he will do very well." My master said he would break me in himself, as he should not like me to be frightened or hurt, and he lost no time about it, for the next day he began.

Everyone may not know what breaking in is, therefore I will describe it. It means to teach a horse to wear a saddle and bridle and to carry on his back a man, woman, or child; to go just the way they wish, and to go quietly. Beside this, he has to learn to wear a collar, a crupper, and a breeching,[1] and to stand still whilst they are put on; then to have a cart or a chaise fixed behind him, so that he cannot walk or trot without dragging it after him: and he must go fast or slow, just as his driver wishes. He must never start at what he sees, nor speak to other horses, nor bite, nor kick, nor have any will of his own; but always do his master's will, even though he may be very tired or hungry; but the worst of all is, when his harness is once on, he may neither jump for joy nor lie down for weariness. So you will see this breaking in is a great thing.

I had of course long been used to a halter and a headstall,[2] and to be led about in the field and lanes quietly, but now I was to

---

1 Parts of harness that secure the horse to a conveyance. The collar goes over the horse's head and enables him to pull the required load, while the crupper and breeching keep the harness from sliding forward.

2 A halter fits over the head of a horse, much a like a bridle but without a bit (see next note); When a rope is attached to it, the horse can be led or tied. In the UK a halter is called a headcollar, which seems to be what is meant here by a headstall.

have a bit and bridle;[1] my master gave me some oats as usual, and after a good deal of coaxing, he got the bit into my mouth, and the bridle fixed, but it was a nasty thing! Those who have never had a bit in their mouths cannot think how bad it feels; a great piece of cold hard steel as thick as a man's finger to be pushed into one's mouth, between one's teeth and over one's tongue, with the ends coming out at the corner of your mouth, and held fast there by straps over your head, under your throat, round your nose, and under your chin; so that no way in the world can you get rid of the nasty hard thing; it is very bad! yes, very bad! at least I thought so; but I knew my mother always wore one when she went out, and all horses did when they were grown up; and so, what with the nice oats, and what with my master's pats, kind words, and gentle ways, I got to wear my bit and bridle.

Next came the saddle, but that was not half so bad; my master put it on my back very gently, whilst old Daniel held my head; he then made the girths[2] fast under my body, patting and talking to me all the time; then I had a few oats, then a little leading about, and this he did every day till I began to look for the oats and the saddle. At length one morning, my master got on my back and rode me round the meadow on the soft grass. It certainly did feel queer; but I must say I felt rather proud to carry my master, and as he continued to ride me a little every day, I soon became accustomed to it.

The next unpleasant business was putting on the iron shoes; that too was very hard at first. My master went with me to the smith's forge, to see that I was not hurt or got any fright. The blacksmith took my feet in his hand one after the other, and cut away some of the hoof. It did not pain me, so I stood still on three legs till he had done them all. Then he took a piece of iron the shape of my foot, and clapped it on, and drove some nails through the shoe quite into my hoof, so that the shoe was firmly on. My feet felt very stiff and heavy, but in time I got used to it.

And now having got so far, my master went on to break me to harness; there were more new things to wear. First, a stiff heavy collar just on my neck, and a bridle with great side-pieces

---

1 A bridle fits over the head of a horse and is used when riding; it usually includes a metal bit that sits in the mouth, to which reins are attached so the rider can steer.

2 Straps that pass under the horse's belly to secure a saddle or harness and prevent it from slipping sideways.

against my eyes called blinkers, and blinkers indeed they were, for I could not see on either side, but only straight in front of me; next there was a small saddle with a nasty stiff strap that went right under my tail; that was the crupper. I hated the crupper: to have my long tail doubled up and poked through that strap was almost as bad as the bit. I never felt more like kicking, but of course I could not kick such a good master, and so in time I got used to everything, and could do my work as well as my mother.

I must not forget to mention one part of my training, which I have always considered a very great advantage. My master sent me for a fortnight to a neighbouring farmer's, who had a meadow which was skirted on one side by the railway. Here were some sheep and cows, and I was turned in amongst them.

I shall never forget the first train that ran by. I was feeding quietly near the pales which separated the meadow from the railway, when I heard a strange sound at a distance, and before I knew whence it came with a rush and a clatter, and a puffing out of smoke a long black train of something flew by, and was gone almost before I could draw my breath. I turned, and galloped to the further side of the meadow as fast as I could go, and there I stood snorting with astonishment and fear. In the course of the day many other trains went by, some more slowly; these drew up at the station close by, and sometimes made an awful shriek and groan before they stopped.

I thought it very dreadful, but the cows went on eating very quietly, and hardly raised their heads as the black frightful thing came puffing and grinding past.

For the first few days I could not feed in peace; but as I found that this terrible creature never came into the field, or did me any harm, I began to disregard it, and very soon I cared as little about the passing of a train, as the cows and sheep did.

Since then I have seen many horses much alarmed and restive at the sight or sound of a steam engine; but thanks to my good master's care, I am as fearless at railway stations as in my own stable.

Now if anyone wants to break in a young horse well, that is the way.

My master often drove me in double harness with my mother, because she was steady, and could teach me how to go better than a strange horse. She told me the better I behaved, the better I should be treated, and that it was wisest always to do my best to please my master; "but," said she, "there are a great many kinds of men; there are good thoughtful men like our master, that any horse may be proud to serve; but there are bad cruel men, who never ought to have a horse or dog to call their own. Beside, there are a great many foolish men, vain, ignorant, and careless, who never trouble themselves to think; these spoil more horses than all, just for want of sense; they don't mean it, but they do it for all that. I hope you will fall into good hands; but a horse never knows who may buy him, or who may drive him; it is all a chance for us, but still I say, do your best wherever it is, and keep up your good name."

CHAPTER FOUR
BIRTWICK PARK

At this time I used to stand in the stable, and my coat was brushed every day till it shone like a rook's wing. It was early in May, when there came a man from Squire Gordon's, who took me away to the Hall. My master said "Good bye, Darkie; be a good horse, and always do your best." I could not say "good bye," so I put my nose into his hand; he patted me kindly, and I left my first home. As I lived some years with Squire Gordon, I may as well tell something about the place.

Squire Gordon's Park skirted the village of Birtwick. It was entered by a large iron gate, at which stood the first Lodge, and then you trotted along on a smooth road between clumps of large old trees; then another Lodge and another gate, which brought you to the house and the gardens. Beyond this lay the home paddock,[1] the old orchard, and the stables. There was accommodation for many horses and carriages; but I need only describe the stable into which I was taken; this was very roomy, with four good stalls; a large swinging window opened into the yard, which made it pleasant and airy.

The first stall was a large square one, shut in behind with a wooden gate; the others were common stalls, good stalls, but not nearly so large; it had a low rack for hay and a low manger for corn;[2] it was called a loose box, because the horse that was put into it was not tied up, but left loose, to do as he liked. It is a great thing to have a loose box.

Into this fine box the groom put me; it was clean, sweet, and airy. I never was in a better box than that, and the sides were not so high, but that I could see all that went on through the iron rails that were at the top.

He gave me some very nice oats, he patted me, spoke kindly, and then went away.

When I had eaten my corn, I looked round. In the stall next to mine, stood a little fat grey pony, with a thick mane and tail, a very pretty head, and a pert little nose.

I put my head up to the iron rails at the top of my box, and said, "How do you do? what is your name?"

---

1 A fenced outdoor enclosure.
2 In the Victorian era, a term for any grain; oats were the most common feed for horses.

He turned round as far as his halter would allow, held his head up and said, "My name is Merrylegs: I am very handsome, I carry the young ladies on my back, and sometimes I take our mistress out in the low chair. They think a great deal of me, and so does James. Are you going to live next door to me in the box?" I said "Yes."

"Well then," he said, "I hope you are good-tempered; I do not like anyone next door who bites."

Just then a horse's head looked over from the stall beyond; the ears were laid back, and the eye looked rather ill-tempered. This was a tall chestnut mare with a long handsome neck; she looked across to me and said,

"So it is you who have turned me out of my box; it is a very strange thing for a colt like you, to come and turn a lady out of her own home."

"I beg your pardon," I said, "I have turned no one out; the man who brought me put me here, and I had nothing to do with it; and as to my being a colt, I am turned four years old, and am a grown-up horse: I never had words yet with horse or mare, and it is my wish to live at peace."

"Well," she said, "we shall see; of course I do not want to have words with a young thing like you." I said no more.

In the afternoon when she went out, Merrylegs told me all about it.

"The thing is this," said Merrylegs, "Ginger has a bad habit of biting and snapping; that is why they call her Ginger, and when she was in the loose box, she used to snap very much. One day she bit James in the arm and made it bleed, and so Miss Flora and Miss Jessie, who are very fond of me, were afraid to come into the stable. They used to bring me nice things to eat, an apple or a carrot, or a piece of bread, but after Ginger stood in that box, they dare not come, and I missed them very much. I hope they will now come again, if you do not bite or snap."

I told him I never bit anything but grass, hay and corn, and could not think what pleasure Ginger found it.

"Well, I don't think she does find pleasure," says Merrylegs, "it is just a bad habit; she says no one was ever kind to her, and why should she not bite? Of course it is a very bad habit; but I am sure, if all she says be true, she must have been very ill-used before she came here. John does all he can to please her, and James does all he can, and our master never uses a whip if a horse acts right; so I think she might be good-tempered here; you see," he said with a wise look, "I am twelve years old; I know a great deal, and I can tell you there is not a better place for a horse all round the country than this. John is the best groom that ever was, he has been here fourteen years; and you never saw such a kind boy as James is, so that it is all Ginger's own fault that she did not stay in that box."

CHAPTER FIVE
A Fair Start

The name of the coachman was John Manly; he had a wife and one little child, and they lived in the coachman's cottage, very near the stables.

The next morning he took me into the yard and gave me a good grooming, and just as I was going into my box with my coat soft and bright, the Squire came in to look at me, and seemed pleased. "John," he said, "I meant to have tried the new horse this morning, but I have other business. You may as well take him a round after breakfast; go by the common and the Highwood, and back by the watermill and the river, that will shew his paces."

"I will, sir," said John. After breakfast he came and fitted me with a bridle. He was very particular in letting out and taking in the straps, to fit my head comfortably; then he brought the saddle, that was not broad enough for my back; he saw it in a minute and went for another, which fitted nicely. He rode me first slowly, then a trot, then a canter, and when we were on the common he gave me a light touch with his whip, and we had a splendid gallop.

"Ho, ho! my boy," he said, as he pulled me up, "you would like to follow the hounds, I think."

As we came back through the Park we met the Squire and Mrs. Gordon walking; they stopped, and John jumped off.

"Well, John, how does he go?"

"First-rate, sir," answered John, "he is as fleet as a deer, and has a fine spirit too; but the lightest touch of the rein will guide him. Down at the end of the common we met one of those travelling carts hung all over with baskets, rugs, and such like; you know, sir, many horses will not pass those carts quietly; he just took a good look at it, and then went on as quiet and pleasant as could be. They were shooting rabbits near the Highwood, and a gun went off close by; he pulled up a little and looked, but did not stir a step to right or left. I just held the rein steady and did not hurry him, and it's my opinion he has not been frightened or ill-used while he was young."

"That's well," said the Squire, "I will try him myself to-morrow."

The next day I was brought up for my master. I remembered my mother's counsel and my good old master's, and I tried to do exactly what he wanted me to do. I found he was a very good rider, and thoughtful for his horse too. When he came home, the lady was at the hall door as he rode up.

"Well, my dear," she said, "how do you like him?"

"He is exactly what John said," he replied, "a pleasanter creature I never wish to mount. What shall we call him?"

"Would you like Ebony?" said she, "he is as black as ebony."

"No, not Ebony."

"Will you call him 'Blackbird,' like your uncle's old horse?"

"No, he is far handsomer than old Blackbird ever was."

"Yes," she said, "he is really quite a beauty, and he has such a sweet good-tempered face and such a fine intelligent eye—what do you say to calling him 'Black Beauty'?"

"Black Beauty, why yes, I think that is a very good name; if you like, it shall be his name," and so it was.

When John went into the stable, he told James that master and mistress had chosen a good sensible English name for me, that meant something, not like Marengo, or Pegasus, or Abdallah.[1] They both laughed, and James said, "If it was not for bringing back the past, I should have named him 'Rob Roy,' for I never saw two horses more alike."

"That's no wonder," said John, "didn't you know that farmer Grey's old Duchess was the mother of them both?"

I had never heard that before, and so poor Rob Roy who was killed at that hunt was my brother! I did not wonder that my mother was so troubled. It seems that horses have no relations; at least, they never know each other after they are sold.

John seemed very proud of me; he used to make my mane and tail almost as smooth as a lady's hair, and he would talk to me a great deal; of course I did not understand all he said, but I learned more and more to know what he meant, and what he wanted me to do. I grew very fond of him, he was so gentle and kind, he seemed to know just how a horse feels, and when he cleaned me, he knew the tender places, and the ticklish places; when he brushed my head, he went as carefully over my eyes as if they were his own, and never stirred up any ill temper.

James Howard, the stable boy, was just as gentle and pleasant in his way, so I thought myself well off. There was another

---

1 Fashionable foreign names for horses. Marengo was Napoleon's horse, Pegasus a mythical Greek winged horse, and Abdallah a famous Arabian stallion.

man who helped in the yard, but he had very little to do with Ginger and me.

A few days after this I had to go out with Ginger in the carriage; I wondered how we should get on together; but except laying her ears back when I was led up to her, she behaved very well. She did her work honestly and did her full share, and I never wish to have a better partner in double harness.

When we came to a hill, instead of slackening her pace, she would throw her weight right into the collar, and pull away straight up. We had both the same sort of courage at our work, and John had oftener to hold us in, than to urge us forward; he never had to use the whip with either of us; then our paces were much the same, and I found it very easy to keep step with her when trotting, which made it pleasant, and master always liked it when we kept step well, and so did John. After we had been out two or three times together we grew quite friendly and sociable, which made me feel very much at home.

As for Merrylegs, he and I soon became great friends; he was such a cheerful, plucky, good-tempered little fellow, that he was a favourite with everyone, and especially with Miss Jessie and Flora, who used to ride him about in the orchard, and have fine games with him and their little dog Frisky.

Our master had two other horses that stood in another stable. One was Justice, a roan cob,[1] used for riding, or for the luggage cart; the other was an old brown hunter, named Sir Oliver; he was past work now, but was a great favourite with the master, who gave him the run of the park; he sometimes did a little light carting on the estate, or carried one of the young ladies when they rode out with their father; for he was very gentle, and could be trusted with a child as well as Merrylegs. The cob was a strong, well-made, good-tempered horse, and we sometimes had a little chat in the paddock, but of course I could not be so intimate with him as with Ginger, who stood in the same stable.

---

1 Roan is a term for a horse whose body has an even mix of white and coloured hairs, while the head, mane, and tail are a single colour. A cob is a horse with a small, sturdy body type.

CHAPTER SIX
LIBERTY

I was quite happy in my new place, and if there was one thing that I missed, it must not be thought I was discontented; all who had to do with me were good, and I had a light airy stable and the best of food. What more could I want? Why, liberty! For three years and a half of my life I had had all the liberty I could wish for; but now, week after week, month after month, and no doubt year after year, I must stand up in a stable night and day except when I am wanted, and then I must be just as steady and quiet as any old horse who has worked twenty years. Straps here and straps there, a bit in my mouth, and blinkers over my eyes. Now, I am not complaining, for I know it must be so. I only mean to say that for a young horse full of strength and spirits who has been used to some large field or plain, where he can fling up his head, and toss up his tail and gallop away at full speed, then round and back again with a snort to his companions—I say it is hard never to have a bit more liberty to do as you like. Sometimes, when I have had less exercise than usual, I have felt so full of life and spring, that when John has taken me out to exercise, I really could not keep quiet; do what I would, it seemed as if I must jump, or dance, or prance, and many a good shake I know I must have given him, specially at the first; but he was always good and patient.

"Steady, steady, my boy," he would say, "wait a bit, and we'll have a good swing, and soon get the tickle out of your feet." Then as soon as we were out of the village, he would give me a few miles at a spanking trot, and then bring me back as fresh as before, only clear of the fidgets, as he called them. Spirited horses, when not enough exercised, are often called skittish, when it is only play; and some grooms will punish them, but our John did not, he knew it was only high spirits. Still, he had his own ways of making me understand by the tone of his voice, or the touch of the rein. If he was very serious and quite determined, I always knew it by his voice, and that had more power with me than anything else, for I was very fond of him.

I ought to say, that sometimes we had our liberty for a few hours; this used to be on fine Sundays in the summer-time. The carriage never went out on Sundays, because the church was not far off.

It was a great treat to us to be turned out into the Home Paddock or the old orchard. The grass was so cool and soft to our feet; the air so sweet, and the freedom to do as we liked was so pleasant; to gallop, to lie down, and roll over on our backs, or to nibble the sweet grass. Then it was a very good time for talking, as we stood together under the shade of the large chestnut tree.

One day when Ginger and I were standing alone in the shade we had a great deal of talk; she wanted to know all about my bringing up and breaking in, and I told her.

"Well," said she, "if I had had your bringing up I might have been as good a temper as you are, but now I don't believe I ever shall."

"Why not?" I said.

"Because it has been all so different with me," she replied; "I never had anyone, horse or man, that was kind to me, or that I cared to please, for in the first place I was taken from my mother as soon as I was weaned, and put with a lot of other young colts; none of them cared for me, and I cared for none of them. There was no kind master like yours to look after me, and talk to me, and bring me nice things to eat. The man that had the care of us never gave me a kind word in my life. I do not mean that he ill-used me, but he did not care for us one bit further than to see that we had plenty to eat and shelter in the winter. A footpath ran through our field, and very often the great boys passing through, would fling stones to make us gallop. I was never hit, but one fine young colt was badly cut in the face, and I should think it would be a scar for life. We did not care for them, but of course it made us more wild, and we settled it in our minds that boys were our enemies. We had very good fun in the free meadows, galloping up and down and chasing each other round and round the field; then standing still under the shade of the trees. But when it came to breaking in, that was a bad time for me; several men came to catch me, and when at last they closed me in at one corner of the field, one caught me by the forelock, another caught me by the nose, and held it so tight I could hardly draw my breath; then another took my under jaw in his hard hand and wrenched my mouth open, and so by force they got on the halter and the bar into my mouth; then one dragged me along by the halter, another flogging behind, and this was the first experience I had of men's kindness, it was all force; they did not give me a chance to know what they wanted. I was high bred and had a great deal of spirit, and was very wild, no doubt, and gave them I daresay plenty of trouble, but then it was dreadful to be shut up in a stall day after day instead of having my liberty, and I fretted and pined and wanted to get loose. You know yourself, it's bad enough when you have a kind master and plenty of coaxing, but there was nothing of that sort for me.

"There was one—the old master, Mr Ryder, who I think could soon have brought me round, and could have done anything with me, but he had given up all the hard part of the trade to his son and to another experienced man, and he only came at times to oversee. His son was a strong, tall, bold man; they called him Samson,[1] and he used to boast that he had never found a horse that could throw him. There was no gentleness in him as there was in his father, but only hardness, a hard voice, a hard eye, a hard hand, and I felt from the first that what he wanted was to wear all the spirit out of me, and just make me into a quiet, humble, obedient piece of horse-flesh. 'Horse-flesh!' Yes, that is all that he thought about,"—and Ginger stamped her foot as if the very thought of him made her angry. And she went on; "If I did not do exactly what he wanted, he would get put out, and make me run round with that long rein in the training field till he had tired me out. I think he drank a good deal, and I am quite sure that the oftener he drank the worse it was for me. One day he had worked me hard in every way he could, and when I laid down I was tired and miserable, and angry; it all seemed so hard. The next morning he came for me early, and ran me round again for a long time. I had scarcely had an hour's rest, when he came again for me with a saddle and bridle and a new kind of bit. I could never quite tell how it came about; he had only just mounted me on the training ground, when something I did put him out of temper, and he chucked me hard with the rein. The new bit was very painful, and I reared up suddenly, which angered him still more, and he began to flog me. I felt my whole spirit set against him, and I began to kick, and plunge, and rear as I had never done before, and we had a regular fight: for a long time he stuck to the saddle and punished me cruelly with his whip and spurs, but my blood was thoroughly up, and I cared for nothing he could do if only I could get him off. At last, after a terrible struggle, I threw him off backwards. I heard him fall heavily on the turf, and without looking behind me, I galloped off to the other end of the field; there I turned round and saw

---

1 A biblical character associated with superhuman strength and unsound judgement.

my persecutor slowly rising from the ground and going into the stable. I stood under an oak tree and watched, but no one came to catch me. The time went on, the sun was very hot, the flies swarmed round me, and settled on my bleeding flanks where the spurs had dug in. I felt hungry, for I had not eaten since the early morning, but there was not enough grass in that meadow for a goose to live on. I wanted to lie down and rest, but with the saddle strapped tightly on, there was no comfort, and there was not a drop of water to drink. The afternoon wore on, and the sun got low. I saw the other colts led in, and I knew they were having a good feed.

"At last, just as the sun went down, I saw the old master come out with a sieve in his hand. He was a very fine old gentleman with quite white hair, but his voice was what I should know him by amongst a thousand. It was not high, nor yet low, but full, and clear, and kind, and when he gave orders it was so steady and decided, that everyone knew, both horses and men, that he expected to be obeyed. He came quietly along, now and then shaking the oats about that he had in the sieve, and speaking cheerfully and gently to me, 'Come along, lassie, come along, lassie; come along, come along.' I stood still and let him come up; he held the oats to me and I began to eat without fear; his voice took all my fear away. He stood by, patting and stroking me whilst I was eating, and seeing the clots of blood on my side he seemed very vexed; 'Poor lassie! it was a bad business, a bad business!' then he quietly took the rein and led me to the stable; just at the door stood Samson. I laid my ears back and snapt at him. 'Stand back,' said the master, 'and keep out of her way; you've done a bad day's work for this filly.' He growled out something about a vicious brute. 'Hark ye,' said the father, 'a bad-tempered man will never make a good-tempered horse. You've not learned your trade yet, Samson.' Then he led me into my box, took off the saddle and bridle with his own hands and tied me up; then he called for a pail of warm water and a sponge, took off his coat, and while the stable man held the pail, he sponged my sides a good while so tenderly that I was sure he knew how sore and bruised they were. 'Whoa! my pretty one,' he said, 'stand still, stand still.' His very voice did me good, and the bathing was very comfortable. The skin was so broken at the corners of my mouth that I could not eat the hay, the stalks hurt me. He looked closely at it, shook his head, and told the man to fetch a good bran mash and put some meal into it. How good that mash was! and so soft and healing to my mouth. He stood by all the time I was eating, stroking me and talking to the man. 'If a high-mettled creature like this,' said he, 'can't be broken in by fair means, she will never be good for anything.'

"After that he often came to see me, and when my mouth was healed, the other breaker, Job,[1] they called him, went on training me; he was steady and thoughtful, and I soon learned what he wanted."

---

1 A biblical character associated with persistence and patience in the face of suffering.

CHAPTER EIGHT
GINGER'S STORY CONTINUED

The next time that Ginger and I were together in the paddock, she told me about her first place. "After my breaking in," she said, "I was bought by a dealer to match another chestnut horse. For some weeks he drove us together, and then we were sold to a fashionable gentleman, and were sent up to London. I had been driven with a bearing rein[1] by the dealer, and I hated it worse than anything else; but in this place we were reined far tighter; the coachman and his master thinking we looked more stylish so. We were often driven about in the Park and other fashionable places. You who never had a bearing rein on, don't know what it is, but I can tell you it is dreadful.

"I like to toss my head about, and hold it as high as any horse; but fancy now yourself, if you tossed your head up high and were obliged to hold it there, and that for hours together, not able to move it at all, except with a jerk still higher, your neck aching till you did not know how to bear it. Beside that, to have two bits instead of one; and mine was a sharp one, it hurt my tongue and my jaw, and the blood from my tongue coloured the froth that kept flying from my lips, as I chafed and fretted at the bits and rein; it was worst when we had to stand by the hour waiting for our mistress at some grand party or entertainment; and if I fretted or stamped with impatience the whip was laid on. It was enough to drive one mad."

"Did not your master take any thought for you?" I said.

"No," said she, "he only cared to have a stylish turn-out, as they call it; I think he knew very little about horses, he left that to his coachman, who told him I was an irritable temper; that I had not been well broken to the bearing rein, but I should soon get used to it; but *he* was not the man to do it, for when I was in the stable, miserable and angry, instead of being soothed and quieted by kindness, I got only a surly word or a blow. If he had been civil, I would have tried to bear it. I was willing to work, and ready to work hard too; but to be tormented for nothing but their fancies, angered me. What right had they to make me suffer

---

1   A central focus of Sewell's critique of horse management, the bearing rein is used as leverage to force the horse's head to stay high when in harness. For a full description see Appendix E3.

like that? Beside the soreness in my mouth and the pain in my neck, it always made my windpipe feel bad, and if I had stopped there long, I know it would have spoiled my breathing; but I grew more and more restless and irritable, I could not help it; and I began to snap and kick when anyone came to harness me; for this the groom beat me, and one day, as they had just buckled us into the carriage, and were straining my head up with that rein, I began to plunge and kick with all my might. I soon broke a lot of harness, and kicked myself clear; so that was an end of that place.

"After this, I was sent to Tattersals[1] to be sold; of course I could not be warranted free from vice, so nothing was said about that. My handsome appearance and good paces soon brought gentlemen to bid for me, and I was bought by another dealer; he tried me in all kinds of ways and with different bits, and he soon found out what I could not bear. At last he drove me quite without a bearing rein, and then sold me as a perfectly quiet horse to a gentleman in the country; he was a good master, and I was getting on very well, but his old groom left him and a new one came. This man was as hard-tempered and hard-handed as Samson; he always spoke in a rough impatient voice, and if I did not move in the stall the moment he wanted me, he would hit me above the hocks[2] with the stable broom or the fork, whichever he might have in his hand. Everything he did was rough, and I began to hate him; he wanted to make me afraid of him, but I was too high-mettled for that; and one day when he had aggravated me more than usual, I bit him, which of course put him in a great rage, and he began to hit me about the head with a riding whip. After that, he never dared to come into my stall again, either my heels or my teeth were ready for him, and he knew it. I was quite quiet with my master, but of course he listened to what the man said, and so I was sold again.

"The same dealer heard of me and said he thought he knew one place where I should do well. 'Twas a pity,' he said, 'that such a fine horse should go to the bad, for want of a real good chance,' and the end of it was that I came here not long before you did; but I had then made up my mind, that men were my natural enemies, and that I must defend myself. Of course it is

---

1 The most prestigious sales yard and horse auction in Victorian England. It remains a world-leader today.
2 The major bending joint of the hind leg.

very different here, but who knows how long it will last? I wish I could think about things as you do; but I can't after all I have gone through."

"Well," I said, "I think it would be a real shame if you were to bite or kick John or James."

"I don't mean to," she said, "while they are good to me. I did bite James once pretty sharp, but John said, 'Try her with kindness,' and instead of punishing me as I expected, James came to me with his arm bound up, and brought me a bran mash and stroked me; and I have never snapped at him since, and I won't either."

I was sorry for Ginger, but of course I knew very little then, and I thought most likely she made the worst of it; however, I found that as the weeks went on, she grew much more gentle and cheerful, and had lost the watchful, defiant look that she used to turn on any strange person who came near her; and one day James said, "I do believe that mare is getting fond of me, she quite whinnied after me this morning when I had been rubbing her forehead."

"Aye, aye, Jim, 'tis the Birtwick balls,"[1] said John, "she'll be as good as Black Beauty by and bye; kindness is all the physic she wants, poor thing!" Master noticed the change too, and one day when he got out of the carriage and came to speak to us as he often did, he stroked her beautiful neck, "Well, my pretty one, well, how do things go with you now? you are a good bit happier than when you came to us, I think."

She put her nose up to him in a friendly trustful way, while he rubbed it gently.

"We shall make a cure of her, John," he said.

"Yes, sir, she's wonderfully improved, she's not the same creature that she was; it's the Birtwick balls, sir," said John, laughing.

This was a little joke of John's; he used to say that a regular course of the Birtwick horse-balls would cure almost any vicious horse; these balls he said were made up of patience and gentleness, firmness and petting, one pound of each to be mixed up with half-a-pint of common sense, and given to the horse every day.

---

1   Horse balls were a preparation concocted by veterinarians to administer medicine; the meaning of "Birtwick balls" is explained in the chapter's final paragraph.

CHAPTER NINE
MERRYLEGS

Mr. Blomefield, the Vicar, had a large family of boys and girls; sometimes they used to come and play with Miss Jessie and Flora, one of the girls was as old as Miss Jessie; two of the boys were older, and there were several little ones. When they came, there was plenty of work for Merrylegs, for nothing pleased them so much as getting on him by turns and riding him all about the orchard and the home paddock, and this they would do by the hour together.

One afternoon he had been out with them a long time, and when James brought him in and put on his halter, he said,

"There, you rogue, mind how you behave yourself, or we shall get into trouble."

"What have you been doing, Merrylegs?" I asked.

"Oh!" said he, tossing his little head, "I have only been giving those young people a lesson, they did not know when they had had enough, nor when I had had enough, so I just pitched them off back-wards, that was the only thing they could understand."

"What?" said I, "you threw the children off? I thought you did know better than that! Did you throw Miss Jessie or Miss Flora?"

He looked very much offended, and said:—

"Of course not, I would not do such a thing for the best oats that ever came into the stable; why I am as careful of our young ladies as the master could be, and as for the little ones, it is I who teach them to ride. When they seem frightened or a little unsteady on my back, I go as smooth and as quiet as old pussy when she is after a bird; and when they are all right, I go on again faster you see, just to use them to it; so don't you trouble yourself preaching to me; I am the best friend, and the best riding master those children have. It is not them, it is the boys; boys," said he, shaking his mane, "are quite different; they must be broken in, as we were broken in when we were colts, and just be taught what's what. The other children had ridden me about for nearly two hours, and then the boys thought it was their turn, and so it was, and I was quite agreeable. They rode me by turns, and I galloped them about up and down the fields and all about the orchard for a good hour. They had each cut a great hazel stick for a riding whip, and laid it on a little too hard; but I took it in good part, till at last I thought we had had enough, so I stopped two or three times by way of a hint. Boys, you see, think a horse or pony is like a steam engine or a thrashing machine, and can go on as long and as fast as they please; they never think that a pony can get tired, or have any feelings; so as the one who was whipping me could not understand, I just rose up on my hind legs and let him slip off behind—that was all; he mounted me again and I did the same. Then the other boy got up, and as soon as he began to use his stick I laid him on the grass, and so on, till they were able to understand, that was all. They are not bad boys; they don't wish to be cruel. I like them very well; but you see I had to give them a lesson. When they brought me to James and told him, I think he was very angry to see such big sticks. He said they were only fit for drovers or gipsies, and not for young gentlemen."

"If I had been you," said Ginger, "I would have given those boys a good kick, and that would have given them a lesson."

"No doubt you would," said Merrylegs, "but then I am not quite such a fool, (begging your pardon) as to anger our master or make James ashamed of me; besides those children are under my charge when they are riding; I tell you they are trusted to me. Why, only the other day I heard our master say to Mrs. Blomefield, 'My dear madam, you need not be anxious about the children, my old Merrylegs will take as much care of them as you or I could: I assure you I would not sell that pony for any money, he is so perfectly good-tempered and trustworthy;' and do you think I am such an ungrateful brute, as to forget all the kind treatment I have had here for five years, and all the trust they place in me, and turn vicious because a couple of ignorant boys used me badly? No! no! you never had a good place where they were kind to you; and so you don't know, and I'm sorry for you, but I can tell you good places make good horses. I wouldn't vex our people for anything; I love them, I do," said Merrylegs, and he gave a low, "ho, ho, ho" through his nose, as he used to do in the morning when he heard James's footstep at the door.

"Besides," he went on, "if I took to kicking, where should I be? why, sold off in a jiffy, and no character,[1] and I might find myself slaved about under a butcher's boy, or worked to death at some seaside place where no one cared for me, except to find out how fast I could go, or be flogged along in some cart with three or four great men in it going out for a Sunday spree, as I have often seen in the place I lived in before I came here; no," said he, shaking his head, "I hope I shall never come to that."

---

1 A term used in relation to servants, referring to a good reference from a previous employer.

CHAPTER TEN
A TALK IN THE ORCHARD

Ginger and I were not of the regular tall carriage horse breed, we had more of the racing blood in us. We stood about fifteen and a half hands high; we were therefore just as good for riding as we were for driving, and our master used to say that he disliked either horse or man that could do but one thing; and as he did not want to show off in the London Parks, he preferred a more active and useful kind of horse. As for us, our greatest pleasure was when we were saddled for a riding party; the master on Ginger, the mistress on me, and the young ladies on Sir Oliver and Merrylegs. It was so cheerful to be trotting and cantering all together, that it always put us in high spirits. I had the best of it, for I always carried the mistress; her weight was little, her voice was sweet, and her hand was so light on the rein, that I was guided almost without feeling it.

Oh! if people knew what a comfort to horses a light hand is, and how it keeps a good mouth and a good temper, they surely would not chuck, and drag, and pull at the rein as they often do. Our mouths are so tender, that where they have not been spoiled or hardened with bad or ignorant treatment, they feel the slightest movement of the driver's hand, and we know in an instant what is required of us. My mouth had never been spoiled, and I believe that was why the mistress preferred me to Ginger, although her paces were certainly quite as good. She used often to envy me, and said it was all the fault of the breaking in, and the gag bit[1] in London, that her mouth was not so perfect as mine; and then old Sir Oliver would say, "There, there! don't vex yourself; you have the greatest honour; a mare that can carry a tall man of our master's weight, with all your spring and sprightly action, does not need to hold her head down because she does not carry the lady; we horses must take things as they come, and always be contented and willing so long as we are kindly used."

I had often wondered how it was, that Sir Oliver had such a

---

1   A very severe bit that uses leverage to offer a high level of control
    and elevate the horse's head. For a full description see Appendix
    E3.

very short tail;[1] it really was only six or seven inches long, with a tassel of hair hanging from it; and on one of our holidays in the orchard I ventured to ask him by what accident it was that he had lost his tail. "Accident!" he snorted with a fierce look, "it was no accident! it was a cruel, shameful, cold-blooded act! When I was young I was taken to a place where these cruel things were done; I was tied up, and made fast so that I could not stir, and then they came and cut off my long beautiful tail, through the flesh, and through the bone, and took it away."

"How dreadful!" I exclaimed.

"Dreadful! ah! it was dreadful; but it was not only the pain, though that was terrible and lasted a long time; it was not only the indignity of having my best ornament taken from me, though that was bad; but it was this, how could I ever brush the flies off my sides and my hind legs any more? You who have tails just whisk the flies off without thinking about it, and you can't tell what a torment it is to have them settle upon you and sting and sting, and have nothing in the world to lash them off with. I tell you it is a life-long wrong, and a life-long loss; but thank Heaven! they don't do it now."

"What did they do it for then?" said Ginger.

"For fashion!" said the old horse with a stamp of his foot; "for fashion! if you know what that means; there was not a well-bred young horse in my time that had not his tail docked in that shameful way, just as if the good God that made us, did not know what we wanted and what looked best."

"I suppose it is fashion that makes them strap our heads up with those horrid bits that I was tortured with in London," said Ginger.

"Of course it is," said he; "to my mind, fashion is one of the wickedest things in the world. Now look, for instance, at the way they serve dogs, cutting off their tails to make them look plucky, and shearing up their pretty little ears to a point to make them look sharp, forsooth. I had a dear friend once, a brown terrier; 'Skye,' they called her, she was so fond of me, that she never would sleep out of my stall; she made her bed

---

1 Docking, or partial amputation of the tail, was intermittently fashionable for carriage horses, hunters, polo ponies, and cavalry mounts in the eighteenth and nineteenth centuries. It was also performed on draft horses to keep the tail from getting caught in the harness.

under the manger, and there she had a litter of five as pretty little puppies as need be; none were drowned, for they were a valuable kind, and how pleased she was with them! and when they got their eyes open and crawled about, it was a real pretty sight; but one day the man came and took them all away; I thought he might be afraid I should tread upon them. But it was not so; in the evening poor Skye brought them back again, one by one in her mouth; not the happy little things that they were, but bleeding and crying pitifully; they had all had a piece of their tails cut off, and the soft flap of their pretty little ears was cut quite off. How their mother licked them, and how troubled she was, poor thing! I never forgot it. They healed in time, and they forgot the pain, but the nice soft flap that of course was intended to protect the delicate part of theirs ears from dust and injury, was gone for ever. Why don't they cut their own children's ears into points to make them look sharp? why don't they cut the end off their noses to make them look plucky? one would be just as sensible as the other. What right have they to torment and disfigure God's creatures?"

Sir Oliver, though he was so gentle, was a fiery old fellow, and what he said was all so new to me and so dreadful, that I found a bitter feeling toward men rise up in my mind that I never had before. Of course Ginger was much excited; she flung up her head with flashing eyes, and distended nostrils, declaring that men were both brutes and blockheads.

"Who talks about blockheads?" said Merrylegs, who just came up from the old apple tree, where he had been rubbing himself against the low branch; "Who talks about blockheads? I believe that is a bad word."

"Bad words were made for bad things," said Ginger, and she told him what Sir Oliver had said. "It is all true," said Merrylegs sadly, "and I've seen that about the dogs over and over again where I lived first; but we won't talk about it here. You know that master, and John, and James are always good to us, and talking against men in such a place as this, doesn't seem fair or grateful, and you know there are good masters and good grooms besides ours, though of course ours are the best." This wise speech of good little Merrylegs, which we knew was quite true, cooled us all down, specially Sir Oliver, who was dearly fond of his master; and to turn the subject I said, "Can anyone tell me the use of blinkers?"

"No!" said Sir Oliver shortly, "because they are no use."

"They are supposed," said Justice in his calm way, "to prevent horses from shying and starting, and getting so frightened as to cause accidents."

"Then what is the reason they do not put them on riding horses; especially ladies' horses?" said I.

"There is no reason at all," said he quietly, "except the fashion: they say that a horse would be so frightened to see the wheels of his own cart or carriage coming behind him, that he would be sure to run away, although of course when he is ridden, he sees them all about him if the streets are crowded. I admit they do sometimes come too close to be pleasant, but we don't run away; we are used to it, and understand it, and if we had never blinkers put on, we should never want them; we should see what was there, and know what was what, and be much less frightened than by only seeing bits of things, that we can't understand."

Of course there may be some nervous horses who have been hurt or frightened when they were young, and may be the better for them, but as I never was nervous, I can't judge.

"I consider," said Sir Oliver, "that blinkers are dangerous things in the night; we horses can see much better in the dark than men can, and many an accident would never have happened if horses might have had the full use of their eyes. Some years ago, I remember, there was a hearse with two horses returning one dark night, and just by farmer Sparrow's house, where the pond is close to the road, the wheels went too near the edge, and the hearse was overturned into the water; both the horses were drowned, and the driver hardly escaped. Of course after this accident a stout white rail was put up that might be easily seen, but if those horses had not been partly blinded, they would of themselves have kept farther from the edge, and no accident would have happened. When our master's carriage was overturned, before you came here, it was said, that if the lamp on the left side had not gone out, John would have seen the great hole that the road makers had left; and so he might, but if old Colin had not had blinkers on, he would have seen it, lamp or no lamp, for he was far too knowing an old horse to run into danger. As it was, he was very much hurt, the carriage was broken, and how John escaped nobody knew."

"I should say," said Ginger, curling her nostril, "that these men, who are so wise, had better give orders, that in future, all foals should be born with their eyes set just in the middle of their foreheads, instead of on the side; they always think they can improve upon nature and mend what God has made."

Things were getting rather sore again, when Merrylegs held up his knowing little face and said, "I'll tell you a secret; I believe John does not approve of blinkers, I heard him talking with master about it one day. The master said, that 'if horses had been used to them, it might be dangerous in some cases to leave them off,' and John said he thought it would be a good thing if all colts were broken in without blinkers, as was the case in some foreign countries; so let us cheer up, and have a run to the other end of the orchard; I believe the wind has blown down some apples, and we might just as well eat them as the slugs."

Merrylegs could not be resisted, so we broke off our long conversation, and got up our spirits by munching some very sweet apples which lay scattered on the grass.

CHAPTER ELEVEN
PLAIN SPEAKING

The longer I lived at Birtwick, the more proud and happy I felt at having such a place. Our master and mistress were respected and beloved by all who knew them; they were good and kind to everybody, and everything; not only men and women, but horses and donkeys, dogs and cats, cattle and birds; there was no oppressed or ill-used creature that had not a friend in them, and their servants took the same tone. If any of the village children were known to treat any creature cruelly, they soon heard about it from the Hall.

The Squire and farmer Grey had worked together as they said, for more than twenty years, to get bearing reins on the cart horses done away with, and in our parts you seldom saw them; but sometimes if mistress met a heavily-laden horse, with his head strained up, she would stop the carriage and get out, and reason with the driver in her sweet serious voice, and try to shew him how foolish and cruel it was.

I don't think any man could withstand our mistress. I wish all ladies were like her. Our master too, used to come down very heavy sometimes; I remember he was riding me towards home one morning, when we saw a powerful man driving towards us in a light pony chaise, with a beautiful little bay pony, with slender legs, and a high-bred sensitive head and face. Just as he came to the Park gates, the little thing turned towards them; the man without word or warning, wrenched the creature's head round with such force and suddenness, that he nearly threw it on its haunches: recovering itself, it was going on when he began to lash it furiously; the pony plunged forward, but the strong heavy hand held the pretty creature back with force almost enough to break its jaw, whilst the whip still cut into him. It was a dreadful sight to me, for I knew what fearful pain it gave that delicate little mouth; but master gave me the word, and we were up with him in a second. "Sawyer," he cried in a stern voice, "is that pony made of flesh and blood?"

"Flesh and blood and temper" he said, "he's too fond of his own will, and that won't suit me." He spoke as if he was in a strong passion; he was a builder who had often been to the Park on business. "And do you think," said master sternly, "that treatment like this, will make him fond of your will?"

"He had no business to make that turn; his road was straight on!" said the man roughly.

"You have often driven that pony up to my place," said master, "it only shews the creature's memory and intelligence; how did he know that you were not going there again? but that has little to do with it. I must say, Mr. Sawyer, that more unmanly, brutal treatment of a little pony, it was never my painful lot to witness; and by giving way to such passion, you injure your own character as much, nay more, than you injure your horse, and remember, we shall all have to be judged according to our works, whether they be towards man or towards beast."

Master rode me home slowly, and I could tell by his voice how the thing had grieved him. He was just as free to speak to gentlemen of his own rank as to those below him; for another day, when we were out, we met a Captain Langley, a friend of our master's; he was driving a splendid pair of greys in a kind of break. After a little conversation the Captain said,

"What do you think of my new team, Mr. Douglas? you know, you are the judge of horses in these parts, and I should like your opinion."

The master backed me a little, so as to get a good view of them. "They are an uncommonly handsome pair," he said, "and if they are as good as they look, I am sure you need not wish for anything better; but I see you yet hold to that pet scheme of yours for worrying your horses and lessening their power."

"What do you mean," said the other, "the bearing reins? Oh, ah! I know that's a hobby of yours; well, the fact is, I like to see my horses hold their heads up."

"So do I," said master, "as well as any man, but I don't like to see them held up; that takes all the shine out of it. Now you are a military man, Langley, and no doubt like to see your regiment look well on parade, 'Heads up,' and all that; but you would not take much credit for your drill, if all your men had their heads tied to a backboard! It might not be much harm on parade, except to worry and fatigue them, but how would it be in a bayonet charge against the enemy, when they want the free use of every muscle, and all their strength thrown forward? I would not give much for their chance of victory, and it is just the same with horses; you fret and worry their tempers, and decrease their power, you will not let them throw their weight against their work, and so they have to do too much with their joints and muscles, and of course it wears them up faster. You may depend upon it, horses were intended to have their heads free, as free as men's are; and if we could act a little more according to common sense, and a good deal less according to fashion, we should find many things work easier; besides, you know as well as I, that if a horse makes a false step, he has much less chance of recovering himself if his head and neck are fastened back. And now," said the master, laughing, "I have given my hobby a good trot out, can't you make up your mind to mount him too, Captain? your example would go a long way."

"I believe you are right in theory," said the other, "and that's rather a hard hit about the soldiers; but—well—I'll think about it," and so they parted.

CHAPTER TWELVE
A STORMY DAY

One day late in the autumn, my master had a long journey to go on business. I was put into the dog-cart, and John went with his master. I always liked to go in the dog-cart, it was so light, and the high wheels ran along so pleasantly. There had been a great deal of rain, and now the wind was very high, and blew the dry leaves across the road in a shower. We went along merrily till we came to the toll-bar,[1] and the low wooden bridge. The river banks were rather high, and the bridge, instead of rising, went across just level, so that in the middle, if the river was full, the water would be nearly up to the woodwork and planks; but as there were good substantial rails on each side, people did not mind it.

The man at the gate said the river was rising fast, and he feared it would be a bad night. Many of the meadows were under water, and in one low part of the road, the water was half way up to my knees; the bottom was good, and master drove gently, so it was no matter.

When we got to the town, of course I had a good bait,[2] but as the master's business engaged him a long time, we did not start for home till rather late in the afternoon. The wind was then much higher, and I heard the master say to John, he had never been out in such a storm; and so I thought, as we went along the skirts of a wood, where great branches were swaying about like twigs, and the rushing sound was terrible.

"I wish we were well out of this wood," said my master, "Yes, sir," said John, "it would be rather awkward if one of these branches came down upon us." The words were scarcely out of his mouth, when there was a groan, and a crack, and a splitting sound, and tearing, crashing down amongst the other trees, came an oak, torn up by the roots, and it fell right across the road just before us. I will never say I was not frightened, for I was. I stopped still, and I believe I trembled; of course I did not turn round or run away; I was not brought up to that. John jumped out and was in a moment at my head.

---

1 Established by an Act of Parliament in 1706, toll bridges and turn-pikes collected user fees to improve and maintain roads.
2 Slang for feed.

"That was a very near touch," said my master, "What's to be done now?" "Well, sir, we can't drive over that tree nor yet get round it; there will be nothing for it, but to go back to the four cross-ways, and that will be a good six miles before we get round to the wooden bridge again; it will make us late, but the horse is fresh." So back we went, and round by the cross roads; but by the time we got to the bridge, it was very nearly dark, we could just see that the water was over the middle of it; but as that happened sometimes when the floods were out, master did not stop. We were going along at a good pace, but the moment my feet touched the first part of the bridge, I felt sure there was something wrong. I dare not go forward, and I made a dead stop. "Go on, Beauty," said my master, and he gave me a touch with the whip, but I dare not stir; he gave me a sharp cut, I jumped, but I dare not go forward.

"There's something wrong, sir," said John, and he sprung out of the dog-cart and came to my head and looked all about. He tried to lead me forward, "Come on, Beauty, what's the matter?" Of course I could not tell him; but I knew very well that the bridge was not safe.

Just then, the man at the toll-gate on the other side ran out of the house, tossing a torch about like one mad. "Hoy, hoy, hoy, halloo, stop!" he cried. "What's the matter?" shouted my master, "The bridge is broken in the middle, and part of it is carried away; if you come on you'll be into the river."

"Thank God!" said my master. "You Beauty!" said John, and took the bridle and gently turned me round to the right-hand road by the river side.

The sun had set some time, the wind seemed to have lulled off after that furious blast which tore up the tree. It grew darker and darker, stiller and stiller. I trotted quietly along, the wheels hardly making a sound on the soft road. For a good while neither master nor John spoke, and then master began in a serious voice. I could not understand much of what they said, but I found they thought, if I had gone on as the master wanted me, most likely the bridge would have given way under us, and horse, chaise, master and man would have fallen into the river; and as the current was flowing very strongly, and there was no light and no help at hand, it was more than likely we should all have been drowned. Master said, God had given men reason by which they could find out things for themselves, but He had given animals knowledge which did not depend on reason, and which was much more prompt and perfect in its way, and by which they had often saved the lives of men. John had many stories to tell of dogs and horses, and the wonderful things they had done; he thought people did not value their animals half enough, nor make friends of them as they ought to do. I am sure he makes friends of them if ever a man did.

At last we came to the Park gates, and found the gardener looking out for us. He said that mistress had been in a dreadful way ever since dark, fearing some accident had happened, and that she had sent James off on Justice, the roan cob, towards the wooden bridge to make enquiry after us.

We saw a light at the hall door and at the upper windows, and as we came up, mistress ran out, saying, "Are you really safe, my dear? Oh! I have been so anxious, fancying all sorts of things. Have you had no accident?"

"No, my dear; but if your Black Beauty had not been wiser than we were, we should all have been carried down the river at the wooden bridge." I heard no more, as they went into the house, and John took me to the stable. Oh! what a good supper he gave me that night, a good bran mash and some crushed beans with my oats, and such a thick bed of straw, and I was glad of it, for I was tired.

CHAPTER THIRTEEN
The Devil's Trade Mark

One day when John and I had been out on some business of our master's, and were returning gently on a long straight road, at some distance we saw a boy trying to leap a pony over a gate; the pony would not take the leap, and the boy cut him with the whip, but he only turned off on one side; he whipped him again, but the pony turned off on the other side. Then the boy got off and gave him a hard thrashing, and knocked him about the head; then he got up again and tried to make him leap the gate, kicking him all the time shamefully, but still the pony refused. When we were nearly at the spot, the pony put down his head and threw up his heels and sent the boy neatly over into a broad quickset hedge, and with the rein dangling from his head, he set off home at a full gallop. John laughed out quite loud, "Served him right," he said.

"Oh! oh! oh!" cried the boy, as he straggled about amongst the thorns; "I say, come and help me out."

"Thank ye," said John, "I think you are quite in the right place, and maybe a little scratching will teach you not to leap a pony over a gate that is too high for him," and so with that John rode off. "It may be," said he to himself, "that young fellow is a liar as well as a cruel one; we'll just go home by farmer Bushby's, Beauty, and then if anybody wants to know, you and I can tell 'em, ye see;" so we turned off to the right, and soon came up to the stack yard, and within sight of the house. The farmer was hurrying out into the road, and his wife was standing at the gate, looking very frightened.

"Have you seen my boy?" said Mr. Bushby, as we came up, "he went out an hour ago on my black pony, and the creature is just come back without a rider."

"I should think, sir," said John, "he had better be without a rider, unless he can be ridden properly."

"What do you mean?" said the farmer.

"Well, sir, I saw your son whipping, and kicking, and knocking that good little pony about shamefully, because he would not leap a gate that was too high for him. The pony behaved well, sir, and shewed no vice; but at last he just threw up his heels, and tipped the young gentleman into the thorn hedge; he wanted me to help him out; but I hope you will excuse me, sir, I did not feel inclined to do so. There's no bones broken, sir, he'll only get a few scratches. I love horses, and it roiles me to see them badly used; it is a bad plan to aggravate an animal till he uses his heels; the first time is not always the last."

During this time the mother began to cry, "Oh! my poor Bill, I must go and meet him, he must be hurt."

"You had better go into the house, wife," said the farmer; "Bill wants a lesson about this, and I must see that he gets it; this is not the first time nor the second that he has illused that pony, and I shall stop it. I am much obliged to you, Manly. Good evening."

So we went on, John chuckling all the way home, then he told James about it, who laughed and said, "Serve him right. I knew that boy at school; he took great airs on himself because he was a farmer's son; he used to swagger about and bully the little boys; of course we elder ones would not have any of that nonsense, and let him know that in the school and the playground, farmers' sons and labourers' sons were all alike. I well remember one day, just before afternoon school, I found him at the large window catching flies and pulling off their wings. He did not see me, and I gave him a box on the ears that laid him sprawling on the floor. Well, angry as I was, I was almost frightened, he roared and bellowed in such a style. The boys rushed in from the playground, and the master ran in from the road to see who was being murdered. Of course I said fair and square at once what I had done, and why; then I shewed the master the poor flies, some crushed and some crawling about helpless, and I shewed him the wings on the window sill. I never saw him so angry before; but as Bill was still howling and whining, like the coward that he was, he did not give him any more punishment of that kind, but set him up on a stool for the rest of the afternoon, and said that he should not go out to play for that week. Then he talked to all the boys very seriously about cruelty, and said how hard-hearted and cowardly it was to hurt the weak and the helpless; but what stuck in my mind was this, he said that cruelty was the Devil's own trade mark, and if we saw anyone who took pleasure in cruelty, we might know who he belonged to, for the devil was a murderer from the beginning, and a tormentor to the end. On the other hand, where we saw people who loved their neighbours, and were kind to man and beast, we might know that was God's mark, for 'God is Love.'"

"Your master never taught you a truer thing," said John; "there is no religion without love, and people may talk as much as they like about their religion, but if it does not teach them to be good and kind to man and beast, it is all a sham—all a sham, James, and it won't stand when things come to be turned inside out and put down for what they are."

CHAPTER FOURTEEN
JAMES HOWARD

One morning early in December, John had just led me into my box after my daily exercise, and was strapping my cloth on, and James was coming in from the corn chamber with some oats, when the master came into the stable; he looked rather serious, and held an open letter in his hand. John fastened the door of my box, touched his cap, and waited for orders.

"Good morning, John," said the master; "I want to know if you have any complaint to make of James."

"Complaint, sir? No, sir."

"Is he industrious at his work and respectful to you?"

"Yes, sir, always."

"You never find he slights his work when your back is turned?"

"Never, sir."

"That's well; but I must put another question; have you no reason to suspect when he goes out with the horses to exercise them, or to take a message, that he stops about talking to his acquaintances, or goes into houses where he has no business, leaving the horses outside?"

"No, sir, certainly not, and if anybody has been saying that about James, I don't believe it, and I don't mean to believe it unless I have it fairly proved before witnesses; it's not for me to say who has been trying to take away James' character, but I will say this, sir, that a steadier, pleasanter, honester, smarter young fellow I never had in this stable. I can trust his word and I can trust his work; he is gentle and clever with the horses, and I would rather have them in charge with him, than with half the young fellows I know of in laced hats and liveries; and whoever wants a character of James Howard," said John, with a decided jerk of his head, "let them come to John Manly."

The master stood all this time grave and attentive, but as John finished his speech, a broad smile spread over his face, and looking kindly across at James, who, all this time had stood still at the door, he said, "James, my lad, set down the oats and come here; I am very glad to find that John's opinion of your character agrees so exactly with my own. John is a cautious man," he said, with a droll smile, "and it is not always easy to get his opinion about people, so I thought if I beat the bush on this side, the birds would fly out, and I should learn what I wanted to know quickly; so now we will come to business. I have a letter from my brother-in-law, Sir Clifford Williams, of Clifford Hall; he wants me to find him a trustworthy young groom, about twenty or twenty-one, who knows his business. His old coachman, who has lived with him thirty years, is getting feeble, and he wants a man to work with him and get into his ways, who would be able, when the old man was pensioned off, to step into his place. He would have eighteen shillings a week at first, a stable suit, a driving suit, a bedroom over the coach-house, and a boy under him. Sir Clifford is a good master, and if you could get the place, it would be a good start for you. I don't want to part with you, and if you left us, I know John would lose his right hand."

"That I should, sir," said John, "but I would not stand in his light for the world."

"How old are you, James?" said master.

"Nineteen next May, sir."

"That's young; what do you think, John?"

"Well, sir, it is young: but he is as steady as a man, and is strong, and well grown, and though he has not had much experience in driving, he has a light firm hand, and a quick eye, and he is very careful, and I am quite sure no horse of his will be ruined for want of having his feet and shoes looked after."

"Your word will go the furthest, John," said the master, "for Sir Clifford adds in a postscript, 'If I could find a man trained by your John, I should like him better than any other'; so James, lad, think it over, talk to your mother at dinner time, and then let me know what you wish."

In a few days after this conversation, it was fully settled that James should go to Clifford Hall in a month or six weeks, as it suited his master, and in the meantime he was to get all the practice in driving that could be given to him. I never knew the carriage go out so often before: when the mistress did not go out, the master drove himself in the two-wheeled chaise; but now, whether it was master or the young ladies, or only an errand, Ginger and I were put into the carriage and James drove us. At the first, John rode with him on the box, telling him this and that, and after that James drove alone.

Then it was wonderful what a number of places the master would go to in the city on Saturday, and what queer streets we were driven through. He was sure to go to the railway station just as the train was coming in, and cabs and carriages, carts and omnibusses were all trying to get over the bridge together; that bridge wanted good horses and good drivers when the railway bell was ringing, for it was narrow, and there was a very sharp turn up to the station, where it would not have been at all difficult for people to run into each other, if they did not look sharp and keep their wits about them.

CHAPTER FIFTEEN
The Old Ostler

After this, it was decided by my master and mistress to pay a visit to some friends who lived about forty-six miles from our home, and James was to drive them. The first day we travelled thirty-two miles; there were some long heavy hills, but James drove so carefully and thoughtfully that we were not at all harassed. He never forgot to put on the drag[1] as we went downhill, nor to take it off at the right place. He kept our feet on the smoothest part of the road, and if the uphill was very long, he set the carriage wheels a little across the road, so as not to run back, and gave us a breathing. All these little things help a horse very much, particularly if they get kind words into the bargain.

We stopped once or twice on the road, and just as the sun was going down, we reached the town where we were to spend the night. We stopped at the principal hotel, which was in the Market Place; it was a very large one; we drove under an archway into a long yard, at the further end of which were the stables and coach-houses. Two ostlers[2] came to take us out. The head ostler was a pleasant, active little man, with a crooked leg, and a yellow striped waistcoat. I never saw a man unbuckle harness so quickly as he did, and with a pat and a good word he led me to a long stable, with six or eight stalls in it, and two or three horses. The other man brought Ginger; James stood by whilst we were rubbed down and cleaned.

I never was cleaned so lightly and quickly as by that little old man. When he had done, James stepped up and felt me over, as if he thought I could not be thoroughly done, but he found my coat as clean and smooth as silk.

"Well," he said, "I thought I was pretty quick, and our John quicker still, but you do beat all I ever saw for being quick and thorough at the same time."

"Practice makes perfect," said the crooked little ostler, "and 'twould be a pity if it didn't; forty years' practice, and not perfect! ha, ha! that would be a pity; and as to being quick, why, bless you! that is only a matter of habit; if you get into the habit

---

1 A skid that functions as a brake by retarding the forward motion of the wheels.
2 Stablemen employed to look after the horses of people staying at an inn.

of being quick, it is just as easy as being slow; easier, I should say; in fact, it don't agree with my health to be hulking about over a job twice as long as it need take. Bless you! I couldn't whistle if I crawled over my work as some folks do! You see, I have been about horses ever since I was twelve years old, in hunting stables, and racing stables; and being small, ye see, I was a jockey for several years; but at the Goodwood,[1] ye see, the turf was very slippery and my poor Larkspur got a fall, and I broke my knee, and so of course I was of no more use there; but I could not live without horses, of course I couldn't, so I took to the Hotels, and I can tell ye it is a downright pleasure to handle an animal like this, well-bred, well-mannered, well-cared for; bless ye! I can tell how a horse is treated. Give me the handling of a horse for twenty minutes, and I'll tell you what sort of a groom he has had; look at this one, pleasant, quiet, turns about just as you want him, holds up his feet to be cleaned out, or anything else you please to wish; then you'll find another, fidgetty, fretty, won't move the right way, or starts across the stall, tosses up his head as soon as you come near him, lays his ears, and seems afraid of you; or else squares about at you with his heels. Poor things! I know what sort of treatment they have had. If they are timid, it makes them start or shy; if they are high-mettled, it makes them vicious or dangerous; their tempers are mostly made when they are young. Bless you! they are like children, train 'em up in the way they should go, as the good book says, and when they are old they will not depart from it, if they have a chance, that is."

"I like to hear you talk," said James, "that's the way we lay it down at home, at our master's."

"Who is your master, young man? if it be a proper question. I should judge he is a good one, from what I see."

"He is Squire Gordon, of Birtwick Park, the other side the Beacon hills," said James.

"Ah! so, so, I have heard tell of him; fine judge of horses, ain't he? the best rider in the county?"

"I believe he is," said James, "but he rides very little now, since the poor young master was killed."

"Ah! poor gentleman; I read all about it in the paper at the time; a bad job it was; a fine horse killed too, wasn't there?"

---

1 A prestigious venue for horse racing established in 1802 by the Duke of Richmond on the grounds of Goodwood Estate.

"Yes," said James, "he was a splendid creature, brother to this one, and just like him."

"Pity! pity!" said the old man, "'twas a bad place to leap, if I remember; a thin fence at top, a steep bank down to the stream, wasn't it? no chance for a horse to see where he is going. Now, I am for bold riding as much as any man, but still there are some leaps that only a very knowing old huntsman has any right to take; a man's life and a horse's life are worth more than a fox's tail, at least I should say they ought to be."

During this time the other man had finished Ginger, and had brought our corn, and James and the old man left the stable together.

CHAPTER SIXTEEN
THE FIRE!

Later on in the evening, a traveller's horse was brought in by the second ostler, and whilst he was cleaning him, a young man with a pipe in his mouth lounged into the stable to gossip.

"I say, Towler," said the ostler, "just run up the ladder into the loft and put some hay down into this horse's rack, will you? only lay down your pipe."

"All right," said the other, and went up through the trap door; and I heard him step across the floor overhead and put down the hay. James came in to look at us the last thing, and then the door was locked.

I cannot say how long I had slept, nor what time in the night it was, but I woke up very uncomfortable, though I hardly knew why. I got up, the air seemed all thick and choking. I heard Ginger coughing, and one of the other horses seemed very restless; it was quite dark, and I could see nothing, but the stable seemed full of smoke and I hardly knew how to breathe. The trap door had been left open, and I thought that was the place it came through. I listened and heard a soft rushing sort of noise, and a low crackling and snapping. I did not know what it was, but there was something in the sound so strange, that it made me tremble all over. The other horses were now all awake, some were pulling at their halters, others were stamping.

At last I heard steps outside, and the ostler who had put up the traveller's horse, burst into the stable with a lantern, and began to untie the horses, and try to lead them out; but he seemed in such a hurry, and so frightened himself that he frightened me still more. The first horse would not go with him; he tried the second and third, they too would not stir. He came to me next and tried to drag me out of the stall by force; of course that was no use. He tried us all by turns and then left the stable.

No doubt we were very foolish, but danger seemed to be all round, and there was nobody we knew to trust in, and all was strange and uncertain. The fresh air that had come in through the open door made it easier to breathe, but the rushing sound overhead grew louder, and as I looked upward, through the bars of my empty rack, I saw a red light flickering on the wall. Then I heard a cry of "Fire" outside, and the old ostler quietly and quickly came in; he got one horse out, and went to another, but the flames were playing round the trap door, and the roaring overhead was dreadful.

The next thing I heard was James's voice, quiet and cheery, as it always was.

"Come, my beauties, it is time for us to be off, so wake up and come along." I stood nearest the door, so he came to me first, patting me as he came in.

"Come, Beauty, on with your bridle, my boy, we'll soon be out of this smother." It was on in no time; then he took the scarf off his neck, and tied it lightly over my eyes, and patting and coaxing he led me out of the stable. Safe in the yard, he slipped the scarf off my eyes, and shouted, "Here, somebody! take this horse while I go back for the other."

A tall broad man stepped forward and took me, and James darted back into the stable. I set up a shrill whinny as I saw him go. Ginger told me afterwards, that whinny was the best thing I could have done for her, for had she not heard me outside, she would never have had courage to come out.

There was much confusion in the yard; the horses being got out of other stables, and the carriages and gigs being pulled out of houses and sheds, lest the flames should spread further. On the other side of the yard, windows were thrown up, and people were shouting all sorts of things; but I kept my eye fixed on the stable door, where the smoke poured out thicker than ever, and I could see flashes of red light; presently I heard above all the stir and din a loud clear voice, which I knew was master's:—

"James Howard! James Howard! are you there?" There was no answer, but I heard a crash of something falling in the stable, and the next moment I gave a loud joyful neigh, for I saw James coming through the smoke leading Ginger with him; she was coughing violently and he was not able to speak.

"My brave lad!" said master, laying his hand on his shoulder, "are you hurt?"

James shook his head, for he could not yet speak.

"Aye," said the big man who held me; "he is a brave lad and no mistake."

"And now," said master, "when you have got your breath, James, we'll get out of this place as quickly as we can," and we were moving towards the entry, when from the Market Place there came a sound of galloping feet and loud rumbling wheels.

"'Tis the fire engine! the fire engine!" shouted two or three voices, "stand back, make way!" and clattering and thundering over the stones two horses dashed into the yard with the heavy engine behind them. The fireman[1] leaped to the ground; there was no need to ask where the fire was—it was torching up in a great blaze from the roof.

We got out as fast as we could into the broad quiet Market Place: the stars were shining, and except the noise behind us, all was still. Master led the way to a large Hotel on the other side, and as soon as the ostler came, he said, "James, I must now hasten to your mistress; I trust the horses entirely to you, order whatever you think is needed," and with that he was gone. The master did not run, but I never saw mortal man walk so fast as he did that night.

There was a dreadful sound before we got into our stalls; the shrieks of those poor horses that were left burning to death in the stable—it was very terrible! and made both Ginger and me feel very bad. We, however, were taken in and well done by.

The next morning the master came to see how we were and to speak to James. I did not hear much, for the ostler was rubbing me down, but I could see that James looked very happy, and I thought the master was proud of him. Our mistress had been so much alarmed in the night, that the journey was put off till the afternoon, so James had the morning on hand, and went first to the Inn to see about our harness and the carriage, and then to hear more about the fire. When he came back, we heard him tell the ostler about it. At first no one could guess how the fire had been caused, but at last a man said he saw Dick Towler go into the stable with a pipe in his mouth, and when he came out he had not one, and went to the tap[2] for another. Then the under ostler said he had asked Dick to go up the ladder to put down some hay, but told him to lay down his pipe first. Dick denied taking the pipe with him, but no one believed him. I remembered our John Manly's rule, never to allow a pipe in the stable, and thought it ought to be the rule everywhere.

James said the roof and floor had all fallen in, and that only the black walls were standing; the two poor horses that could not be got out, were buried under the burnt rafters and tiles.

---

1 Victorian fire engines had small crews; the director secured help from bystanders at the scene to work the engine while the rest of the brigade manned the hoses.
2 Slang for taphouse, or pub.

CHAPTER SEVENTEEN
JOHN MANLY'S TALK

The rest of our journey was very easy, and a little after sunset we reached the house of my master's friend. We were taken into a clean snug stable; there was a kind coachman, who made us very comfortable, and who seemed to think a good deal of James when he heard about the fire.

"There is one thing quite clear, young man," he said; "your horses know who they can trust; it is one of the hardest things in the world to get horses out of a stable, when there is either fire or flood. I don't know why they won't come out, but they won't—not one in twenty."

We stopped two or three days at this place and then returned home. All went well on the journey; we were glad to be in our own stable again, and John was equally glad to see us.

Before he and James left us for the night, James said, "I wonder who is coming in my place."

"Little Joe Green at the Lodge," said John.

"Little Joe Green! why he's a child!"

"He is fourteen and a half," said John.

"But he is such a little chap!"

"Yes, he is small, but he is quick, and willing, and kind-hearted too, and then he wishes very much to come, and his father would like it; and I know the master would like to give him the chance. He said, if I thought he would not do, he would look out for a bigger boy; but I said I was quite agreeable to try him for six weeks."

"Six weeks!" said James, "why it will be six months before he can be of much use! it will make you a deal of work, John."

"Well," said John with a laugh, "work and I are very good friends; I never was afraid of work yet."

"You are a very good man," said James, "I wish I may ever be like you."

"I don't often speak of myself," said John, "but as you are going away from us out into the world, to shift for yourself, I'll just tell you how I look on these things. I was just as old as Joseph when my father and mother died of the fever, within ten days of each other, and left me and my crippled sister Nelly alone in the world, without a relation that we could look to for help. I was a farmer's boy, not earning enough to keep myself, much less both of us, and she must have gone to the workhouse, but for our mistress (Nelly calls her, her angel, and she has good right to do so). She went and hired a room for her with old widow Mallet, and she gave her knitting and needlework, when she was able to do it; and when she was ill, she sent her dinners and many nice comfortable things, and was like a mother to her. Then the master, he took me into the stable under old Norman, the coachman that was then. I had my food at the house, and my bed in the loft, and a suit of clothes and three shillings a week, so that I could help Nelly. Then there was Norman, he might have turned round and said, at his age he could not be troubled with a raw boy from the ploughtail,[1] but he was like a father to me, and took no end of pains with me. When the old man died some years after, I stepped into his place, and now of course I have top wages, and can lay by for a rainy day or a sunny day as it may happen, and Nelly is as happy as a bird. So you see, James, I am not the man that should turn up his nose at a little boy, and vex a good kind master. No! no! I shall miss you very much, James, but we shall pull through, and there's nothing like doing a kindness when 'tis put in your way, and I am glad I can do it."

"Then," said James, "you don't hold with that saying, 'Everybody look after himself, and take care of number one.'"

"No, indeed," said John, "where should I and Nelly have been, if master and mistress and old Norman had only taken care of number one? Why—she in the workhouse and I hoeing turnips! Where would Black Beauty and Ginger have been if you had only thought of number one? why, roasted to death! No, Jim, no! that is a selfish heathenish saying, whoever uses it, and any man who thinks he has nothing to do, but take care of number one, why, it's pity but what he had been drowned like a puppy or a kitten, before he got his eyes open, that's what I think," said John, with a very decided jerk of his head.

James laughed at this; but there was a thickness in his voice when he said, "You have been my best friend except my mother; I hope you won't forget me."

"No, lad, no!" said John, "and if ever I can do you a good turn, I hope you won't forget me."

The next day Joe came to the stables to learn all he could before James left. He learned to sweep the stable, to bring in the

---

1 The handles on a plough.

straw and hay; he began to clean the harness, and helped to wash the carriage, as he was quite too short to do anything in the way of grooming Ginger and me, James taught him upon Merrylegs, for he was to have full charge of him; under John. He was a nice little bright fellow, and always came whistling to his work.

Merrylegs was a good deal put out, at being "mauled about," as he said, "by a boy who knew nothing;" but towards the end of the second week, he told me confidentially, that he thought the boy would turn out well.

At last the day came when James had to leave us: cheerful as he always was, he looked quite downhearted that morning.

"You see," he said to John, "I am leaving a great deal behind; my mother and Betsey, and you, and a good master and mistress, and then the horses, and my old Merrylegs. At the new place, there will not be a soul that I shall know. If it were not that I shall get a higher place, and be able to help my mother better, I don't think I should have made up my mind to it: it is a real pinch, John."

"Aye James, lad, so it is, but I should not think much of you, if you could leave your home for the first time and not feel it; cheer up, you'll make friends there, and if you get on well—as I'm sure you will, it will be a fine thing for your mother, and she will be proud enough that you have got into such a good place as that."

So John cheered him up, but everyone was sorry to lose James; as for Merrylegs, he pined after him for several days, and went quite off his appetite. So John took him out several mornings with a leading rein, when he exercised me, and trotting and galloping by my side, got up the little fellow's spirits again, and he was soon all right.

Joe's father would often come in and give a little help, as he understood the work, and Joe took a great deal of pains to learn, and John was quite encouraged about him.

CHAPTER EIGHTEEN
Going for the Doctor

One night, a few days after James had left, I had eaten my hay
and was laid down in my straw fast asleep, when I was suddenly
awoke by the stable bell ringing very loud. I heard the door of
John's house open, and his feet running up to the Hall. He was
back again in no time; he unlocked the stable door, and came
in, calling out, "Wake up, Beauty, you must go well now, if ever
you did;" and almost before I could think, he had got the saddle
on my back and the bridle on my head; he just ran round for his
coat, and then took me at a quick trot up to the Hall door. The
Squire stood there with a lamp in his hand.

"Now John," he said, "ride for your life, that is, for your
mistress's life; there is not a moment to lose; give this note to
Dr. White; give your horse a rest at the Inn, and be back as soon
as you can."

John said, "Yes, sir," and was on my back in a minute. The
gardener who lived at the lodge had heard the bell ring, and was
ready with the gate open, and away we went through the Park, and
through the village, and down the hill till we came to the toll-gate.
John called very loud and thumped upon the door: the man was
soon out and flung open the gate. "Now," said John, "do you keep
the gate open for the Doctor; here's the money," and off we went
again. There was before us a long piece of level road by the river
side; John said to me, "Now Beauty, do your best," and so I did; I
wanted no whip nor spur, and for two miles I galloped as fast as I
could lay my feet to the ground; I don't believe that my old grandfather who won the race at Newmarket, could have gone faster.
When we came to the bridge, John pulled me up a little and patted
my neck. "Well done, Beauty! good old fellow," he said. He would
have let me go slower, but my spirit was up, and I was off again as
fast as before. The air was frosty, the moon was bright, it was very
pleasant; we came through a village, then through a dark wood,
then uphill, then downhill, till after an eight miles run we came to
the town, through the streets and into the Market Place. It was all
quite still except the clatter of my feet on the stones—everybody
was asleep. The church clock struck three as we drew up at Doctor
White's door. John rung the bell twice, and then knocked at the
door like thunder. A window was thrown up, and Doctor White
in his nightcap, put his head out and said, "What do you want?"

"Mrs. Gordon is very ill, sir; master wants you to go at once, he thinks she will die if you cannot get there—here is a note."

"Wait," he said, "I will come."

He shut the window and was soon at the door. "The worst of it is," he said, "that my horse has been out all day and is quite done up; my son has just been sent for and he has taken the other. What is to be done? can I have your horse?"

"He has come at a gallop nearly all the way, sir, and I was to give him a rest here; but I think my master would not be against it if you think fit, sir."

"All right," he said, "I will soon be ready."

John stood by me and stroked my neck, I was very hot. The Doctor came out with his riding whip, "You need not take that, sir," said John, "Black Beauty will go till he drops; take care of him, sir, if you can; I should not like harm to come to him."

"No! no! John," said the Doctor, "I hope not," and in a minute we had left John far behind.

I will not tell about our way back; the Doctor was a heavier man than John, and not so good a rider; however, I did my very best. The man at the toll-gate had it open. When we came to the hill, the Doctor drew me up, "Now, my good fellow," he said, "take some breath." I was glad he did, for I was nearly spent, but that breathing helped me on, and soon we were in the Park. Joe was at the lodge gate, my master was at the Hall door, for he had heard us coming. He spoke not a word; the Doctor went into the house with him, and Joe led me to the stable. I was glad to get home, my legs shook under me, and I could only stand and pant. I had not a dry hair on my body, the water ran down my legs, and I steamed all over—Joe used to say, like a pot on the fire. Poor Joe! He was young and small, and as yet, he knew very little, and his father, who would have helped him, had been sent to the next village; but I am sure he did the very best he knew. He rubbed my legs and my chest, but he did not put my warm cloth on me; he thought I was so hot I should not like it, then he gave me a pail full of water to drink; it was cold and very good, and I drank it all; then he gave me some hay and some corn, and thinking he had done all right, he went away. Soon I began to shake and tremble, and turned deadly cold, my legs ached, and my loins ached, and my chest ached, and I felt sore all over. Oh! how I wished for my warm thick cloth as I stood and trembled. I wished for John, but he had eight miles to walk, so I laid down in my straw and tried to go to sleep. After a long while I heard John at the door; I gave a low moan, for I was in great pain. He was at my side in a moment, stooping down by me; I could not tell him how I felt; but he seemed to know it all; he covered me up with two or three warm cloths, and then ran to the house for some hot water; he made me some warm gruel which I drank, and then I think I went to sleep.

John seemed to be very much put out. I heard him say to himself, over and over again, "Stupid boy! stupid boy! no cloth put on, and I dare say the water was cold too; boys are no good," but Joe was a good boy after all.

I was now very ill; a strong inflammation had attacked my lungs, and I could not draw my breath without pain. John nursed me night and day, he would get up two or three times in the night to come to me; my master too, often came to see me. "My poor Beauty," he said one day, "my good horse, you saved your mistress's life, Beauty! yes, you saved her life." I was very glad to hear that, for it seems the Doctor had said if we had been a little longer it would have been too late. John told my master, he never saw a horse go so fast in his life, it seemed as if the horse knew what was the matter. Of course I did, though John thought not; at least I knew as much as this, that John and I must go at the top of our speed, and that it was for the sake of the mistress.

CHAPTER NINETEEN
Only Ignorance

I do not know how long I was ill. Mr. Bond, the horse Doctor, came every day. One day he bled me; John held a pail for the blood; I felt very faint after it, and thought I should die, and I believe they all thought so too.

Ginger and Merrylegs had been moved into the other stable, so that I might be quiet, for the fever made me very quick of hearing; any little noise seemed quite loud, and I could tell everyone's footstep going to and from the house. I knew all that was going on. One night John had to give me a draught; Thomas Green came in to help him. After I had taken it and John had made me as comfortable as he could, he said he should stay half-an-hour to see how the medicine settled. Thomas said he would stay with him, so they went and sat down on a bench that had been brought into Merrylegs' stall, and put down the lantern at their feet, that I might not be disturbed with the light.

For a while both men sat silent, and then Tom Green said in a low voice,

"I wish, John, you'd say a bit of a kind word to Joe, the boy is quite broken-hearted, he can't eat his meals, and he can't smile, he says he knows it was all his fault, though he is sure he did the best he knew, and he says, if Beauty dies, no one will ever speak to him again; it goes to my heart to hear him; I think you might give him just a word, he is not a bad boy."

After a short pause, John said slowly, "You must not be too hard upon me, Tom. I know he meant no harm, I never said he did; I know he is not a bad boy, but you see I am sore myself; that horse is the pride of my heart, to say nothing of his being such a favourite with the master and mistress; and to think that his life may be flung away in this manner, is more than I can bear; but if you think I am hard on the boy, I will try to give him a good word to-morrow—that is, I mean if Beauty is better."

"Well, John! thank you, I knew you did not wish to be too hard, and I am glad you see it was only ignorance."

John's voice almost startled me as he answered, "*Only* ignorance! only *ignorance!* how can you talk about *only* ignorance? don't you know that it is the worst thing in the world, next to wickedness—and which does the most mischief heaven only knows. If people can say, Oh! I did not know, I did not mean any harm, they think it is all right. I suppose Martha Mulwash did not mean to kill that baby, when she dosed it with Dalby and soothing syrups; but she did kill it, and was tried for manslaughter."[1]

"And serve her right too," said Tom, "a woman should not undertake to nurse a tender little child without knowing what is good and what is bad for it."

"Bill Starkey," continued John, "did not mean to frighten his brother into fits, when he dressed up like a ghost, and ran after him in the moonlight; but he did; and that bright handsome little fellow, that might have been the pride of any mother's heart, is just no better than an idiot, and never will be, if he live to be eighty years old. You were a good deal cut up yourself, Tom, two weeks ago, when those young ladies left your hothouse door open, with a frosty east wind blowing right in; you said it killed a good many of your plants."

"A good many!" said Tom, "there was not one of the tender cuttings that was not nipped off; I shall have to strike all over again, and the worst of it is, that I don't know where to go to get fresh ones. I was nearly mad when I came in and saw what was done."

"And yet," said John, "I am sure the young ladies did not mean it, it was only ignorance!"

I heard no more of this conversation, for the medicine did well and sent me to sleep, and in the morning I felt much better: but I often thought of John's words when I came to know more of the world.

---

1   The use of soothing syrups that contained alcohol and narcotics was common and unregulated in the Victorian era. Incorrectly dosed, a product such as Dalby's (which contained opium) could kill an infant.

CHAPTER TWENTY
JOE GREEN

Joe Green went on very well, he learned quickly, and was so attentive and careful, that John began to trust him in many things; but as I have said, he was small of his age, and it was seldom that he was allowed to exercise either Ginger or me; but it so happened one morning that John was out with "Justice" in the luggage cart, and the master wanted a note to be taken immediately to a gentleman's house, about three miles distant, and sent his orders for Joe to saddle me and take it; adding the caution that he was to ride steadily.

The note was delivered, and we were quietly returning till we came to the brickfield; here we saw a cart heavily laden with bricks; the wheels had stuck fast in the stiff mud of some deep ruts; and the carter was shouting and flogging the two horses unmercifully. Joe pulled up. It was a sad sight. There were the two horses straining and struggling with all their might to drag the cart out, but they could not move it; the sweat streamed from their legs and flanks, their sides heaved, and every muscle was strained, whilst the man, fiercely pulling at the head of the forehorse, swore and lashed most brutally.

"Hold hard," said Joe, "don't go on flogging the horses like that, the wheels are so stuck, that they cannot move the cart." The man took no heed, but went on lashing.

"Stop! pray stop," said Joe, "I'll help you to lighten the cart, they can't move it now."

"Mind your own business, you impudent young rascal, and I'll mind mine." The man was in a towering passion, and the worse for drink, and laid on the whip again. Joe turned my head, and the next moment we were going at a round gallop towards the house of the master brickmaker. I cannot say if John would have approved of our pace, but Joe and I were both of one mind, and so angry, that we could not have gone slower.

The house stood close by the roadside. Joe knocked at the door and shouted, "Hulloa! is Mr. Clay at home?" The door was opened, and Mr. Clay himself came out.

"Hulloa! young man! you seem in a hurry; any orders from the Squire this morning?"

"No, Mr. Clay, but there's a fellow in your brickyard flogging two horses to death. I told him to stop and he wouldn't; I said I'd help him to lighten the cart, and he wouldn't; so I've come to tell you; pray sir, go." Joe's voice shook with excitement.

"Thank ye, my lad," said the man, running in for his hat; then pausing for a moment— "Will you give evidence of what you saw if I should bring the fellow up before a magistrate?"

"That I will," said Joe, "and glad too." The man was gone; and we were on our way home at a smart trot.

"Why, what's the matter with you, Joe? you look angry all over," said John, as the boy flung himself from the saddle.

"I am angry all over, I can tell you," said the boy, and then in hurried excited words he told all that had happened. Joe was usually such a quiet gentle little fellow, that it was wonderful to see him so roused.

"Right, Joe! you did right, my boy, whether the fellow gets a summons or not. Many folks would have ridden by and said 'twas not their business to interfere. Now I say, that with cruelty and oppression, it is everybody's business to interfere when they see it; you did right, my boy."

Joe was quite calm by this time, and proud that John approved of him, and he cleaned out my feet, and rubbed me down with a firmer hand than usual.

They were just going home to dinner when the footman came down to the stable to say, that, Joe was wanted directly in master's private room; there was a man brought up for ill-using horses, and Joe's evidence was wanted. The boy flushed up to his forehead, and his eyes sparkled. "They shall have it," said he.

"Put yourself a bit straight," said John. Joe gave a pull at his necktie and a twitch at his jacket, and was off in a moment. Our master being one of the county magistrates, cases were often brought to him to settle, or say what should be done. In the stable we heard no more for some time, as it was the men's dinner hour, but when Joe came next into the stable I saw he was in high spirits; he gave me a good-natured slap and said, "We won't see such things done, will we, old fellow?" We heard afterwards, that he had given his evidence so clearly, and the horses were in such an exhausted state, bearing marks of such brutal usage, that the carter was committed to take his trial, and might possibly be sentenced to two or three months in prison.

It was wonderful what a change had come over Joe. John laughed and said, he had grown an inch taller in that week, and I believe he had. He was just as kind and gentle as before, but there was more purpose and determination in all that he did—as if he had jumped at once from a boy into a man.

CHAPTER TWENTY ONE
The Parting

I had now lived in this happy place three years, but sad changes were about to come over us. We heard from time to time that our mistress was ill. The Doctor was often at the house, and the master looked grave and anxious. Then we heard that she must leave her home at once and go to a warm country for two or three years. The news fell upon the household like the tolling of a death-bell, everybody was sorry; but the master began directly to make arrangements for breaking up his establishment and leaving England. We used to hear it talked about in our stable; indeed nothing else was talked about.

John went about his work silent and sad, and Joe scarcely whistled. There was a great deal of coming and going; Ginger and I had full work.

The first of the party who went were Miss Jessie and Flora with their governess. They came to bid us good bye. They hugged poor Merrylegs like an old friend, and so indeed he was. Then we heard what had been arranged for us. Master had sold Ginger and me to his old friend the Earl of W—, for he thought we should have a good place there. Merrylegs he had given to the Vicar, who was wanting a pony for Mrs. Blomefield, but it was on the condition, that he should never be sold, and when he was past work that he should be shot and buried.[1]

Joe was engaged to take care of him, and to help in the house, so I thought that Merrylegs was well off. John had the offer of several good places, but he said he should wait a little and look round.

The evening before they left, the master came into the stable to give some directions and to give his horses the last pat. He seemed very low-spirited; I knew that by his voice. I believe we horses can tell more by the voice than many men can.

"Have you decided what to do, John?" he said. "I find you have not accepted either of those offers."

---

1 Euthanizing horses in this manner was considered a kind alternative to selling them to be slaughtered and their carcasses rendered into products such as pet food, bone meal fertilizer, and hides for the furniture trade.

"No, sir, I have made up my mind that if I could get a situation with some first-rate colt-breaker and horse-trainer, that it would be the right thing for me. Many young animals are frightened and spoiled by wrong treatment, which need not be, if the right man took them in hand. I always get on well with horses, and if I could help some of them to a fair start, I should feel as if I was doing some good. What do you think of it, sir?"

"I don't know a man anywhere," said master, "that I should think so suitable for it as yourself. You understand horses, and somehow they understand you, and in time you might set up for yourself; I think you could not do better. If in any way I can help you, write to me; I shall speak to my agent in London, and leave your character with him."

Master gave John the name and address, and then he thanked him for his long and faithful service; but that was too much for John. "Pray don't, sir, I can't hear it; you and my dear mistress have done so much for me that I could never repay it; but we shall never forget you, sir, and please God we may someday see mistress back again like herself; we must keep up hope, sir." Master gave John his hand, but he did not speak, and they both left the stable.

The last sad day had come; the footman and the heavy luggage had gone off the day before, and there was only master and mistress and her maid. Ginger and I brought the carriage up to the Hall door for the last time. The servants brought out cushions and rugs and many other things, and when all were arranged, master came down the steps carrying the mistress in his arms (I was on the side next the house and could see all that went on); he placed her carefully in the carriage, while the house servants stood round crying. "Good bye again," he said, "we shall not forget any of you," and he got in—"Drive on, John." Joe jumped up, and we trotted slowly through the Park, and through the village, where the people were standing at their doors to have a last look and to say, "God bless them."

When we reached the railway station, I think mistress walked from the carriage to the waiting room. I heard her say in her own sweet voice, "Good bye, John, God bless you." I felt the rein twitch, but John made no answer, perhaps he could not speak. As soon as Joe had taken the things out of the carriage, John called him to stand by the horses, while he went on the platform. Poor Joe! he stood close up to our heads to hide his tears. Very soon the train came puffing up into the station; then two or three minutes, and the doors were slammed to; the guard whistled and the train glided away, leaving behind it only clouds of white smoke, and some very heavy hearts.

When it was quite out of sight, John came back—"We shall never see her again," he said, "never." He took the reins, mounted the box, and with Joe drove slowly home; but it was not our home now.

PART II.

CHAPTER TWENTY TWO
EARLSHALL

The next morning after breakfast, Joe put Merrylegs into the mistress's low chaise to take him to the vicarage; he came first and said good bye to us, and Merrylegs neighed to us from the yard. Then John put the saddle on Ginger and the leading rein on me, and rode us across the country, about fifteen miles to Earlshall Park, where the Earl of W— lived. There was a very fine house and a great deal of stabling; we went into the yard through a stone gateway, and John asked for Mr. York. It was some time before he came. He was a fine-looking middle-aged man, and his voice said at once that he expected to be obeyed. He was very friendly and polite to John, and after giving us a slight look, he called a groom to take us to our boxes, and invited John to take some refreshment.

We were taken to a light airy stable, and placed in boxes adjoining each other, where we were rubbed down and fed. In about half-an-hour John and Mr. York, who was to be our new coachman, came in to see us. "Now Mr. Manly," he said, after carefully looking at us both, "I can see no fault in these horses, but we all know that horses have their peculiarities as well as men, and that sometimes they need different treatment; I should like to know if there is anything particular in either of these, that you would like to mention."

"Well," said John, "I don't believe there is a better pair of horses in the country, and right grieved I am to part with them, but they are not alike; the black one is the most perfect temper I ever knew; I suppose he has never known a hard word or a blow since he was foaled, and all his pleasure seems to be to do what you wish; but the chestnut I fancy must have had bad treatment; we heard as much from the dealer. She came to us snappish and suspicious, but when she found what sort of place ours was, it all went off by degrees; for three years I have never seen the smallest sign of temper, and if she is well treated there is not a better, more willing animal than she is; but she is naturally a more irritable constitution than the black horse; flies tease her more; anything wrong in the harness frets her more; and if she were ill-used or unfairly treated she would not be unlikely to give tit for tat; you know that many high mettled horses will do so."

"Of course," said York, "I quite understand, but you know it is not easy in stables like these to have all the grooms just what they should be; I do my best, and there I must leave it. I'll remember what you have said about the mare."

They were going out of the stable, when John stopped and said, "I had better mention that we have never used the 'bearing rein' with either of them; the black horse never had one on, and the dealer said it was the gag-bit that spoiled the other's temper."

"Well," said York, "if they come here, they must wear the bearing rein. I prefer a loose rein myself, and his lordship is always very reasonable about horses; but my lady—that's another thing, she will have style; and if her carriage horses are not reined up tight, she wouldn't look at them. I always stand out against the gag-bit, and shall do so, but it must be tight up when my lady rides!"

"I am sorry for it, very sorry," said John, "but I must go now, or I shall lose the train."

He came round to each of us to pat and speak to us for the last time; his voice sounded very sad.

I held my face close to him, that was all I could do to say good bye; and then he was gone, and I have never seen him since.

The next day Lord W— came to look at us; he seemed pleased with our appearance.

"I have great confidence in these horses," he said, "from the character my friend Mr. Gordon has given me of them. Of course they are not a match in colour, but my idea is, that they will do very well for the carriage whilst we are in the country. Before we go to London I must try to match Baron; the black horse, I believe, is perfect for riding."

York then told him what John had said about us. "Well," said he, "you must keep an eye to the mare, and put the bearing rein easy; I dare say they will do very well with a little humouring at first. I'll mention it to your lady."

In the afternoon we were harnessed and put in the carriage, and as the stable clock struck three we were led round to the front of the house. It was all very grand, and three or four times as large as the old house at Birtwick, but not half so pleasant, if a horse may have an opinion. Two footmen were standing ready, dressed in drab livery, with scarlet breeches and white stockings.

Presently we heard the rustling sound of silk as my lady came down the flight of stone steps. She stepped round to look at us; she was a tall, proud-looking woman, and did not seem pleased about something, but she said nothing, and got into the carriage. This was the first time of wearing a bearing rein, and I must say though it certainly was a nuisance not to be able to get my head down now and then, it did not pull my head higher than I was accustomed to carry it. I felt anxious about Ginger, but she seemed to be quiet and content.

The next day at three o'clock we were again at the door, and the footmen as before; we heard the silk dress rustle, and the lady came down the steps and in an imperious voice, she said, "York, you must put those horses' heads higher, they are not fit to be seen." York got down and said very respectfully, "I beg your pardon, my lady, but these horses have not been reined up for three years, and my lord said it would be safer to bring them to it by degrees; but if your ladyship pleases, I can take them up a little more."

"Do so," she said.

York came round to our heads and shortened the rein himself, one hole I think; every little makes a difference, be it for better or worse, and that day we had a steep hill to go up. Then I began to understand what I had heard of. Of course I wanted to put my head forward and take the carriage up with a will, as we had been used to do; but no, I had to pull with my head up now, and that took all the spirit out of me, and the strain came on my back and legs. When we came in, Ginger said, "Now you see what it is like, but this is not bad, and if it does not get much worse than this, I shall say nothing about it, for we are very well treated here; but if they strain me up tight, why, let 'em look out! I can't bear it, and I won't."

Day by day, hole by hole our bearing reins were shortened, and instead of looking forward with pleasure to having my harness put on as I used to do, I began to dread it. Ginger too seemed restless, though she said very little. At last I thought the worst was over; for several days there was no more shortening, and I determined to make the best of it and do my duty, though it was now a constant harass instead of a pleasure; but the worst was not come.

CHAPTER TWENTY THREE

A STRIKE FOR LIBERTY

One day my lady came down later than usual, and the silk rustled more than ever.

"Drive to the Duchess of B's," she said, and then after a pause—"Are you never going to get those horses' heads up, York? Raise them up at once, and let us have no more of this humouring and nonsense."

York came to me first, whilst the groom stood at Ginger's head. He drew my head back and fixed the rein so tight that it was almost intolerable; then he went to Ginger, who was impatiently jerking her head up and down against the bit, as was her way now. She had a good idea of what was coming, and the moment York took the rein off the terret[1] in order to shorten it, she took her opportunity, and reared up so suddenly, that York had his nose roughly hit, and his hat knocked off; the groom was nearly thrown off his legs. At once they both flew to her head, but she was a match for them, and went on plunging, rearing, and kicking in a most desperate manner; at last she kicked right over the carriage pole and fell down, after giving me a severe blow on my near quarter. There is no knowing what further mischief she might have done, had not York promptly sat himself down flat on her head, to prevent her struggling, at the same time calling out, "Unbuckle the black horse! run for the winch and unscrew the carriage pole; cut the trace here—somebody, if you can't unhitch it." One of the footmen ran for the winch, and another brought a knife from the house. The groom soon set me free from Ginger and the carriage, and led me to my box. He just turned me in as I was, and ran back to York. I was much excited by what had happened, and if I had ever been used to kick or rear, I am sure I should have done it then; but I never had, and there I stood angry, sore in my leg, my head still strained up to the terret on the saddle, and no power to get it down. I was very miserable, and felt much inclined to kick the first person who came near me.

Before long, however, Ginger was led in by two grooms, a good deal knocked about and bruised. York came with her and gave his orders, and then came to look at me. In a moment he let down my head.

---

1 Metal loops on the harness through which the reins are threaded to keep them from tangling.

"Confound these bearing reins!" he said to himself; "I thought we should have some mischief soon—master will be sorely vexed; but there—if a woman's husband can't rule her, of course a servant can't; so I wash my hands of it, and if she can't get to the Duchess' garden party, I can't help it." York did not say this before the men; he always spoke respectfully when they were by. Now, he felt me all over, and soon found the place above my hock where I had been kicked. It was swelled and painful; he ordered it to be sponged with hot water, and then some lotion was put on.

Lord W— was much put out when he learned what had happened; he blamed York for giving way to his mistress, to which he replied, that in future he would much prefer to receive his orders only from his lordship; but I think nothing came of it, for things went on the same as before. I thought York might have stood up better for his horses, but perhaps I am no judge.

Ginger was never put into the carriage again, but when she was well of her bruises, one of Lord W's younger sons said he should like to have her; he was sure she would make a good hunter. As for me, I was obliged still to go in the carriage, and had a fresh partner called Max; he had always been used to the tight rein. I asked him how it was he bore it. "Well," he said, "I bear it because I must, but it is shortening my life, and so it will yours, if you have to stick to it."

"Do you think," I said, "that our masters know how bad it is for us?"

"I can't say," he replied, "but the dealers and the horse doctors know it very well. I was at a dealer's once, who was training me and another horse to go as a pair; he was getting our heads up as he said, a little higher and a little higher every day. A gentleman who was there asked him why he did so; 'Because,' said he, 'people won't buy them unless we do. The London people always want their horses to carry their heads high, and to step high; of course it is very bad for the horses, but then it is good for trade. The horses soon wear up, or get diseased, and they come for another pair. That," said Max, "is what he said in my hearing, and you can judge for yourself."

What I suffered with that rein for four long months in my lady's carriage, it would be hard to describe, but I am quite sure that, had it lasted much longer, either my health or my temper would have given way. Before that, I never knew what it was to foam at the mouth, but now the action of the sharp bit on my tongue and jaw, and the constrained position of my head and throat, always caused me to froth at the mouth more or less. Some people think it very fine to see this, and say, "What fine-spirited creatures!" But it is just as unnatural for horses as for men, to foam at the mouth. It is a sure sign of something wrong, and generally proceeds from suffering. Besides this, there was a pressure on my windpipe, which often made my breathing very uncomfortable; when I returned from my work, my neck and chest were strained and painful, my mouth and tongue tender, and I felt worn and depressed.

In my old home, I always knew that John and my master were my friends; but here, although in many ways I was well treated, I had no friend. York might have known, and very likely did know, how that rein harassed me; but I suppose he took it as a matter of course that could not be helped; at any rate nothing was done to relieve me.

CHAPTER TWENTY FOUR
THE LADY ANNE, OR A RUNAWAY HORSE

Early in the spring, Lord W— and part of his family went up to London, and took York with them. I and Ginger and some other horses were left at home for use, and the head groom was left in charge.

The Lady Harriet, who remained at the Hall, was a great invalid, and never went out in the carriage, and the Lady Anne preferred riding on horseback with her brother, or cousins. She was a perfect horse-woman, and as gay and gentle as she was beautiful. She chose me for her horse, and named me "Black Auster."[1] I enjoyed these rides very much in the clear cold air, sometimes with Ginger, sometimes with Lizzie. This Lizzie was a bright bay mare, almost thoroughbred, and a great favourite with the gentlemen, on account of her fine action and lively spirit; but Ginger, who knew more of her than I did, told me she was rather nervous.

There was a gentleman of the name of Blantyre staying at the Hall; he always rode Lizzie, and praised her so much, that one day Lady Anne ordered the side-saddle to be put on her, and the other saddle on me. When we came to the door, the gentleman seemed very uneasy. "How is this?" he said, "are you tired of your good Black Auster?"

"Oh! no, not at all," she replied, "but I am amiable enough to let you ride him for once, and I will try your charming Lizzie. You must confess that in size and appearance she is far more like a lady's horse than my own favourite."

"Do let me advise you not to mount her," he said; "she is a charming creature, but she is too nervous for a lady. I assure you she is not perfectly safe; let me beg you to have the saddles changed."

"My dear cousin," said Lady Anne, laughing, "pray do not trouble your good careful head about me; I have been a horse-woman ever since I was a baby, and I have followed the hounds a great many times, though I know you do not approve of ladies hunting; but still that is the fact, and I intend to try this Lizzie that you gentlemen are all so fond of; so please help me to mount like a good friend as you are."

---

1 In Roman mythology, the embodiment of sirocco, or south wind, that brings storms.

There was no more to be said, he placed her carefully on the saddle, looked to the bit and curb, gave the reins gently into her hand, and then mounted me. Just as we were moving off, a footman came out with a slip of paper and message from the Lady Harriet—"Would they ask this question for her at Dr. Ashley's, and bring the answer?"

The village was about a mile off, and the Doctor's house was the last in it. We went along gaily enough till we came to his gate. There was a short drive up to the house between tall evergreens. Blantyre alighted at the gate and was going to open it for Lady Anne, but she said, "I will wait for you here, and you can hang Auster's rein on the gate."

He looked at her doubtfully—"I will not be five minutes," he said.

"Oh, do not hurry yourself; Lizzie and I shall not run away from you."

He hung my rein on one of the iron spikes, and was soon hidden amongst the trees. Lizzie was standing quietly by the side of the road a few paces off, with her back to me. My young mistress was sitting easily with a loose rein, humming a little song. I listened to my rider's footsteps until they reached the house, and heard him knock at the door. There was a meadow on the opposite side of the road, the gate of which stood open; just then, some cart horses and several young colts came trotting out in a very disorderly manner, whilst a boy behind was cracking a great whip. The colts were wild and frolicksome, and one of them bolted across the road, and blundered up against Lizzie's hind legs; and whether it was the stupid colt, or the loud cracking of the whip, or both together, I cannot say, but she gave a violent kick, and dashed off into a headlong gallop. It was so sudden, that Lady Anne was nearly unseated, but she soon recovered herself. I gave a loud shrill neigh for help: again and again I neighed, pawing the ground impatiently, and tossing my head to get the rein loose. I had not long to wait. Blantyre came running to the gate; he looked anxiously about, and just caught sight of the flying figure, now, far away on the road. In an instant he sprang to the saddle. I needed no whip, or spur, for I was as eager as my rider: he saw it, and giving me a free rein, and leaning a little forward, we dashed after them.

For about a mile and a half, the road ran straight, and then bent to the right, after which it divided into two roads. Long before we came to the bend, she was out of sight. Which way had she turned? A woman was standing at her garden gate, shading her eyes with her hand, and looking eagerly up the road. Scarcely drawing the rein, Blantyre shouted, "Which way?" "To the right," cried the woman, pointing with her hand, and away we went up the right-hand road; then, for a moment we caught sight of her; another bend, and she was hidden again. Several times we caught glimpses, and then lost them. We scarcely seemed to gain ground upon them at all. An old road-mender was standing near a heap of stones—his shovel dropped, and his hands raised. As we came near he made a sign to speak. Blantyre drew the rein a little. "To the common, to the common, sir; she has turned off there." I knew this common very well; it was for the most part very uneven ground, covered with heather and dark green furze bushes, with here and there a scrubby old thorn tree; there were also open spaces of fine short grass, with anthills and mole turns everywhere; the worst place I ever knew for a headlong gallop.

We had hardly turned on the common, when we caught sight again of the green habit flying on before us. My lady's hat was gone, and her long brown hair was streaming behind her. Her head and body were thrown back, as if she were pulling with all her remaining strength, and as if that strength were nearly exhausted. It was clear that the roughness of the ground had very much lessened Lizzie's speed, and there seemed a chance that we might overtake her.

Whilst we were on the high road, Blantyre had given me my head; but now with a light hand and a practised eye, he guided me over the ground in such a masterly manner, that my pace was scarcely slackened, and we were decidedly gaining on them.

About half way across the heath there had been a wide dyke recently cut, and the earth from the cutting was cast up roughly on the other side.

Surely this would stop them! but no; with scarcely a pause Lizzie took the leap, stumbled among the rough clods, and fell. Blantyre groaned, "Now Auster, do your best!" he gave me a steady rein, I gathered myself well together, and with one determined leap cleared both dyke and bank.

Motionless among the heather, with her face to the earth, lay my poor young mistress. Blantyre kneeled down and called her name—there was no sound; gently he turned her face upward, it was ghastly white, and the eyes were closed. "Annie, dear Annie, do speak!" but there was no answer. He unbuttoned her habit, loosened her collar, felt her hands and wrist, then started up and looked wildly round him for help.

At no great distance there were two men cutting turf, who seeing Lizzie running wild without a rider had left their work to catch her.

Blantyre's halloo soon brought them to the spot. The foremost man seemed much troubled at the sight, and asked what he could do.

"Can you ride?"

"Well, sir, I bean't much of a horseman, but I'd risk my neck for the Lady Anne; she was uncommon good to my wife in the winter."

"Then mount this horse, my friend; your neck will be quite safe, and ride to the Doctor's, and ask him to come instantly—then on to the Hall—tell them all that you know, and bid them send the carriage with Lady Anne's maid and help. I shall stay here."

"All right, sir, I'll do my best, and I pray God the dear young lady may open her eyes soon." Then seeing the other man, he called out, "Here, Joe, run for some water, and tell my missis to come as quick as she can to the Lady Anne." He then somehow scrambled into the saddle, and with a "Gee up" and a clap on my sides with both his legs, he started on his journey, making a little circuit to avoid the dyke. He had no whip, which seemed to trouble him, but my pace soon cured that difficulty, and he found the best thing he could do was to stick to the saddle, and hold me in, which he did manfully. I shook him as little as I could help, but once or twice on the rough ground he called out, "Steady! Woah! Steady." On the high road we were all right; and at the Doctor's, and the Hall, he did his errand like a good man and true. They asked him in to take a drop of something. "No! no," he said, "I'll be back to 'em again by a short cut through the fields, and be there afore the carriage."

There was a great deal of hurry and excitement after the news became known. I was just turned into my box, the saddle and bridle were taken off, and a cloth thrown over me.

Ginger was saddled and sent off in great haste for Lord George, and I soon heard the carriage roll out of the yard.

It seemed a long time before Ginger came back, and before we were left alone; then she told me all that she had seen.

"I can't tell much," she said; "we went a gallop nearly all the way, and got there just as the Doctor rode up. There was a woman sitting on the ground with the lady's head in her lap. The Doctor poured something into her mouth, but all that I heard was, "she is not dead." Then I was led off by a man to a little distance. After a while she was taken to the carriage, and we came home together. I heard my master say to a gentleman who stopped him to enquire, that he hoped no bones were broken, but that she had not spoken yet."

When Lord George took Ginger for hunting, York shook his head; he said it ought to be a steady hand to train a horse for the first season, and not a random rider like Lord George.

Ginger used to like it very much, but sometimes when she came back, I could see that she had been very much strained, and now and then she gave a short cough. She had too much spirit to complain, but I could not help feeling anxious about her.

Two days after the accident, Blantyre paid me a visit: he patted me and praised me very much, he told Lord George that he was sure the horse knew of Annie's danger as well as he did. "I could not have held him in, if I would," said he; "she ought never to ride any other horse." I found by their conversation, that my young mistress was now out of danger, and would soon be able to ride again. This was good news to me, and I looked forward to a happy life.

I must now say a little about Reuben Smith, who was left in charge of the stables when York went to London. No one more thoroughly understood his business than he did, and when he was all right, there could not be a more faithful or valuable man. He was gentle and very clever in his management of horses, and could doctor them almost as well as a farrier, for he had lived two years with a veterinary surgeon. He was a first-rate driver; he could take a four-in-hand, or a tandem,[1] as easily as a pair. He was a handsome man, a good scholar, and had very pleasant manners. I believe everybody liked him; certainly the horses did; the only wonder was, that he should be in an under situation, and not in the place of a head coachman like York: but he had one great fault, and that was the love of drink. He was not like some men, always at it; he used to keep steady for weeks or months together, and then he would break out and have a "bout" of it, as York called it, and be a disgrace to himself, a terror to his wife, and a nuisance to all that had to do with him. He was, however, so useful, that two or three times York had hushed the matter up, and kept it from the Earl's knowledge; but one night, when Reuben had to drive a party home from a ball, he was so drunk that he could not hold the reins, and a gentleman of the party had to mount the box and drive the ladies home. Of course this could not be hidden, and Reuben was at once dismissed; his poor wife and little children had to turn out of the pretty cottage by the Park gate and go where they could. Old Max told me all this, for it happened a good while ago; but shortly before Ginger and I came, Smith had been taken back again. York had interceded for him with the Earl, who is very kind-hearted, and the man had promised faithfully that he would never taste another drop as long as he lived there. He had kept his promise so well, that York thought he might be safely trusted to fill his place whilst he was away, and he was so clever and honest, that no one else seemed so well fitted for it.

It was now early in April, and the family was expected home sometime in May. The light brougham was to be fresh done up, and as Colonel Blantyre was obliged to return to his regiment, it was arranged that Smith should drive him to the town in it, and

---

1 Both forms of driving require great skill.

ride back; for this purpose, he took the saddle with him, and I was chosen for the journey. At the station the Colonel put some money into Smith's hand and bid him good bye, saying, "Take care of your young mistress, Reuben, and don't let Black Auster be hacked about by any random young prig that wants to ride him—keep him for the lady."

We left the carriage at the maker's, and Smith rode me to the White Lion, and ordered the ostler to feed me well and have me ready for him at four o'clock. A nail in one of my front shoes had started as I came along, but the ostler did not notice it till just about four o'clock. Smith did not come into the yard till five, and then he said he should not leave till six, as he had met with some old friends. The man then told him of the nail and asked if he should have the shoe looked to. "No," said Smith, "that will be all right till we get home." He spoke in a very loud off-hand way, and I thought it very unlike him, not to see about the shoe, as he was generally wonderfully particular about loose nails in their shoes. He did not come at six, nor seven, nor eight, and it was nearly nine o'clock before he called for me, and then it was with a loud rough voice. He seemed in a very bad temper, and abused the ostler, though I could not tell what for.

The landlord stood at the door and said, "Have a care, Mr. Smith!" but he answered angrily with an oath; and almost before he was out of the town he began to gallop, frequently giving me a sharp cut with his whip, though I was going at full speed. The moon had not yet risen, and it was very dark. The roads were stony, having been recently mended; going over them at this pace, my shoe soon became looser, and when we were near the turnpike gate, it came off.

If Smith had been in his right senses, he would have been sensible of something wrong in my pace; but he was too madly drunk to notice anything.

Beyond the turnpike was a long piece of road, upon which fresh stones had just been laid; large sharp stones, over which no horse could be driven quickly without risk of danger. Over this road, with one shoe gone, I was forced to gallop at my utmost speed, my rider meanwhile cutting into me with his whip, and with wild curses urging me to go still faster. Of course my shoe-less foot suffered dreadfully; the hoof was broken and split down to the very quick, and the inside was terribly cut by the sharpness of the stones.

This could not go on; no horse could keep his footing under such circumstances, the pain was too great. I stumbled, and fell with violence on both my knees. Smith was flung off by my fall, and owing to the speed I was going at, he must have fallen with great force. I soon recovered my feet and limped to the side of the road, where it was free from stones. The moon had just risen above the hedge, and by its light I could see Smith lying a few yards beyond me. He did not rise, he made one slight effort to do so, and then, there was a heavy groan. I could have groaned too, for I was suffering intense pain both from my foot and knees; but horses are used to bear their pain in silence. I uttered no sound, but I stood there and listened. One more heavy groan from Smith; but though he now lay in the full moonlight, I could see no motion. I could do nothing for him nor myself, but, oh! how I listened for the sound of horse, or wheels, or footsteps. The road was not much frequented, and at this time of the night, we might stay for hours before help came to us. I stood watching and listening. It was a calm sweet April night; there were no sounds, but a few low notes of a nightingale, and nothing moved but the white clouds near the moon, and a brown owl that flitted over the hedge. It made me think of the summer nights long ago, when I used to lie beside my mother in the green pleasant meadow at Farmer Grey's.

CHAPTER TWENTY SIX
How It Ended

It must have been nearly midnight, when I heard at a great distance the sound of a horse's feet. Sometimes the sound died away, then it grew clearer again and nearer. The road to Earlshall led through plantations that belonged to the Earl: the sound came in that direction, and I hoped it might be someone coming in search of us. As the sound came nearer and nearer, I was almost sure I could distinguish Ginger's step; a little nearer still, and I could tell she was in the dog-cart. I neighed loudly, and was overjoyed to hear an answering neigh from Ginger, and men's voices. They came slowly over the stones, and stopped at the dark figure that lay upon the ground.

One of the men jumped out, and stooped down over it. "It is Reuben!" he said, "and he does not stir."

The other man followed and bent over him, "He's dead," he said; "feel how cold his hands are." They raised him up, but there was no life, and his hair was soaked with blood. They laid him down again and came and looked at me. They soon saw my cut knees.

"Why, the horse has been down and thrown him! who would have thought the black horse would have done that? nobody thought he could fall. Reuben must have been lying here for hours! Odd too, that the horse has not moved from the place."

Robert then attempted to lead me forward. I made a step, but almost fell again. "Halloo! he's bad in his foot as well as his knees; look here—his hoof is cut all to pieces, he might well come down, poor fellow! I tell you what, Ned, I'm afraid it hasn't been all right with Reuben! Just think of him riding a horse over these stones without a shoe! why, if he had been in his right senses, he would just as soon have tried to ride him over the moon; I'm afraid it has been the old thing over again. Poor Susan! she looked awfully pale when she came to my house to ask if he had not come home. She made believe she was not a bit anxious, and talked of a lot of things that might have kept him. But for all that, she begged me to go and meet him—but what must we do? There's the horse to get home as well as the body—and that will be no easy matter."

Then followed a conversation between them, till it was

agreed that Robert as the groom should lead me, and that Ned must take the body. It was a hard job to get it into the dog-cart, for there was no one to hold Ginger; but she knew as well as I did, what was going on, and stood as still as a stone. I noticed that, because, if she had a fault, it was that she was impatient in standing.

Ned started off very slowly with his sad load, and Robert came and looked at my foot again; then he took his handkerchief and bound it closely round, and so he led me home. I shall never forget that night walk; it was more than three miles. Robert led me on very slowly, and I limped and hobbled on as well as I could with great pain. I am sure he was sorry for me, for he often patted and encouraged me, talking to me in a pleasant voice.

At last I reached my own box, and had some corn, and after Robert had wrapped up my knees in wet cloths, he tied up my foot in a bran poultice to draw out the heat, and cleanse it before the horse doctor saw it in the morning, and I managed to get myself down on the straw, and slept in spite of the pain.

The next day, after the farrier had examined my wounds, he said he hoped the joint was not injured, and if so, I should not be spoiled for work, but I should never lose the blemish. I believe they did the best to make a good cure, but it was a long and painful one; proud flesh, as they called it, came up in my knees, and was burnt out with caustic,[1] and when at last it was healed, they put a blistering fluid over the front of both knees to bring all the hair off: they had some reason for this, and I suppose it was all right.

As Smith's death had been so sudden and no one was there to see it, there was an inquest held. The landlord and ostler at the White Lion, with several other people, gave evidence that he was intoxicated when he started from the inn. The keeper of the toll-gate said he rode at a hard gallop through the gate; and my shoe was picked up amongst the stones, so that the case was quite plain to them, and I was cleared of all blame.

Everybody pitied Susan; she was nearly out of her mind: she kept saying over and over again, "Oh! he was so good— so good! it was all that cursed drink; why will they sell that

---

1 An irritant used in the practice of blistering, which draws heat to an injury to promote healing. The practice generally causes scars.

cursed drink? Oh Reuben, Reuben!" so she went on till after he was buried; and then, as she had no home or relations, she, with her six little children, were obliged once more to leave the pleasant home by the tall oak trees, and go into that great gloomy Union House.[1]

---

1   Part of the workhouse system inaugurated by the Poor Law amendment of 1834. These institutions were built to house those on relief—such as the impoverished, orphans, the sick, and the elderly—who could not support themselves. In return for basic sustenance, inmates submitted to prison-like conditions, including hard labour. The intent of the system was to provide an option so undesirable that it would only be considered as a final resort for those in need. "Union" houses were built by groups of parishes too small to maintain a dedicated workhouse on their own.

As soon as my knees were sufficiently healed, I was turned into a small meadow for a month or two; no other creature was there, and though I enjoyed the liberty and the sweet grass, yet I had been so long used to society that I felt very lonely. Ginger and I had become fast friends, and now I missed her company extremely. I often neighed when I heard horses' feet passing in the road, but I seldom got an answer; till one morning the gate was opened, and who should come in but dear old Ginger. The man slipped off her halter and left her there. With a joyful whinny I trotted up to her; we were both glad to meet, but I soon found that it was not for our pleasure that she was brought to be with me. Her story would be too long to tell, but the end of it was that she had been ruined by hard riding, and was now turned off to see what rest would do.

Lord George was young and would take no warning; he was a hard rider, and would hunt whenever he could get the chance, quite careless of his horse. Soon after I left the stable there was a steeple chase, and he determined to ride, though the groom told him she was a little strained, and was not fit for the race. He did not believe it, and on the day of the race, urged Ginger to keep up with the foremost riders. With her high spirit, she strained herself to the utmost; she came in with the first three horses, but her wind was touched, beside which, he was too heavy for her, and her back was strained; "And so," she said, "here we are—ruined in the prime of our youth and strength—you by a drunkard, and I by a fool; it is very hard." We both felt in ourselves that we were not what we had been. However, that did not spoil the pleasure we had in each other's company; we did not gallop about as we once did, but we used to feed, and lie down together, and stand for hours under one of the shady lime trees with our heads close to each other; and so we passed our time till the family returned from town.

One day we saw the Earl come into the meadow, and York was with him. Seeing who it was, we stood still under our lime tree, and let them come up to us. They examined us carefully. The Earl seemed much annoyed. "There is three hundred pounds flung away for no earthly use," said he, "but what I care most for is, that these horses of my old friend, who thought they would find a good home with me, are ruined. The mare shall have a twelve-month's run, and we shall see what that will do for her; but the black one, he must be sold: 'tis a great pity, but I could not have knees like these in my stables."

"No, my lord, of course not," said York, "but he might get a place where appearance is not of much consequence, and still be well treated. I know a man in Bath, the master of some livery stables, who often wants a good horse at a low figure; I know he looks well after his horses. The inquest cleared the horse's character, and your lordship's recommendation, or mine, would be sufficient warrant for him."

"You had better write to him, York: I should be more particular about the place than the money he would fetch." After this they left us.

"They'll soon take you away," said Ginger, and I shall lose the only friend I have, and most likely we shall never see each other again; 'tis a hard world!"

About a week after this, Robert came into the field with a halter, which he slipped over my head and led me away. There was no leave-taking of Ginger; we neighed to each other as I was led off, and she trotted anxiously along by the hedge, calling to me as long as she could hear the sound of my feet.

Through the recommendation of York, I was bought by the master of the livery stables. I had to go by Train, which was new to me, and required a good deal of courage the first time; but as I found the puffing, rushing, whistling, and more than all, the trembling of the horse box in which I stood did me no real harm, I soon took it quietly.

When I reached the end of my journey, I found myself in a tolerably comfortable stable and well attended to. These stables were not so airy and pleasant as those I had been used to. The stalls were laid on a slope instead of being level, and as my head was kept tied to the manger I was obliged always to stand on the slope, which was very fatiguing. Men do not seem to know yet, that horses can do more work if they can stand comfortably and can turn about: however, I was well fed and well cleaned, and on the whole, I think our master took as much care of us as he could. He kept a good many horses and carriages of different kinds, for hire. Sometimes his own men drove them; at others, the horse and chaise were let to gentlemen or ladies who drove themselves.

CHAPTER TWENTY EIGHT
A Job Horse, and His Drivers

Hitherto I had always been driven by people who at least knew how to drive; but in this place, I was to get my experience of all the different kinds of bad and ignorant driving to which we horses are subjected; for I was a "job-horse," and was let out to all sorts of people, who wished to hire me; and as I was good-tempered and gentle, I think I was oftener let out to the ignorant drivers, than some of the other horses, because I could be depended upon. It would take a long time to tell of all the different styles in which I was driven, but I will mention a few of them.

First, there were the tight-rein drivers—men, who seemed to think that all depended on holding the reins as hard as they could, never relaxing the pull on the horse's mouth, or giving him the least liberty of movement. They are always talking about "keeping the horse well in hand," and "holding a horse up," just as if a horse was not made to hold himself up.

Some poor broken-down horses, whose mouths have been made hard and insensible by just such drivers as these, may, perhaps, find some support in it: but, for a horse who can depend upon his own legs, and who has a tender mouth, and is easily guided, it is not only tormenting, but it is stupid.

Then there are the loose-rein drivers, who let the reins lie easily on our backs, and their own hand rest lazily on their knees. Of course, such gentlemen have no control over a horse, if anything happens suddenly. If a horse shies, or starts, or stumbles, they are nowhere, and cannot help the horse or themselves, till the mischief is done. Of course, for myself, I had no objection to it, as I was not in the habit either of starting or stumbling, and had only been used to depend on my driver for guidance and encouragement; still, one likes to feel the rein a little in going down-hill, and likes to know, that one's driver is not gone to sleep.

Besides, a slovenly way of driving gets a horse into bad, and often lazy habits; and when he changes hands, he has to be whipped out of them with more or less pain and trouble. Squire Gordon always kept us to our best paces, and our best manners. He said that spoiling a horse, and letting him get into bad habits, was just as cruel as spoiling a child, and both had to suffer for it afterwards.

Besides, these drivers are often careless altogether, and will attend to anything else more than their horses. I went out in the phaeton one day with one of them; he had a lady, and two children behind. He flopped the reins about as we started, and of course, gave me several unmeaning cuts with the whip, though I was fairly off. There had been a good deal of road-mending going on, and even where the stones were not freshly laid down, there were a great many loose ones about. My driver was laughing and joking with the lady and the children, and talking about the country to the right and the left; but he never thought it worthwhile to keep an eye on his horse, or to drive on the smoothest parts of the road; and so it easily happened, that I got a stone in one of my fore feet.

Now if Mr. Gordon, or John, or in fact, any good driver had been there, he would have seen that something was wrong, before I had gone three paces. Or even if it had been dark, a practised hand would have felt by the rein that there was something wrong in the step, and they would have got down and picked out the stone. But this man went on laughing and talking, whilst at every step the stone became more firmly wedged between my shoe and the frog of my foot.[1] The stone was sharp on the inside and round on the outside, which as everyone knows, is the most dangerous kind that a horse can pick up; at the same time cutting his foot, and making him most liable to stumble and fall.

Whether the man was partly blind, or only very careless, I can't say; but he drove me with that stone in my foot for a good half mile before he saw anything. By that time I was going so lame with the pain, that at last he saw it and called out, "Well, here's a go! Why they have sent us out with a lame horse! What a shame!"

He then chucked the reins and nipped about with the whip, saying, "Now then, it's no use playing the old soldier with me; there's the journey to go, and it's no use turning lame and lazy."

Just at this time a farmer came riding up on a brown cob; he lifted his hat and pulled up. "I beg your pardon, sir," he said, "but I think there is something the matter with your horse, he goes very much as if he had a stone in his shoe. If you will allow me, I will look at his feet; these loose scattered stones are confounded dangerous things for the horses."

---

1 The triangular wedge of soft tissue on the bottom of the horse's hoof.

"He's a hired horse," said my driver; "I don't know what's the matter with him, but it is a great shame to send out a lame beast like this."

The farmer dismounted, and slipping his rein over his arm, at once took up my near foot. "Bless me, there's a stone! lame! I should think so!"

At first he tried to dislodge it with his hand, but, as it was now very tightly wedged, he drew a stone-pick out of his pocket, and very carefully, and with some trouble, got it out. Then holding it up, he said, "There, that's the stone your horse had picked up; it is a wonder he did not fall down and break his knees into the bargain!"

"Well, to be sure!" said my driver, "that is a queer thing! I never knew that horses picked up stones before."

"Didn't you?" said the farmer, rather contemptuously; "but they do, though, and the best of them will do it, and can't help it sometimes on such roads as these. And if you don't want to lame your horse, you must look sharp and get them out quickly. This foot is very much bruised," he said, setting it gently down and patting me. "If I might advise, sir, you had better drive him gently for a while; the foot is a good deal hurt, and the lameness will not go off directly." Then, mounting his cob and raising his hat to the lady, he trotted off.

When he was gone, my driver began to flop the reins about, and whip the harness, by which I understood that I was to go on, which of course I did, glad that the stone had gone; but still in a good deal of pain.

This was the sort of experience we job-horses often came in for.

CHAPTER TWENTY NINE
COCKNEYS

Then there is the steam-engine style of driving; these drivers were mostly people from towns, who never had a horse of their own, and generally travelled by rail.

They always seemed to think that a horse was something like a steam-engine, only smaller. At any rate, they think that if only they pay for it, a horse is bound to go just as far, and just as fast, and with just as heavy a load as they please. And be the roads heavy and muddy, or dry and good; be they stony or smooth, up-hill or down-hill, it is all the same—on, on, on, one must go at the same pace, with no relief, and no consideration.

These people never think of getting out to walk up a steep hill. Oh, no, they have paid to ride, and ride they will! The horse? Oh, he's used to it! What were horses made for, if not to drag people up-hill? Walk! A good joke indeed! And so the whip is plied and the rein is chucked, and often a rough scolding voice cries out; "Go along, you lazy beast!" And then another slash of the whip, when all the time we are doing our very best to get along, uncomplaining and obedient, though often sorely harassed and down-hearted.

This steam-engine style of driving wears us up faster than any other kind. I would far rather go twenty miles with a good considerate driver, than I would go ten with some of these; it would take less out of me.

Another thing—they scarcely ever put on the drag, however steep the down-hill may be, and thus bad accidents sometimes happen; or if they do put it on, they often forget to take it off at the bottom of the hill: and more than once, I have had to pull half way up the next hill, with one of the wheels lodged fast in the drag-shoe, before my driver chose to think about it; and that is a terrible strain on a horse.

Then these Cockneys,[1] instead of starting at an easy pace as a gentleman would do, generally set off at full speed from the very stable yard; and when they want to stop, they first whip us, and then pull up so suddenly, that we are nearly thrown on our haunches, and our mouths jagged with the bit; they call that

---

1 Working-class Londoners.

pulling up with a dash! and when they turn a corner, they do it as sharply as if there were no right side or wrong side of the road.

I well remember one spring evening I and Rory had been out for the day. (Rory was the horse that mostly went with me when a pair was ordered, and a good honest fellow he was.) We had our own driver, and as he was always considerate and gentle with us, we had a very pleasant day. We were coming home at a good smart pace about twilight; our road turned sharp to the left; but as we were close to the hedge on our own side, and there was plenty of room to pass, our driver did not pull us in. As we neared the corner I heard a horse and two wheels coming rapidly down the hill towards us. The hedge was high and I could see nothing, but the next moment we were upon each other. Happily for me I was on the side next the hedge. Rory was on the right side of the pole, and had not even a shaft to protect him. The man who was driving, was making straight for the corner, and when he came in sight of us, he had no time to pull over to his own side. The whole shock came upon Rory. The gig shaft ran right into the chest, making him stagger back with a cry that I shall never forget. The other horse was thrown upon his haunches, and one shaft broken. It turned out that it was a horse from our own stables, with the high-wheeled gig, that the young men were so fond of.

The driver was one of those random, ignorant fellows, who don't even know which is their own side of the road, or if they know, don't care. And there was poor Rory with his flesh torn open and bleeding, and the blood streaming down. They said if it had been a little more to one side, it would have killed him; and a good thing for him, poor fellow, if it had.

As it was, it was a long time before the wound healed, and then he was sold for coal carting; and what that is, up and down those steep hills, only horses know. Some of the sights I saw there, where a horse had to come down-hill with a heavily-loaded two-wheel cart behind him, on which no drag could be placed, make me sad even now to think of.

After Rory was disabled, I often went in the carriage with a mare named Peggy, who stood in the next stall to mine. She was a strong, well-made animal, of a bright dun colour, beautifully dappled, and with a dark-brown mane and tail. There was no high breeding about her, but she was very pretty, and remarkably sweet-tempered and willing. Still there was an anxious look about her eye, by which I knew that she had some trouble. The first time we went out together I thought she had a very odd pace; she seemed to go partly a trot, partly a canter—three or four paces, and then a little jump forward.

It was very unpleasant for any horse who pulled with her, and made me quite fidgetty. When we got home, I asked her what made her go in that odd, awkward way.

"Ah," she said in a troubled manner, "I know my paces are very bad, but what can I do? it really is not my fault, it is just because my legs are so short. I stand nearly as high as you, but your legs are a good three inches longer above your knee than mine, and of course you can take a much longer step, and go much faster. You see I did not make myself; I wish I could have done so, I would have had long legs then; all my troubles come from my short legs;" said Peggy, in a desponding tone.

"But how is it," I said, "when you are so strong and good-tempered and willing?"

"Why, you see," said she, "men will go so fast, and if one can't keep up to other horses, it is nothing but whip, whip, whip, all the time. And so I have had to keep up as I could, and have got into this ugly shuffling pace. It was not always so; when I lived with my first master I always went a good regular trot, but then he was not in such a hurry. He was a young clergyman in the country, and a good kind master he was. He had two churches a good way apart, and a great deal of work, but he never scolded or whipped me for not going faster. He was very fond of me. I only wish I was with him now; but he had to leave and go to a large town, and then I was sold to a farmer.

"Some farmers, you know, are capital masters; but I think this one was a low sort of man. He cared nothing about good horses, or good driving, he only cared for going fast. I went as fast as I could, but that would not do, and he was always whipping; so I got into this way of making a spring forward to keep up. On market nights he used to stay very late at the inn, and then drive home at a gallop. One dark night he was galloping home as usual, when all on a sudden the wheel came against some great heavy thing in the road, and turned the gig over in a minute. He was thrown out and his arm broken, and some of his ribs, I think. At any rate, it was the end of my living with him, and I was not sorry. But you see it will be the same everywhere for me, if men *must* go so fast. I wish my legs were longer!"

Poor Peggy! I was very sorry for her, and I could not comfort her, for I knew how hard it was upon slow-paced horses to be put with fast ones; all the whipping comes to their share, and they can't help it.

She was often used in the phaeton, and was very much liked by some of the ladies, because she was so gentle; and sometime after this she was sold to two ladies who drove themselves, and wanted a safe good horse.

I met her several times out in the country, going a good steady pace, and looking as gay and contented as a horse could be. I was very glad to see her, for she deserved a good place.

After she left us, another horse came in her stead. He was young, and had a bad name for shying and starting, by which he had lost a good place. I asked him what made him shy.

"Well, I hardly know," he said, "I was timid when I was young, and was a good deal frightened several times, and if I saw anything strange, I used to turn and look at it—you see with our blinkers, one can't see or understand what a thing is unless one looks round; and then my master always gave me a whipping, which of course made me start on, and did not make me less afraid. I think if he would have let me just look at things quietly, and see that there was nothing to hurt me, it would have been all right, and I should have got used to them. One day an old gentleman was riding with him, and a large piece of white paper or rag, blew across just on one side of me; I shied and started forward—my master as usual whipped me smartly, but the old man cried out, 'You're wrong! you're wrong! you should never whip a horse for shying: he shies because he is frightened, and you only frighten him more, and make the habit worse.' So I suppose all men don't do so. I am sure I don't want to shy for the sake of it; but how should one know what is dangerous and what is not, if one is never allowed to get used to anything? I am never afraid of what I know. Now I was brought up in a park where there were deer; of course, I knew them as well as I did a sheep or a cow, but they are not common, and I know many sensible horses who are frightened at them, and who kick up quite a shindy[1] before they will pass a paddock where there are deer."

I knew what my companion said was true, and I wished that every young horse had as good masters as Farmer Grey and Squire Gordon.

---

1 Disturbance or quarrel.

Of course we sometimes came in for good driving here. I remember one morning I was put into the light gig, and taken to a house in Pultney Street. Two gentlemen came out; the taller of them came round to my head, he looked at the bit and bridle, and just shifted the collar with his hand, to see if it fitted comfortably.

"Do you consider this horse wants a curb?" he said to the ostler.

"Well," said the man, "I should say he would go just as well without, he has an uncommon good mouth, and though he has a fine spirit, he has no vice; but we generally find people like the curb."

"I don't like it," said the gentleman; "be so good as to take it off, and put the rein in at the cheek; an easy mouth is a great thing on a long journey, is it not, old fellow?" he said, patting my neck.

Then he took the reins, and they both got up. I can remember now how quietly he turned me round, and then with a light feel of the rein, and drawing the whip gently across my back, we were off.

I arched my neck and set off at my best pace. I found I had someone behind me, who knew how a good horse ought to be driven. It seemed like old times again, and made me feel quite gay.

This gentleman took a great liking to me, and after trying me several times with the saddle, he prevailed upon my master to sell me to a friend of his, who wanted a safe pleasant horse for riding. And so it came to pass that in the summer I was sold to Mr. Barry.

CHAPTER THIRTY
A THIEF!

My new master was an unmarried man. He lived at Bath, and was much engaged in business. His doctor advised him to take horse exercise, and for this purpose he bought me. He hired a stable a short distance from his lodgings, and engaged a man named Filcher as groom. My master knew very little about horses, but he treated me well, and I should have had a good and easy place, but for circumstances of which he was ignorant. He ordered the best hay with plenty of oats, crushed beans, and bran, with vetches, or rye grass, as the man might think needful. I heard the master give the order, so I knew there was plenty of good food, and I thought I was well off.

For a few days all went on well; I found that my groom understood his business. He kept the stable clean and airy, and he groomed me thoroughly; and was never otherwise than gentle. He had been an ostler in one of the great hotels in Bath. He had given that up, and now cultivated fruit and vegetables for the market; and his wife bred and fattened poultry and rabbits for sale. After a while it seemed to me that my oats came very short; I had the beans, but bran was mixed with them instead of oats, of which there were very few; certainly not more than a quarter of what there should have been. In two or three weeks this began to tell upon my strength and spirits. The grass food, though very good, was not the thing to keep up my condition without corn. However, I could not complain, nor make known my wants. So it went on for about two months; and I wondered my master did not see that something was the matter. However, one afternoon he rode out into the country to see a friend of his—a gentleman farmer, who lived on the road to Wells. This gentleman had a very quick eye for horses; and after he had welcomed his friend, he said, casting his eye over me, "It seems to me, Barry, that your horse does not look so well as he did when you first had him; has he been well?"

"Yes, I believe so," said my master, "but he is not nearly so lively as he was; my groom tells me that horses are always dull and weak in the autumn, and that I must expect it."

"Autumn! fiddlestick!" said the farmer; "why this is only August; and with your light work and good food he ought not to go down like this, even if it was autumn. How do you feed him?"

My master told him. The other shook his head slowly, and began to feel me over, "I can't say who eats your corn, my dear fellow, but I am much mistaken if your horse gets it. Have you ridden very fast?"

"No! very gently."

"Then just put your hand here," said he, passing his hand over my neck and shoulder; "he is as warm and damp as a horse just come up from grass. I advise you to look into your stable a little more. I hate to be suspicious, and, thank heaven, I have no cause to be, for I can trust my men, present or absent; but there are mean scoundrels, wicked enough to rob a dumb beast of his food; you must look into it." And turning to his man who had come to take me, "Give this horse a right good feed of bruised oats, and don't stint him."

"Dumb beasts!" yes, we are; but if I could have spoken, I could have told my master where his oats went to. My groom used to come every morning about six o'clock, and with him a little boy, who always had a covered basket with him. He used to go with his father into the harness room where the corn was kept, and I could see them when the door stood ajar, fill a little bag with oats out of the bin, and then he used to be off.

Five or six mornings after this, just as the boy had left the stable, the door was pushed open and a policeman walked in, holding the child tight by the arm; another policeman followed, and locked the door on the inside, saying, "Shew me the place where your father keeps his rabbits' food."

The boy looked very frightened and began to cry; but there was no escape, and he led the way to the corn bin. Here, the policeman found another empty bag like that which was found full of oats in the boy's basket.

Filcher was cleaning my feet at the time, but they soon saw him, and though he blustered a good deal, they walked him off to the "lock-up," and his boy with him. I heard afterwards, that the boy was not held to be guilty, but the man was sentenced to prison for two months.

CHAPTER THIRTY ONE
A Humbug!

My master was not immediately suited,[1] but in a few days my new groom came. He was a tall, good-looking fellow enough; but if ever there was a humbug in the shape of a groom, Alfred Smirk was the man. He was very civil to me, and never used me ill; in fact, he did a great deal of stroking and patting, when his master was there to see it. He always brushed my mane and tail with water, and my hoofs with oil before he brought me to the door, to make me look smart; but as to cleaning my feet, or looking to my shoes, or grooming me thoroughly, he thought no more of that, than if I had been a cow.

He left my bit rusty, my saddle damp, and my crupper stiff.

Alfred Smirk considered himself very handsome; he spent a great deal of time about his hair, whiskers, and necktie, before a little looking-glass in the harness room. When his master was speaking to him, it was always "Yes, sir, yes, sir," touching his hat at every word; and everyone thought he was a very nice young man, and that Mr. Barry was very fortunate to meet with him. I should say he was the laziest, most conceited fellow I ever came near. Of course it was a great thing not to be ill-used, but then a horse wants more than that. I had a loose box, and might have been very comfortable if he had not been too indolent to clean it out. He never took all the straw away, and the smell from what lay underneath was very bad; while the strong vapours that rose up, made my eyes smart and inflame, and I did not feel the same appetite for my food.

One day his master came in and said, "Alfred, the stable smells rather strong; should not you give that stall a good scrub, and throw down plenty of water?"

"Well, sir," he said, touching his cap, "I'll do so if you please, sir, but it is rather dangerous, sir, throwing down water in a horse's box, they are very apt to take cold, sir. I should not like to do him an injury, but I'll do it if you please, sir."

"Well," said his master, "I should not like him to take cold, but I don't like the smell of this stable; do you think the drains are all right?"

"Well, sir, now you mention it, I think the drain does sometimes send back a smell; there may be something wrong, sir."

---

1 Did not immediately find a new servant.

"Then send for the bricklayer and have it seen to," said his master.

"Yes, sir, I will."

The bricklayer came and pulled up a great many bricks, and found nothing amiss; so he put down some lime, and charged the master five shillings, and the smell in my box was as bad as ever: but that was not all—standing as I did on a quantity of moist straw, my feet grew unhealthy, and tender, and the master used to say,

"I don't know what is the matter with this horse, he goes very fumble-footed. I am sometimes afraid he will stumble."

"Yes, sir," said Alfred, "I have noticed the same myself, when I have exercised him."

Now the fact was, that he hardly ever did exercise me, and when the master was busy, I often stood for days together without stretching my legs at all, and yet being fed just as high as if I were at hard work. This often disordered my health, and made me sometimes heavy and dull, but more often restless and feverish. He never even gave me a meal of green meat,[1] or a bran mash,[2] which would have cooled me, for he was altogether as ignorant as he was conceited; and then instead of exercise or change of food, I had to take horse balls and draughts;[3] which, beside the nuisance of having them poured down my throat, used to make me feel ill and uncomfortable.

One day my feet were so tender, that trotting over some fresh stones with my master on my back, I made two such serious stumbles, that as he came down Lansdown[4] into the city, he stopped at the farrier's, and asked him to see what was the matter with me. The man took up my feet one by one and examined them; then standing up and dusting his hands one against the other, he said, "Your horse has got the 'thrush,'[5]

---

1 Vegetable matter such as carrots.

2 A mixture of bran and hot water; "cooling" feed was less rich than oats, and therefore appropriate for a stabled horse not being exercised sufficiently to burn off the extra energy.

3 This represents a significant shift in Beauty's experience, from the metaphoric medicine of kindness, to the need for actual medicine; see above, p. 62, n. 1.

4 A suburb of Bath.

5 A bacterial infection of the frog and hoof caused by exposure to wet, unsanitary conditions such as a dirty stable.

and badly too; his feet are very tender; it is fortunate that he has not been down. I wonder your groom has not seen to it before. This is the sort of thing we find in foul stables, where the litter is never properly cleared out. If you will send him here to-morrow, I will attend to the hoof, and I will direct your man how to apply the liniment which I will give him." The next day I had my feet thoroughly cleansed and stuffed with tow,[1] soaked in some strong lotion; and a very unpleasant business it was.

The farrier ordered all the litter to be taken out of my box day by day, and the floor kept very clean. Then I was to have bran mashes, a little green meat, and not so much corn, till my feet were well again. With this treatment I soon regained my spirits, but Mr. Barry was so much disgusted at being twice deceived by his grooms, that he determined to give up keeping a horse, and to hire when he wanted one. I was therefore kept till my feet were quite sound, and was then sold again.

---

1 Flax or hemp prepared for spinning, in this case used to pack the infected hoof.

PART III.

CHAPTER THIRTY TWO
A Horse Fair

No doubt a horse fair is a very amusing place to those who have nothing to lose; at any rate there is plenty to see.

Long strings of young horses out of the country, fresh from the marshes; and droves of shaggy little Welsh ponies, no higher than Merrylegs; and hundreds of cart horses of all sorts, some of them with their long tails braided up, and tied with scarlet cord; and a good many like myself, handsome and highbred, but fallen into the middle class, through some accident or blemish, unsoundness of wind, or some other complaint. There were some splendid animals quite in their prime, and fit for anything; they were throwing out their legs, and shewing off their paces in high style, as they were trotted out with a leading rein, the groom running by the side. But round in the back ground, there were a number of poor things, sadly broken down with hard work; with their knees knuckling over, and their hind legs swinging out at every step; and there were some very dejected-looking old horses, with the under lip hanging down, and the ears laying back heavily, as if there was no more pleasure in life, and no more hope; there were some so thin, you might see all their ribs, and some with old sores on their backs and hips; these were sad sights for a horse to look upon, who knows not but he may come to the same state.

There was a great deal of bargaining; of running up and beating down, and if a horse may speak his mind so far as he understands, I should say, there were more lies told, and more trickery at that horse fair, than a clever man could give an account of. I was put with two or three other strong useful-looking horses, and a good many people came to look at us. The gentlemen always turned from me when they saw the broken knees;[1] though the man who had me swore it was only a slip in the stall.

---

1 An injury caused by impact, usually from stumbling as in Black Beauty's case. It does not necessarily indicate damage to the bone, but scarring can cause decreased mobility. Stumbling itself can be caused by many factors, but broken knees were regarded with suspicion because they could indicate navicular disease, a debilitating and untreatable condition.

The first thing was to pull my mouth open, then to look at my eyes, then feel all the way down my legs, and give me a hard feel of the skin and flesh, and then try my paces. It was wonderful what a difference there was in the way these things were done. Some did it in a rough off-hand way, as if one was only a piece of wood; while others would take their hands gently over one's body, with a pat now and then, as much as to say, "by your leave." Of course I judged a good deal of the buyers by their manners to myself.

There was one man, I thought, if he would buy me, I should be happy. He was not a gentleman, nor yet one of the loud flashy sort, that called themselves so. He was rather a small man; but well made, and quick in all his motions. I knew in a moment by the way he handled me, that he was used to horses; he spoke gently, and his grey eye had a kindly cheery look in it. It may seem strange to say—but it is true all the same, that the clean fresh smell there was about him made me take to him; no smell of old beer and tobacco, which I hated, but a fresh smell as if he had come out of a hayloft. He offered twenty-three pounds for me; but that was refused, and he walked away. I looked after him, but he was gone, and a very hard-looking loud-voiced man came; I was dreadfully afraid he would have me; but he walked off. One or two more came who did not mean business. Then the hard-faced man came back again and offered twenty-three pounds. A very close bargain was being driven; for my salesman began to think he should not get all he asked, and must come down; but just then the grey-eyed man came back again. I could not help reaching out my head towards him. He stroked my face kindly. "Well, old chap," he said, "I think we should suit each other." "I'll give twenty-four for him."

"Say twenty-five and you shall have him."

"Twenty-four ten," said my friend, in a very decided tone, "and not another sixpence—yes or no?"

"Done," said the salesman, "and you may depend upon it there's a monstrous deal of quality in that horse, and if you want him for cab work, he's a bargain."

The money was paid on the spot, and my new master took my halter, and led me out of the fair to an inn, where he had a saddle and bridle ready. He gave me a good feed of oats, and stood by whilst I ate it, talking to himself, and talking to me. Half-an-hour after we were on our way to London, through pleasant lanes and country roads, until we came into the great

London thoroughfare, on which we travelled steadily, till in the twilight, we reached the great City. The gas lamps were already lighted; there were streets to the right, and streets to the left, and streets crossing each other for mile upon mile. I thought we should never come to the end of them. At last, in passing through one, we came to a long cab stand, when my rider called out in a cheery voice, "Good night, governor!"[1]

"Halloo!" cried a voice, "Have you got a good one?"

"I think so," replied my owner.

"I wish you luck with him."

"Thank ye, governor," and he rode on; we soon turned up one of the side streets, and about half way up that, we turned into a very narrow street, with rather poor-looking houses on one side, and what seemed to be coach-houses and stables on the other.

My owner pulled up at one of the houses and whistled. The door flew open, and a young woman, followed by a little girl and boy, ran out. There was a very lively greeting as my rider dismounted. "Now then, Harry my boy, open the gates, and mother will bring us the lantern." The next minute they were all standing round me in a small stable yard.

"Is he gentle, father?"

"Yes, Dolly, as gentle as your own kitten; come and pat him."

At once the little hand was patting about all over my shoulder without fear; how good it felt!

"Let me get him a bran mash while you rub him down," said the mother.

"Do, Polly, it's just what he wants, and I know you've got a beautiful mash ready for me."

"Sausage dumpling and apple turnover," shouted the boy, which set them all laughing. I was led into a comfortable clean-smelling stall with plenty of dry straw, and after a capital supper, I laid down, thinking I was going to be happy.

---

1 Respectful but informal slang term for "Boss."

CHAPTER THIRTY THREE
A LONDON CAB HORSE

My new master's name was Jeremiah[1] Barker, but as everyone called him Jerry, I shall do the same. Polly, his wife, was just as good a match as a man could have. She was a plump, trim, tidy little woman, with smooth dark hair, dark eyes, and a merry little mouth. The boy was nearly twelve years old; a tall, frank, good-tempered lad; and little Dorothy, (Dolly, they called her), was her mother over again, at eight years old. They were all wonderfully fond of each other; I never knew such a happy, merry family before, or since. Jerry had a cab of his own, and two horses, which he drove and attended to himself. His other horse was a tall, white, rather large-boned animal, called Captain; he was old now, but when he was young, he must have been splendid; he had still a proud way of holding his head, and arching his neck; in fact, he was a high-bred, fine-mannered, noble old horse, every inch of him. He told me that in his early youth he went to the Crimean War;[2] he belonged to an officer in the Cavalry, and used to lead the regiment; I will tell more of that hereafter.

The next morning, when I was well groomed, Polly and Dolly came into the yard to see me, and make friends. Harry had been helping his father since the early morning, and had stated his opinion that I should turn out "a regular brick." Polly brought me a slice of apple, and Dolly a piece of bread, and made as much of me as if I had been the "Black Beauty" of olden time. It was a great treat to be petted again, and talked to in a gentle voice, and I let them see as well as I could that I wished to be friendly. Polly thought I was very handsome, and a great deal too good for a cab, if it was not for the broken knees. "Of course, there's no one to tell us whose fault that was," said Jerry, "and as long as I don't know, I shall give him the benefit of the doubt; for a firmer, neater stepper, I never rode; we'll call him 'Jack,' after the old one shall we, Polly?"

"Do," she said, "for I like to keep a good name going."

---

1 In the Old Testament, a prophet appointed to reveal the sins of the people, who prefigures the covenant with Christ.
2 Waged between Russia and a coalition of British, French, and Turkish armies, 1853–56. In the British popular memory, it was associated with terrible mistakes in management, both on the battlefield and off.

Captain went out in the cab all the morning. Harry came in after school to feed me and give me water. In the afternoon I was put into the cab. Jerry took as much pains to see if the collar and bridle fitted comfortably, as if he had been John Manly over again. When the crupper was let out a hole or two, it all fitted well. There was no bearing rein—no curb—nothing but a plain ring snaffle.[1] What a blessing that was!

After driving through the side street we came to the large cab stand, where Jerry had said "Good-night." On one side of this wide street were high houses with wonderful shop fronts, and on the other, was an old church and churchyard, surrounded by iron pallisades. Alongside these iron rails a number of cabs were drawn up, waiting for passengers: bits of hay were lying about on the ground; some of the men were standing together talking; some were sitting on their boxes reading the newspaper; and one or two were feeding their horses with bits of hay, and a drink of water. We pulled up in the rank at the back of the last cab. Two or three men came round and began to look at me and pass their remarks.

"Very good for a funeral," said one.

"Too smart-looking," said another, shaking his head in a very wise way; "you'll find out something wrong one of these fine mornings, or my name isn't Jones."

"Well," said Jerry pleasantly, "I suppose I need not find it out till it finds me out; eh? and if so, I'll keep up my spirits a little longer." Then came up a broad-faced man, dressed in a great grey coat with great grey capes, and great white buttons, a grey hat, and a blue comforter loosely tied round his neck; his hair was grey too, but he was a jolly-looking fellow, and the other men made way for him. He looked me all over, as if he had been going to buy me; and then straightening himself up with a grunt, he said, "He's the right sort for you, Jerry; I don't care what you gave for him, he'll be worth it." Thus my character was established on the stand.

This man's name was Grant, but he was called "Grey Grant," or "Governor Grant;" he had been the longest on that stand of any of the men, and he took it upon himself to settle matters, and stop disputes. He was generally a good-humoured, sensible man;

---

1 A jointed bit with rings to which the reins are directly attached. The mildest form of bit, it does not use leverage on the horse's jaw.

but if his temper was a little out, as it was sometimes, when he had drank too much, nobody liked to come too near his fist, for he could deal a very heavy blow.

The first week of my life as a cab horse was very trying; I had never been used to London, and the noise, the hurry, the crowds of horses, carts, and carriages, that I had to make my way through, made me feel anxious and harassed; but I soon found that I could perfectly trust my driver, and then I made myself easy, and got used to it.

Jerry was as good a driver as I had ever known; and what was better, he took as much thought for his horses, as he did for himself. He soon found out that I was willing to work, and do my best; and he never laid the whip on me, unless it was gently drawing the end of it over my back, when I was to go on; but generally I knew this quite well by the way in which he took up the reins; and I believe his whip was more frequently stuck up by his side, than in his hand.

In a short time I and my master understood each other, as well as horse and man can do. In the stable too, he did all that he could for our comfort. The stalls were the old-fashioned style, too much on the slope; but he had two moveable bars fixed across the back of our stalls, so that at night, and when we were resting, he just took off our halters, and put up the bars, and thus we could turn about and stand whichever way we pleased; and as the stall divisions were lower at the back, Captain and I were able to touch each other's noses in a friendly way, as we horses always do with those we like.

Jerry kept us very clean, and gave us as much change of food as he could, and always plenty of it. But the best thing we had was, our Sundays for rest; we worked so hard in the week, that I do not think we could have kept up to it, but for that day; besides we had then a little time to enjoy each other's company, and chat a bit. It was on these days that I learned my companion's history.

CHAPTER THIRTY FOUR
An Old War Horse

Captain had been broken in and trained for an army horse; his first owner was an officer of cavalry going out to the Crimean War. He said he quite enjoyed the training with all the other horses, trotting together, turning together, to the right hand or to the left, halting at the word of command, or dashing forward at full speed at the sound of the trumpet, or signal of the officer. He was, when young, a dark dappled iron grey, and considered very handsome. His master, a young, high-spirited gentleman, was very fond of him, and treated him from the first with the greatest care and kindness. He told me he thought the life of an army horse was very pleasant; but when it came to being sent abroad, over the sea in a great ship, he almost changed his mind.

"That part of it," said he, "was dreadful! Of course we could not walk off the land into the ship; so they were obliged to put strong straps under our bodies, and then we were lifted off our legs, in spite of our struggles, and were swung through the air over the water, to the deck of the great vessel. There we were placed in small close stalls, and never for a long time saw the sky, or were able to stretch our legs. The ship sometimes rolled about in high winds, and we were knocked about, and felt bad enough. However, at last, it came to an end, and we were hauled up, and swung over again to the land; we were very glad, and snorted, and neighed for joy, when we once more felt firm ground under our feet.

"We soon found that the country we had come to was very different to our own, and that we had many hardships to endure besides the fighting; but many of the men were so fond of their horses, that they did everything they could to make them comfortable, in spite of snow, wet, and all things out of order."

"But what about the fighting?" said I; "was not that worse than anything else?"

"Well," said he, "I hardly know; we always liked to hear the trumpet sound, and to be called out, and were impatient to start off, though sometimes we had to stand for hours, waiting for the word of command; and when the word was given, we used to spring forward as gaily and eagerly as if there were no cannon balls, bayonets, or bullets. I believe so long as we felt our rider firm in the saddle, and his hand steady on the bridle, not one of us gave way to fear, not even when the terrible bombshells whirled through the air and burst into a thousand pieces.

"I, with my noble master went into many actions together without a wound; and though I saw horses shot down with bullets, pierced through with lance, and gashed with fearful sabre-cuts; though we left them dead on the field, or dying in agony of their wounds, I don't think I feared for myself. My master's cheery voice, as he encouraged his men, made me feel as if he and I could not be killed. I had such perfect trust in him, that whilst he was guiding me, I was ready to charge up to the very cannon's mouth. I saw many brave men cut down, many fall mortally wounded from their saddles. I had heard the cries and groans of the dying, I had cantered over ground slippery with blood, and frequently had to turn aside to avoid trampling on wounded man or horse, but, until one dreadful day, I had never felt terror; that day, I shall never forget."

Here old Captain paused for a while and drew a long breath; I waited, and he went on.

"It was one autumn morning, and as usual, an hour before day-break our cavalry had turned out, ready caparisoned[1] for the day's work, whether it might be fighting or waiting. The men stood by their horses waiting, ready for orders. As the light increased, there seemed to be some excitement among the officers; and before the day was well begun, we heard the firing of the enemy's guns.

"Then one of the officers rode up and gave the word for the men to mount, and in a second, every man was in his saddle, and every horse stood expecting the touch of the rein, or the pressure of his rider's heels, all animated, all eager; but still we had been trained so well, that except by the champing of our bits, and the restive tossing of our heads from time to time, it could not be said that we stirred.

"My dear master and I were at the head of the line, and as all sat motionless and watchful, he took a little stray lock of my mane which had turned over on the wrong side, laid it over on the right, and smoothed it down with his hand; then patting my neck, he said, 'We shall have a day of it to-day, Bayard,[2] my

---

1 Riderless horses in full military ceremonial tack.
2 A magic bay horse in French legend, famous for his spirit.

beauty; but we'll do our duty as we have done.'[1] He stroked my neck that morning, more I think, than he had ever done before; quietly on and on, as if he were thinking of something else. I loved to feel his hand on my neck, and arched my crest proudly and happily; but I stood very still, for I knew all his moods, and when he liked me to be quiet, and when gay.

"I cannot tell all that happened on that day, but I will tell of the last charge that we made together; it was across a valley right in front of the enemy's cannon. By this time we were well used to the roar of heavy guns, the rattle of musket fire, and the flying of shot near us; but never had I been under such a fire as we rode through on that day. From the right, from the left, and from the front, shot and shell poured in upon us. Many a brave man went down, many a horse fell, flinging his rider to the earth; many a horse without a rider ran wildly out of the ranks; then terrified at being alone with no hand to guide him, came pressing in amongst his old companions, to gallop with them to the charge.

"Fearful as it was, no one stopped, no one turned back. Every moment the ranks were thinned, but as our comrades fell, we closed in to keep them together; and instead of being shaken or staggered in our pace, our gallop became faster and faster as we neared the cannon, all clouded in white smoke, while the red fire flashed through it.

"My master, my dear master! was cheering on his comrades with his right arm raised on high, when one of the balls, whizzing close to my head, struck him. I felt him stagger with the shock, though he uttered no cry; I tried to check my speed, but the sword dropped from his right hand, the rein fell loose from the left, and sinking backward from the saddle he fell to the earth; the other riders swept past us, and by the force of their charge I was driven from the spot where he fell.

"I wanted to keep my place by his side, and not leave him under that rush of horses' feet, but it was in vain; and now

---

1   This passage associates Captain with the Charge of the Light Brigade memorialized in a famous poem by Alfred, Lord Tennyson (1809–92). In this episode of the Battle of Balaclava (1854), miscommunication among British commanders led to an ill-fated cavalry charge with high casualties. Tennyson's poem from the same year highlights the bravery and honour of the soldiers, while Captain's account offers a horse's perspective on the senselessness and waste of war.

without a master or friend, I was alone on that great slaughter ground; then, fear took hold on me, and I trembled as I had never trembled before; and I too, as I had seen other horses do, tried to join in the ranks and gallop with them; but I was beaten off by the swords of the soldiers. Just then, a soldier whose horse had been killed under him, caught at my bridle and mounted me; and with this new master I was again going forward: but our gallant company was cruelly overpowered, and those who remained alive after the fierce fight for the guns, came galloping back over the same ground. Some of the horses had been so badly wounded, that they could scarcely move from the loss of blood; other noble creatures were trying on three legs to drag themselves along, and others were struggling to rise on their fore feet, when their hind legs had been shattered by shot. Their groans were piteous to hear, and the beseeching look in their eyes as those who escaped passed by, and left them to their fate, I shall never forget. After the battle the wounded men were brought in, and the dead were buried."

"And what about the wounded horses?" I said; "were they left to die?"

"No, the army farriers went over the field with their pistols, and shot all that were ruined; some that had only slight wounds were brought back and attended to, but the greater part of the noble willing creatures that went out that morning, never came back! In our stables there was only about one in four that returned.

"I never saw my dear master again, I believe he fell dead from the saddle. I never loved any other master so well. I went into many other engagements, but was only once wounded, and then not seriously; and when the war was over, I came back again to England, as sound and strong as when I went out."

I said, "I have heard people talk about war as if it was a very fine thing."

"Ah!" said he, "I should think they never saw it. No doubt it is very fine when there is no enemy, when it is just exercise and parade, and sham-fight. Yes, it is very fine then; but when thousands of good brave men and horses are killed, or crippled for life, it has a very different look."

"Do you know what they fought about?" said I.

"No," he said, "that is more than a horse can understand, but the enemy must have been awfully wicked people, if it was right to go all that way over the sea on purpose to kill them."

CHAPTER THIRTY FIVE
JERRY BARKER

I never knew a better man than my new master; he was kind and good, and as strong for the right as John Manly; and so good-tempered and merry, that very few people could pick a quarrel with him. He was very fond of making little songs, and singing them to himself. One, he was very fond of, was this,

> "Come father and mother,
> And sister and brother,
> Come all of you turn to,
> And help one another."

And so they did; Harry was as clever at stable work as a much older boy, and always wanted to do what he could. Then, Polly and Dolly used to come in the morning to help with the cab—to brush and beat the cushions, and rub the glass, while Jerry was giving us a cleaning in the yard, and Harry was rubbing the harness. There used to be a great deal of laughing and fun between them, and it put Captain and me in much better spirits, than if we had heard scolding and hard words. They were always early in the morning, for Jerry would say,

> "If you in the morning
> Throw minutes away,
> You can't pick them up
> In the course of the day.
> You may hurry and scurry,
> And flurry and worry,
> You've lost them for ever,
> For ever and aye."

He could not bear any careless loitering, and waste of time; and nothing was so near making him angry, as to find people who were always late, wanting a cab-horse to be driven hard, to make up for their idleness.

One day, two wild-looking young men came out of a tavern close by the stand, and called Jerry. "Here cabby! look sharp, we are rather late; put on the steam, will you, and take us to the Victoria in time for the one o'clock train? you shall have a shilling extra."

"I will take you at the regular pace, gentlemen: shillings don't pay for putting on the steam like that."

Larry's cab was standing next to ours; he flung open the door, and said, "I'm your man, gentlemen! take my cab, my horse will get you there all right;" and as he shut them in, with a wink towards Jerry, said, "It's against his conscience to go beyond a jog-trot." Then slashing his jaded horse, he set off as hard as he could. Jerry patted me on the neck—"No, Jack, a shilling would not pay for that sort of thing, would it, old boy?"

Although Jerry was determinately set against hard driving, to please careless people, he always went a good fair pace, and was not against putting on the steam, as he said, if only he knew why.

I well remember one morning, as we were on the stand waiting for a fare, that a young man, carrying a heavy portmanteau, trod on a piece of orange peel which lay on the pavement, and fell down with great force.

Jerry was the first to run and lift him up. He seemed much stunned, and as they led him into a shop, he walked as if he were in great pain. Jerry of course came back to the stand, but in about ten minutes one of the shopmen called him, so we drew up to the pavement.

"Can you take me to the South Eastern railway?" said the young man; "this unlucky fall has made me late, I fear; but it is of great importance that I should not lose the twelve o'clock train. I should be most thankful if you could get me there in time, and will gladly pay you an extra fare."

"I'll do my very best," said Jerry heartily, "if you think you are well enough, sir," for he looked dreadfully white and ill.

"I *must* go," he said earnestly, "please to open the door, and let us lose no time."

The next minute Jerry was on the box; with a cheery chirrup to me, and a twitch of the rein that I well understood—"Now then, Jack, my boy," said he, "spin along, we'll shew them how we can get over the ground, if we only know why."

It is always difficult to drive fast in the city in the middle of the day, when the streets are full of traffic, but we did what could be done; and when a good driver and a good horse, who understand each other, are of one mind, it is wonderful what they can do. I had a very good mouth—that is, I could be guided by the slightest touch of the rein, and that is a great thing in London, amongst carriages, omnibusses, carts, vans, trucks,

cabs, and great wagons creeping along at a walking pace; some
going one way, some another, some going slow, others wanting
to pass them, omnibusses stopping short every few minutes to
take up a passenger, obliging the horse that is coming behind, to
pull up too, or to pass, and get before them; perhaps you try to
pass, but just then, something else comes dashing in through the
narrow opening, and you have to keep in behind the omnibus
again; presently you think you see a chance, and manage to get
to the front, going so near the wheels on each side, that half-an-
inch nearer and they would scrape. Well—you get along for a bit,
but soon find yourself in a long train of carts and carriages all
obliged to go at a walk; perhaps you come to a regular block-up,
and have to stand still for minutes together, till something clears
out into a side street, or the policeman interferes: you have to be
ready for any chance—to dash forward if there be an opening,
and be quick as a rat dog to see if there be room, and if there be
time, lest you get your own wheels locked, or smashed, or the
shaft of some other vehicle run into your chest or shoulder. All
this, is what you have to be ready for. If you want to get through
London fast in the middle of the day, it wants a deal of practice.

Jerry and I were used to it, and no one could beat us at getting
through when we were set upon it. I was quick and bold, and could
always trust my driver; Jerry was quick, and patient at the same
time, and could trust his horse, which was a great thing too. He
very seldom used the whip; I knew by his voice, and his click click,
when he wanted to get on fast, and by the rein where I was to go;
so there was no need for whipping; but I must go back to my story.

The streets were very full that day, but we got on pretty well
as far as the bottom of Cheapside, where there was a block for
three or four minutes. The young man put his head out, and said
anxiously, "I think I had better get out and walk, I shall never get
there if this goes on."

"I'll do all that can be done, sir," said Jerry, "I think we shall
be in time; this block-up cannot last much longer, and your luggage is very heavy for you to carry, sir."

Just then the cart in front of us began to move on, and then
we had a good turn. In and out—in and out we went, as fast as
horseflesh could do it, and for a wonder had a good clear time
on London Bridge, for there was a whole train of cabs and carriages, all going our way at a quick trot—perhaps wanting to
catch that very train; at any rate we whirled into the station with

many more, just as the great clock pointed to eight minutes to twelve o'clock. "Thank God! we are in time," said the young man, "and thank you too, my friend, and your good horse; you have saved me more than money can ever pay for; take this extra half-crown."

"No sir, no, thank you all the same; so glad we hit the time, sir, but don't stay now, sir, the bell is ringing. Here! porter! take this gentleman's luggage—Dover line—twelve o'clock train— that's it," and without waiting for another word, Jerry wheeled me round to make room for other cabs that were dashing up at the last minute, and drew up on one side till the crush was past.

"'So glad!' he said, 'so glad!' poor young fellow! I wonder what it was that made him so anxious!" Jerry often talked to himself quite loud enough for me to hear, when we were not moving.

On Jerry's return to the rank, there was a good deal of laughing and chaffing at him, for driving hard to the train for an extra fare, as they said, all against his principles; and they wanted to know how much he had pocketed. "A good deal more than I generally get," said he, nodding slily; "what he gave me will keep me in little comforts for several days."

"Gammon!" said one.

"He's a humbug," said another, "preaching to us, and then doing the same himself."

"Look here, mates," said Jerry, "the gentleman offered me half-a-crown extra, but I didn't take it; 'twas quite pay enough for me, to see how glad he was to catch that train; and if Jack and I choose to have a quick run now and then, to please ourselves, that's our business and not yours."

"Well," said Larry, "you'll never be a rich man."

"Most likely not," said Jerry, "but I don't know that I shall be the less happy for that. I have heard the commandments read a great many times, and I never noticed that any of them said, 'Thou shalt be rich;' and there are a good many curious things said in the New Testament about rich men, that I think would make me feel rather queer if I was one of them."

"If you ever do get rich," said Governor Gray, looking over his shoulder across the top of his cab, "you'll deserve it, Jerry, and you won't find a curse come with your wealth. As for you, Larry, you'll die poor, you spend too much in whipcord."

"Well," said Larry, "what is a fellow to do if his horse won't go without it?"

"You never take the trouble to see if he will go without it; your whip is always going as if you had the St. Vitus' dance[1] in your arm; and if it does not wear you out, it wears your horse out; you know you are always changing your horses, and why? because you never give them any peace or encouragement."

"Well, I have not had good luck," said Larry, "that's where it is."

"And you never will," said the Governor: "Good Luck is rather particular who she rides with, and mostly prefers those who have got common sense and a good heart: at least, that is my experience." Governor Gray turned round again to his newspaper, and the other men went to their cabs.

---

1 A colloquial term for Sydenham's chorea, a disease in which patients exhibit rapid jerking movements, usually in the face, feet, and hands.

One morning, as Jerry had just put me into the shafts and was fastening the traces, a gentleman walked into the yard; "Your servant, sir," said Jerry.

"Good morning, Mr. Barker," said the gentleman. "I should be glad to make some arrangements with you for taking Mrs. Briggs regularly to church on Sunday morning. We go to the New Church now, and that is rather further than she can walk."

"Thank you, sir," said Jerry, "but I have only taken out a six days' licence,[1] and therefore I could not take a fare on a Sunday, it would not be legal."

"Oh!" said the other, "I did not know yours was a six days' cab; but of course it would be very easy to alter your licence. I would see that you did not lose by it: the fact is, Mrs. Briggs very much prefers you to drive her."

"I should be glad to oblige the lady, sir, but I had a seven days' licence once, and the work was too hard for me, and too hard for my horses. Year in and year out, not a day's rest, and never a Sunday with my wife and children, and never able to go to a place of worship, which I had always been used to do before I took to the driving box; so for the last five years I have only taken a six days' licence, and I find it better all the way round."

"Well, of course," replied Mr. Briggs, "it is very proper that every person should have rest, and be able to go to church on Sundays, but I should have thought you would not have minded such a short distance for the horse, and only once a day: you would have all the afternoon and evening for yourself, and we are very good customers, you know."

"Yes, sir, that is true, and I am grateful for all favours, I am sure, and anything that I could do to oblige you, or the lady, I should be proud and happy to do; but I can't give up my Sundays, sir, indeed I can't. I read that God made man, and He made horses and all the other beasts, and as soon as He had made them, He made a day of rest, and bade that all should rest one day in seven; and I think, sir, He must have known what was

---

1 [Sewell's note:] A few years since the annual charge for a cab licence was very much reduced, and the difference between the six and seven days' cabs was abolished.

good for them, and I am sure it is good for me; I am stronger and healthier altogether, now that I have a day of rest; the horses are fresh too, and do not wear up nearly so fast. The six day drivers all tell me the same, and I have laid by more money in the Savings' Bank than ever I did before; and as for the wife and children, sir—why heart alive! they would not go back to the seven days for all they could see."

"Oh, very well," said the gentleman. "Don't trouble yourself, Mr. Barker, any further, I will enquire somewhere else;" and he walked away.

"Well," says Jerry to me, "we can't help it, Jack, old boy, we must have our Sundays."

"Polly!" he shouted, "Polly! come here." She was there in a minute.

"What is it all about, Jerry?"

"Why, my dear, Mr. Briggs wants me to take Mrs. Briggs to church every Sunday morning. I say, I have only a six days' licence. He says get a seven days' licence, and I'll make it worth your while; and you know, Polly, they are very good customers to us. Mrs. B— often goes out shopping for hours, or making calls, and then she pays down fair and honourable like a lady; there's no beating down, or making three hours into two hours and a half as some folks do; and it is easy work for the horses, not like tearing along to catch trains for people that are always a quarter of an hour too late; and if I don't oblige her in this matter, it is very likely we shall lose them altogether. What do you say, little woman?"

"I say, Jerry," says she, speaking very slowly, "I say, if Mrs. Briggs would give you a sovereign[1] every Sunday morning, I would not have you a seven days' cabman again. We have known what it was to have no Sundays; and now we know what it is to call them our own. Thank God, you earn enough to keep us, though it is sometimes close work to pay for all the oats and hay, the licence, and the rent beside; but Harry will soon be earning something, and I would rather struggle on harder than we do, than go back to those horrid times, when you hardly had a minute to look at your own children, and we never could go to a place of worship together, or have a happy quiet day. God forbid that we should ever turn back to those times: that's what I say, Jerry."

---

1 A gold coin worth one pound (or twenty shillings).

"And that is just what I told Mr. Briggs, my dear," said Jerry, "and what I mean to stick to; so don't go and fret yourself, Polly, (for she had begun to cry,) I would not go back to the old times if I earned twice as much, so that is settled, little woman. Now cheer up, and I'll be off to the stand."

Three weeks had passed away after this conversation, and no order had come from Mrs. Briggs; so there was nothing but taking jobs from the stand.

Jerry took it to heart a good deal, for of course the work was harder for horse and man; but Polly would always cheer him up and say, "Never mind, father, never mind,

> Do your best,
> And leave the rest,
> 'Twill all come right
> Some day or night."

It soon became known that Jerry had lost his best customer, and for what reason; most of the men said he was a fool, but two or three took his part.

"If working men don't stick to their Sunday," said Truman, "they'll soon have none left; it is every man's right and every beast's right. By God's law we have a day of rest, and by the law of England we have a day of rest; and I say we ought to hold to the rights these laws give us, and keep them for our children."

"All very well for you religious chaps to talk so," said Larry, "but I'll turn a shilling when I can. I don't believe in religion, for I don't see that your religious people are any better than the rest."

"If they are not better," put in Jerry, "it is because they are not religious. You might as well say that our country's laws are not good, because some people break them. If a man gives way to his temper, and speaks evil of his neighbour, and does not pay his debts, he is not religious; I don't care how much he goes to church. If some men are shams and humbugs, that does not make religion untrue. Real religion is the best, and the truest thing in the world; and the only thing that can make a man really happy, or make the world any better."

"If religion was good for anything," said Jones, "it would prevent your religious people from making us work on Sundays as you know many of them do, and that's why I say religion is nothing but a sham—why, if it was not for the church and chapel goers it would be hardly worth while our coming out on a Sunday; but they have their privileges as they call them, and I go without. I shall expect them to answer for my soul, if I can't get a chance of saving it."

Several of the men applauded this, till Jerry said, "That may sound well enough, but it won't do: every man must look after his own soul; you can't lay it down at another man's door like a foundling, and expect him to take care of it; and don't you see, if you are always sitting on your box waiting for a fare, they will say, 'If we don't take him, someone else will, and he does not look for any Sunday.' Of course they don't go to the bottom of it, or they would see if they never came for a cab, it would be no use your standing there; but people don't always like to go to the bottom of things; it may not be convenient to do it; but if you Sunday drivers would all strike for a day of rest, the thing would be done."

"And what would all the good people do, if they could not get to their favourite preachers?" said Larry.

"'Tis not for me to lay down plans for other people," said Jerry, "but if they can't walk so far, they can go to what is nearer; and if it should rain they can put on their macintoshes[1] as they do on a week-day. If a thing is right, it can be done, and if it is wrong, it *can be done without*; and a good man will find a way; and that is as true for us cabmen as it is for the church goers."

---

1 A raincoat made of rubberized fabric named for its inventor, Charles Macintosh (1766–1843), who patented a process for waterproofing fabric in 1823.

CHAPTER THIRTY SEVEN
The Golden Rule

Two or three weeks after this, as we came into the yard rather late in the evening, Polly came running across the road with the lantern (she always brought it to him if it was not very wet).

"It has all come right, Jerry; Mrs. Briggs sent her servant this afternoon, to ask you to take her out to-morrow at eleven o'clock. I said 'Yes, I thought so, but we supposed she employed someone else now.'

'Well,' says he, 'the real fact is, master was put out because Mr. Barker refused to come on Sundays, and he has been trying other cabs, but there's something wrong with them all; some drive too fast, and some too slow, and the mistress says, there is not one of them so nice and clean as yours, and nothing will suit her but Mr. Barker's cab again.'"

Polly was almost out of breath, and Jerry broke out into a merry laugh—

"All come right some day or night: you were right, my dear; you generally are. Run in and get the supper, and I'll have Jack's harness off and make him snug and happy in no time."

After this, Mrs. Briggs wanted Jerry's cab quite as often as before, never, however, on a Sunday; but there came a day when we had Sunday work, and this was how it happened. We had all come home on the Saturday night very tired, and very glad to think that the next day would be all rest, but so it was not to be.

On Sunday morning Jerry was cleaning me in the yard, when Polly stepped up to him, looking very full of something.

"What is it?" said Jerry.

"Well, my dear" she said, "poor Dinah Brown has just had a letter brought to say that her mother is dangerously ill, and that she must go directly if she wishes to see her alive. The place is more than ten miles away from here, out in the country, and she says if she takes the train she should still have four miles to walk; and so weak as she is, and the baby only four weeks old, of course that would be impossible; and she wants to know if you would take her in your cab, and she promises to pay you faithfully as she can get the money."

"Tut, tut, we'll see about that. It was not the money I was thinking about, but of losing our Sunday; the horses are tired, and I am tired too—that's where it pinches."

"It pinches all round for that matter," said Polly, "for it's only half Sunday without you, but you know we should do to other people as we should like they should do to us; and I know very well what I should like if my mother was dying; and Jerry, dear, I am sure it won't break the Sabbath; for if pulling a poor beast or a donkey out of a pit would not spoil it, I am quite sure taking poor Dinah would not do it."

"Why, Polly, you are as good as the minister, and so, as I've had my Sunday morning sermon early to-day, you may go and tell Dinah that I'll be ready for her as the clock strikes ten; but stop—just step round to butcher Braydon's with my compliments, and ask him if he would lend me his light trap; I know he never uses it on Sunday, and it would make a wonderful difference to the horse."

Away she went, and soon returned saying that he could have the trap and welcome. "All right," said he, "now put me up a bit of bread and cheese, and I'll be back in the afternoon as soon as I can."

"And I'll have the meat pie ready for an early tea instead of for dinner," said Polly, and away she went, whilst he made his preparations to the tune of "Polly's the woman and no mistake," of which tune he was very fond.

I was selected for the journey, and at ten o'clock we started, in a light high-wheeled gig, which ran so easily, that after the four-wheeled cab, it seemed like nothing.

It was a fine May day, and as soon as we were out of the town, the sweet air, the smell of the fresh grass, and the soft country roads were as pleasant as they used to be in the old times, and I soon began to feel quite fresh.

Dinah's family lived in a small farm house, up a green lane, and close by a meadow with some fine shady trees: there were two cows feeding in it. A young man asked Jerry to bring his trap into the meadow, and he would tie me up in the cowshed; he wished he had a better stable to offer.

"If your cows would not be offended," said Jerry, "there is nothing my horse would like so well as to have an hour or two in your beautiful meadow; he's quiet, and it would be a rare treat for him."

"Do and welcome," said the young man; "the best we have is at your service for your kindness to my sister; we shall be having some dinner in an hour, and I hope you'll come in, though with mother so ill, we are all out of sorts in the house."

Jerry thanked him kindly, but said as he had some dinner with him, there was nothing he should like so well as walking about in the meadow.

When my harness was taken off, I did not know what I should do first—whether to eat the grass, or roll over on my back, or lie down and rest, or have a gallop across the meadow out of sheer spirits at being free; and I did all by turns. Jerry seemed to be quite as happy as I was; he sat down by a bank under a shady tree, and listened to the birds, then he sang himself, and read out of the little brown book he is so fond of, then wandered round the meadow and down by a little brook, where he picked the flowers and the hawthorn, and tied them up with long sprays of ivy; then he gave me a good feed of the oats which he had brought with him; but the time seemed all too short—I had not been in a field since I left poor Ginger at Earlshall.

We came home gently, and Jerry's first words as we came into the yard were, "Well, Polly, I have not lost my Sunday after all, for the birds were singing hymns in every bush, and I joined in the service; and as for Jack, he was like a young colt." When he handed Dolly the flowers, she jumped about for joy.

CHAPTER THIRTY EIGHT
DOLLY AND A REAL GENTLEMAN

The winter came in early, with a great deal of cold and wet. There was snow, or sleet, or rain, almost every day for weeks, changing only for keen driving winds, or sharp frosts. The horses all felt it very much. When it is a dry cold, a couple of good thick rugs will keep the warmth in us; but when it is soaking rain, they soon get wet through and are no good. Some of the drivers had a waterproof cover to throw over, which was a fine thing; but some of the men were so poor that they could not protect either themselves or their horses, and many of them suffered very much that winter. When we horses had worked half the day we went to our dry stables, and could rest; whilst they had to sit on their boxes, sometimes staying out as late as one or two o'clock in the morning, if they had a party to wait for. When the streets were slippery with frost or snow, that was the worst of all for us horses; one mile of such travelling, with a weight to draw, and no firm footing, would take more out of us than four on a good road; every nerve and muscle of our bodies is on the strain to keep our balance; and added to this, the fear of falling is more exhausting than anything else. If the roads are very bad indeed, our shoes are roughed, but that makes us feel nervous at first.

When the weather was very bad, many of the men would go and sit in the tavern close by, and get someone to watch for them; but they often lost a fare in that way, and could not, as Jerry said, be there without spending money. He never went to the "Rising Sun;" there was a coffee-shop near, where he now and then went—or he bought of an old man, who came to our rank with tins of hot coffee and pies. It was his opinion that spirits and beer made a man colder afterwards, and that dry clothes, good food, cheerfulness, and a comfortable wife at home, were the best things to keep a cabman warm.

Polly always supplied him with something to eat when he could not get home, and sometimes he would see little Dolly peeping from the corner of the street, to make sure if "Father" was on the stand. If she saw him, she would run off at full speed, and soon come back with something in a tin, or basket—some hot soup, or pudding that Polly had ready. It was wonderful how such a little thing could get safely across the street, often thronged with horses and carriages; but she was a brave little maid, and felt it quite an honour to bring "father's first course," as he used to call it. She was a general favourite on the stand, and there was not a man who would not have seen her safely across the street, if Jerry had not been able to do it.

One cold windy day, Dolly had brought Jerry a basin of something hot, and was standing by him whilst he ate it. He had scarcely begun, when a gentleman, walking towards us very fast, held up his umbrella. Jerry touched his hat in return, gave the basin to Dolly, and was taking off my cloth, when the gentleman, hastening up, cried out, "No, no, finish your soup, my friend; I have not much time to spare, but I can wait till you have done, and set your little girl safe on the pavement." So saying, he seated himself in the cab. Jerry thanked him kindly, and came back to Dolly.

"There Dolly, that's a gentleman; that's a real gentleman, Dolly, he has got time and thought for the comfort of a poor cabman and a little girl."

Jerry finished his soup, set the child across, and then took his orders to drive to "Clapham Rise." Several times after that, the same gentleman took our cab. I think he was very fond of dogs and horses, for whenever we took him to his own door, two or three dogs would come bounding out to meet him. Sometimes he came round and patted me, saying in his quiet, pleasant way, "This horse has got a good master, and he deserves it." It was a very rare thing for anyone to notice the horse that had been working for him. I have known ladies do it now and then, and this gentleman, and one or two others have given me a pat and a kind word; but ninety-nine out of a hundred, would as soon think of patting the steam engine that drew the train.

This gentleman was not young, and there was a forward stoop in his shoulders as if he was always going at something. His lips were thin, and close shut, though they had a very pleasant smile; his eye was keen, and there was something in his jaw and the motion of his head, that made one think he was very determined in anything he set about. His voice was pleasant and kind; any horse would trust that voice, though it was just as decided as everything else about him.

One day, he and another gentleman took our cab; they stopped at a shop in R— Street, and whilst his friend went in, he stood at the door. A little ahead of us on the other side of the street, a cart with two very fine horses was standing before some wine vaults;

the carter was not with them, and I cannot tell how long they had been standing, but they seemed to think they had waited long enough, and began to move off. Before they had gone many paces, the carter came running out and caught them. He seemed furious at their having moved, and with whip and rein punished them brutally, even beating them about the head. Our gentleman saw it all, and stepping quickly across the street, said in a decided voice,

"If you don't stop that directly, I'll have you summoned for leaving your horses, and for brutal conduct."

The man, who had clearly been drinking, poured forth some abusive language, but he left off knocking the horses about, and taking the reins, got into his cart; meantime our friend had quietly taken a note-book from his pocket, and looking at the name and address painted on the cart, he wrote something down.

"What do you want with that?" growled the carter, as he cracked his whip and was moving on; a nod, and a grim smile, was the only answer he got.

On returning to the cab, our friend was joined by his companion, who said laughingly, "I should have thought, Wright, you had enough business of your own to look after, without troubling yourself about other people's horses and servants."

Our friend stood still for a moment, and throwing his head a little back, "Do you know why this world is as bad as it is?"

"No," said the other.

"Then I'll tell you; it is because people think only about their own business, and won't trouble themselves to stand up for the oppressed, nor bring the wrong-doer to light. I never see a wicked thing like this without doing what I can, and many a master has thanked me for letting him know how his horses have been used."

"I wish there were more gentlemen like you, sir," said Jerry, "for they are wanted badly enough in this city."

After this we continued our journey, and as they got out of the cab, our friend was saying, "My doctrine is this, that if we see cruelty or wrong that we have the power to stop, and do nothing, we make ourselves sharers in the guilt."

CHAPTER THIRTY NINE
SEEDY SAM

I should say, that for a cab-horse I was very well off indeed; my driver was my owner, and it was his interest to treat me well, and not overwork me, even had he not been so good a man as he was; but there were a great many horses which belonged to the large cab-owners, who let them out to their drivers for so much money a day. As the horses did not belong to these men, the only thing they thought of was, how to get their money out of them, first, to pay the master, and then to provide for their own living, and a dreadful time some of these horses had of it. Of course I understood but little, but it was often talked over on the stand, and the Governor, who was a kind-hearted man, and fond of horses, would sometimes speak up if one came in very much jaded or ill-used.

One day, a shabby, miserable-looking driver, who went by the name of "Seedy Sam," brought in his horse looking dreadfully beat, and the Governor said, "You and your horse look more fit for the police station than for this rank."

The man flung his tattered rug over the horse, turned full round upon the Governor, and said, in a voice that sounded almost desperate, "If the police have any business with the matter, it ought to be with the masters who charge us so much, or with the fares that are fixed so low. If a man has to pay eighteen shillings a day for the use of a cab and two horses, as many of us have to do in the season,[1] and must make that up before we earn a penny for ourselves—I say 'tis more than hard work; nine shillings a day to get out of each horse, before you begin to get your own living; you know that's true, and if the horses don't work we must starve, and I and my children have known what that is before now. I've six of 'em and only one earns anything; I am on the stand fourteen or sixteen hours a day, and I haven't had a Sunday these ten or twelve weeks; you know Skinner never gives a day if he can help it, and if I don't work hard, tell me who does! I want a warm coat and a macintosh, but with so many to feed, how can a man get it? I had to pledge[2] my clock a week ago to pay Skinner, and I shall never see it again."

---

1 Corresponding with the sitting of Parliament, the time of year between January and late June when society's elite took up residence in London in order to participate in exclusive social events.
2 Pawn.

Some of the other drivers stood round nodding their heads, and saying he was right; the man went on—

"You that have your own horses and cabs, or drive for good masters, have a chance of getting on, and a chance of doing right; I haven't. We can't charge more than sixpence a mile after the first, within the four mile radius.[1] This very morning I had to go a clear six miles and only took three shillings. I could not get a return fare, and had to come all the way back; there's twelve miles for the horse and three shillings for me. After that I had a three-mile fare, and there were bags and boxes enough to have brought in a good many twopences if they had been put outside; but you know how people do; all that could be piled up inside on the front seat, were put in, and three heavy boxes went on the top, that was sixpence, and the fare one and sixpence; then I got a return for a shilling; now that makes eighteen miles for the horse and six shillings for me; there's three shillings still for that horse to earn, and nine shillings for the afternoon horse before I touch a penny. Of course it is not always so bad as that, but you know it often is, and I say 'tis a mockery to tell a man that he must not overwork his horse, for when a beast is downright tired, there's nothing but the whip that will keep his legs agoing—you can't help yourself—you must put your wife and children before the horse, the masters must look to that, we can't. I don't ill-use my horse for the sake of it, none of you can say I do; there's wrong lays somewhere—never a day's rest—never a quiet hour with the wife and children. I often feel like an old man though I'm only forty-five. You know how quick some of the gentry are to suspect us of cheating, and over-charging; why, they stand with their purses in their hands, counting it over to a penny, and looking at us as if we were pick-pockets. I wish some of 'em had got to sit on my box sixteen hours a day, and get a living out of it, and eighteen shillings beside, and that in all weathers; they would not be so uncommon particular never to give us a sixpence over, or to cram all the luggage inside. Of course, some of 'em tip us pretty handsome now and then, or else we could not live, but you can't depend upon that."

---

1 Victorian cab fares were regulated to six pence per mile within a four-mile radius of Charing Cross (at the centre of London), and one shilling per mile beyond this radius.

The men who stood round, much approved this speech, and one of them said, "It is desperate hard, and if a man sometimes does what is wrong, it is no wonder, and if he gets a dram too much, who's to blow him up?"

Jerry had taken no part in this conversation, but I never saw his face look so sad before. The Governor had stood with both his hands in his pockets; now he took his handkerchief out of his hat, and wiped his forehead.

"You've beaten me, Sam," he said, "for it's all true, and I won't cast it up to you any more about the police; it was the look in that horse's eye that came over me. It is hard lines for man, and it's hard lines for beast, and who's to mend it I don't know; but any way you might tell the poor beast that you were sorry to take it out of him in that way. Sometimes a kind word is all we can give 'em, poor brutes, and 'tis wonderful what they do understand."

A few mornings after this talk, a new man came on the stand with Sam's cab.

"Halloo!" said one, "what's up with Seedy Sam?"

"He's ill in bed," said the man, "he was taken last night in the yard, and could scarcely crawl home. His wife sent a boy this morning to say, his father was in a high fever and could not get out; so I'm here instead."

The next morning the same man came again. "How is Sam?" enquired the Governor, "He's gone," said the man.

"What? Gone! you don't mean to say he's dead?"

"Just snuffed out," said the other; "he died at four o'clock this morning; all yesterday he was raving about Skinner, and having no Sundays. 'I never had a Sunday's rest,' these were his last words."

No one spoke for a while, and then the Governor said, "I tell you what, mates, this is a warning for us."

CHAPTER FORTY
Poor Ginger

One day, whilst our cab and many others were waiting outside one of the Parks, where music was playing, a shabby old cab drove up beside ours. The horse was an old worn-out chestnut, with an ill-kept coat and bones that shewed plainly through it, the knees knuckled over, and the forelegs were very unsteady. I had been eating some hay, the wind rolled a little lock of it that way, and the poor creature put out her long thin neck and picked it up, and then turned round and looked about for more. There was a hopeless look in the dull eye that I could not help noticing, and then, as I was thinking where I had seen that horse before, she looked full at me and said, "Black Beauty, is that you?"

It was Ginger! but how changed! The beautifully arched and glossy neck was now straight, and lank, and fallen in, the clean straight legs and delicate fetlocks were swelled; the joints were grown out of shape with hard work; the face, that was once so full of spirit and life, was now full of suffering, and I could tell by the heaving of her sides, and her frequent cough, how bad her breath was.

Our drivers were standing together a little way off, so I sided up to her a step or two, that we might have a little quiet talk. It was a sad tale that she had to tell.

After a twelvemonth's run off at Earlshall, she was considered to be fit for work again, and was sold to a gentleman. For a little while she got on very well, but after a longer gallop than usual, the old strain returned, and after being rested and doctored, she was again sold. In this way she changed hands several times, but always getting lower down. "And so at last," said she, "I was bought by a man who keeps a number of cabs and horses, and lets them out. You look well off, and I am glad of it, but I could not tell you what my life has been. When they found out my weakness, they said I was not worth what they gave for me, and that I must go into one of the low cabs, and just be used up; that is what they are doing, whipping and working with never one thought of what I suffer—they paid for me, and must get it out of me, they say. The man who hires me now, pays a deal of money to the owner every day, and so he has to get it out of me too; and so it's all the week round and round, with never a Sunday rest."

I said, "You used to stand up for yourself if you were ill-used."

"Ah!" she said, "I did once, but it's no use; men are strongest, and if they are cruel and have no feeling, there is nothing that we can do, but just bear it, bear it on and on to the end. I wish the end was come, I wish I was dead. I have seen dead horses, and I am sure they do not suffer pain; I wish I may drop down dead at my work, and not be sent off to the knacker's."[1]

I was very much troubled, and I put my nose up to hers, but I could say nothing to comfort her. I think she was pleased to see me, for she said, "You are the only friend I ever had."

Just then her driver came up, and with a tug at her mouth, backed her out of the line and drove off, leaving me very sad indeed.

A short time after this, a cart with a dead horse in it passed our cab-stand. The head hung out of the cart-tail, the lifeless tongue was slowly dropping with blood; and the sunken eyes! but I can't speak of them, the sight was too dreadful. It was a chestnut horse with a long thin neck. I saw a white streak down the forehead. I believe it was Ginger; I hoped it was, for then her troubles would be over. Oh! if men were more merciful, they would shoot us before we came to such misery.[2]

---

1 Slang term for a person who slaughters animals unfit for work in order to make use of their body parts for products such as dog food and glue.

2 Repeated references to the kindness of euthanasia highlight the horrors associated with working a horse to death; see above, p. 98, n. 1.

CHAPTER FORTY ONE
The Butcher

I saw a great deal of trouble amongst the horses in London, and much of it that might have been prevented by a little common sense. We horses do not mind hard work if we are treated reasonably; and I am sure there are many driven by quite poor men who have a happier life than I had, when I used to go in the Countess of W——s carriage, with my silver-mounted harness and high feeding.[1]

It often went to my heart to see how the little ponies were used, straining along with heavy loads, or staggering under heavy blows from some low cruel boy. Once I saw a little grey pony with a thick mane and a pretty head, and so much like Merrylegs, that if I had not been in harness, I should have neighed to him. He was doing his best to pull a heavy cart, while a strong rough boy was cutting him under the belly with his whip, and chucking cruelly at his little mouth. Could it be Merrylegs? It was just like him; but then Mr. Blomefield was never to sell him, and I think he would not do it; but this might have been quite as good a little fellow, and had as happy a place when he was young.

I often noticed the great speed at which butchers' horses were made to go, though I did not know why it was so, till one day when we had to wait some time in "St. John's Wood."[2] There was a butcher's shop next door, and as we were standing, a butcher's cart came dashing up at a great pace. The horse was hot, and much exhausted; he hung his head down, while his heaving sides and trembling legs showed how hard he had been driven. The lad jumped out of the cart and was getting the basket, when the master came out of the shop much displeased. After looking at the horse, he turned angrily to the lad; "How many times shall I tell you not to drive in this way? you ruined the last horse, and broke his wind, and you are going to ruin this in the same way. If you were not my own son, I would dismiss you on the spot; it is a disgrace to have a horse brought to the shop in a condition like that; you are liable to be taken up by the police for such driving, and if you are, you need not look to me for bail, for I have spoken to you till I am tired; you must look out for yourself."

---

1 A rich diet of oats intended to make the horse energetic and spirited.
2 A fashionable residential district in northwest London.

During this speech, the boy had stood by, sullen and dogged, but when his father ceased, he broke out angrily. It wasn't his fault, and he wouldn't take the blame, he was only going by orders all the time. "You always say, 'Now be quick, now look sharp!' and when I go to the houses, one wants a leg of mutton for an early dinner, and I must be back with it in a quarter of an hour. Another cook had forgotten to order the beef; I must go and fetch it and be back in no time, or the mistress will scold; and the housekeeper says they have company coming unexpected, and must have some chops sent up directly; and the lady at No. 4 in the Crescent, never orders her dinner till the meat comes in for lunch, and it's nothing but hurry, hurry, all the time. If the gentry would think of what they want, and order their meat the day before, there need not be this blow up!"

"I wish to goodness they would," said the butcher; "'twould save me a wonderful deal of harass, and I could suit my customers much better if I knew beforehand—but there—what's the use of talking—who ever thinks of a butcher's convenience, or a butcher's horse? Now then, take him in, and look to him well: mind, he does not go out again to-day, and if anything else is wanted, you must carry it yourself in the basket." With that he went in, and the horse was led away.

But all boys are not cruel. I have seen some as fond of their pony or donkey as if it had been a favourite dog, and the little creatures have worked away as cheerfully and willingly for their young drivers as I work for Jerry. It may be hard work sometimes, but a friend's hand and voice makes it easy.

There was a young coster-boy who came up our street with greens and potatoes; he had an old pony, not very handsome, but the cheerfullest and pluckiest little thing I ever saw, and to see how fond those two were of each other, was a treat. The pony followed his master like a dog, and when he got into his cart, would trot off without a whip or a word, and rattle down the street as merrily as if he had come out of the Queen's stables. Jerry liked the boy, and called him "Prince Charlie," for he said he would make a king of drivers someday.

There was an old man, too, who used to come up our street with a little coal cart; he wore a coal-heaver's hat, and looked rough and black. He and his old horse used to plod together along the street, like two good partners who understood each other; the horse would stop of his own accord, at the doors where they took coal of him: he used to keep one ear bent towards his master. The old man's cry could be heard up the street long before he came near. I never knew what he said, but the children called him "Old Ba-a-ar Hoo," for it sounded like that. Polly took her coal of him, and was very friendly, and Jerry said it was a comfort to think how happy an old horse might be in a poor place.

CHAPTER FORTY TWO
The Election

As we came into the yard one afternoon, Polly came out, "Jerry! I've had Mr. B— here asking about your vote, and he wants to hire your cab for the election: he will call for an answer."

"Well, Polly, you may say that my cab will be otherwise engaged; I should not like to have it pasted over with their great bills, and as to make Jack and Captain race about to the public-houses to bring up half-drunken voters, why, I think 'twould be an insult to the horses. No, I shan't do it."

"I suppose you'll vote for the gentleman? he said he was of your politics."

"So he is in some things, but I shall not vote for him, Polly; you know what his trade is?"

"Yes."

"Well, a man who gets rich by that trade, may be all very well in some ways, but he is blind as to what working men want: I could not in my conscience send him up to make the laws. I dare say they'll be angry, but every man must do what he thinks to be the best for his country."

On the morning before the election, Jerry was putting me into the shafts, when Dolly came into the yard sobbing and crying, with her little blue frock and white pinafore spattered all over with mud.

"Why, Dolly, what is the matter?"

"Those naughty boys," she sobbed, "have thrown the dirt all over me, and called me a little ragga—ragga—"

"They called her a little blue raggamuffin, father," said Harry, who ran in, looking very angry; "but I have given it to them, they won't insult my sister again. I have given them a thrashing they will remember; a set of cowardly, rascally, orange[1] black-guards!"

Jerry kissed the child and said, "Run in to mother, my pet, and tell her I think you had better stay at home to-day and help her."

Then turning gravely to Harry—"My boy, I hope you will always defend your sister, and give anybody who insults her a good thrashing—that is as it should be; but mind, I won't have

---

1 The colours blue and orange were worn to signify support for conservative and liberal political parties respectively.

any election blackguarding on my premises. There are as many blue blackguards as there are orange, and as many white as there are purple, or any other colour, and I won't have any of my family mixed up with it. Even women and children are ready to quarrel for the sake of a colour, and not one in ten of them knows what it is about."

"Why, father, I thought blue was for Liberty."

"My boy, Liberty does not come from colours, they only show party, and all the liberty you can get out of them is, liberty to get drunk at other people's expense, liberty to ride to the poll in a dirty old cab, liberty to abuse anyone that does not wear your colour, and to shout yourself hoarse at what you only half understand—that's your liberty!"

"Oh, father, you are laughing."

"No, Harry, I am serious, and I am ashamed to see how men go on that ought to know better. An election is a very serious thing; at least it ought to be, and every man ought to vote according to his conscience, and let his neighbour do the same."

CHAPTER FORTY THREE
A FRIEND IN NEED

At last came the election day; there was no lack of work for Jerry and me. First, came a stout puffy gentleman with a carpet bag; he wanted to go to the Bishopsgate Station: then we were called by a party who wished to be taken to the Regent's Park; and next we were wanted in a side street where a timid anxious old lady was waiting to be taken to the Bank: there we had to stop to take her back again, and just as we had set her down, a red-faced gentleman with a handful of papers, came running up out of breath, and before Jerry could get down, he had opened the door, popped himself in, and called out "Bow Street Police Station, quick!" so, off we went with him, and when, after another turn or two we came back, there was no other cab on the stand.

Jerry put on my nose-bag, for as he said, "We must eat when we can on such days as these; so munch away, Jack, and make the best of your time, old boy."

I found I had a good feed of crushed oats wetted up with a little bran; this would be a treat any day, but very refreshing then. Jerry was so thoughtful and kind—what horse would not do his best for such a master? Then he took out one of Polly's meat pies, and standing near me, he began to eat it. The streets were very full, and the cabs with the Candidates' colours on them, were dashing about through the crowds as if life and limb were of no consequence; we saw two people knocked down that day, and one was a woman. The horses were having a bad time of it, poor things! but the voters inside thought nothing of that, many of them were half drunk, hurrahing out of the cab windows if their own party came by. It was the first election I had seen, and I don't want to be in another, though I have heard things are better now.

Jerry and I had not eaten many mouthfuls, before a poor young woman, carrying a heavy child, came along the street. She was looking this way, and that way, and seemed quite bewildered. Presently she made her way up to Jerry, and asked if he could tell her the way to St. Thomas's Hospital, and how far it was to get there. She had come from the country that morning, she said, in a market cart; she did not know about the election, and was quite a stranger in London. She had got an order for the Hospital for her little boy. The child was crying with a feeble pining cry. "Poor little fellow!" she said, "he suffers a deal of pain, he is four years old, and can't walk any more than a baby; but the Doctor said if I could get him into the Hospital, he might get well; pray, sir, how far is it? and which way is it?"

"Why, missis," said Jerry, "you can't get there walking through crowds like this! why, it is three miles away, and that child is heavy."

"Yes, bless him, he is, but I am strong, thank God, and if I knew the way, I think I should get on somehow: please tell me the way."

"You can't do it," said Jerry, "you might be knocked down and the child be run over. Now, look here, just get into this cab, and I'll drive you safe to the Hospital: don't you see the rain is coming on?"

"No sir, no, I can't do that, thank you, I have only just money enough to get back with: please tell me the way."

"Look you here, missis," said Jerry, "I've got a wife and dear children at home, and I know a father's feelings: now get you into that cab, and I'll take you there for nothing; I'd be ashamed of myself to let a woman and a sick child run a risk like that."

"Heaven bless you!" said the woman, and burst into tears.

"There, there, cheer up, my dear, I'll soon take you there; come, let me put you inside."

As Jerry went to open the door, two men with colours in their hats and button-holes, ran up, calling out, "Cab!"

"Engaged," cried Jerry; but one of the men pushing past the woman, sprang into the cab, followed by the other. Jerry looked as stern as a policeman: "This cab is already engaged, gentlemen, by that lady."

"Lady!" said one of them; "oh! she can wait: our business is very important, beside we were in first, it is our right, and we shall stay in."

A droll smile came over Jerry's face as he shut the door upon them. "All right, gentlemen, pray stay in as long as it suits you: I can wait whilst you rest yourselves;" and turning his back on them, he walked up to the young woman, who was standing near me. "They'll soon be gone," he said, laughing, "don't trouble yourself, my dear."

And they soon were gone, for when they understood Jerry's

dodge, they got out, calling him all sorts of bad names, and blustering about his number, and getting a summons. After this little stoppage we were soon on our way to the Hospital, going as much as possible through bye streets. Jerry rung the great bell, and helped the young woman out.

"Thank you a thousand times," she said; "I could never have got here alone."

"You're kindly welcome, and I hope the dear child will soon be better."

He watched her go in at the door, and gently he said to himself—"Inasmuch as ye have done it to one of the least of these,"[1] then he patted my neck, which was always his way when anything pleased him.

The rain was now coming down fast, and just as we were leaving the Hospital, the door opened again, and the porter called out, "Cab!" We stopped, and a lady came down the steps. Jerry seemed to know her at once; she put back her veil and said, "Barker! Jeremiah Barker! is it you? I am very glad to find you here; you are just the friend I want, for it is very difficult to get a cab in this part of London today."

"I shall be proud to serve you, ma'am, I am right glad I happened to be here; where may I take you to, ma'am?"

"To the Paddington Station, and then if we are in good time, as I think we shall be, you shall tell me all about Mary[2] and the children."

We got to the station in good time, and being under shelter, the lady stood a good while talking to Jerry. I found she had been Polly's mistress, and after many enquiries about her, she said, "How do you find the cab-work suit you in winter? I know Mary was rather anxious about you last year."

"Yes, ma'am, she was; I had a bad cough that followed me up quite into the warm weather, and when I am kept out late, she does worry herself a good deal. You see, ma'am, it is all hours and all weathers, and that does try a man's constitution; but I am getting on pretty well, and I should feel quite lost if I had not horses to look after. I was brought up to it, and I am afraid I should not do so well at anything else."

---

1 Jerry is quoting the Bible (Matthew 25:40).
2 Polly is a nickname for Mary.

"Well, Barker," she said, "it would be a great pity that you should seriously risk your health in this work, not only for your own, but for Mary and the children's sake: there are many places, where good drivers or good grooms are wanted; and if ever you think you ought to give up this cab-work, let me know." Then sending some kind messages to Mary she put something into his hand, saying, "There is five shillings each for the two children; Mary will know how to spend it." Jerry thanked her and seemed much pleased, and turning out of the station, we at last reached home, and I, at least, was tired.

CHAPTER FORTY FOUR
OLD CAPTAIN AND HIS SUCCESSOR

Captain and I were great friends. He was a noble old fellow, and he was very good company. I never thought that he would have to leave his home and go down the hill, but his turn came: and this was how it happened. I was not there, but I heard all about it.

He and Jerry had taken a party to the great railway station over London Bridge, and were coming back, somewhere between the Bridge and the Monument,[1] when Jerry saw a brewer's empty dray coming along, drawn by two powerful horses. The drayman was lashing his horses with his heavy whip; the dray was light, and they started off at a furious rate; the man had no control over them, and the street was full of traffic; one young girl was knocked down and run over, and the next moment they dashed up against our cab; both the wheels were torn off, and the cab was thrown over. Captain was dragged down, the shafts splintered, and one of them ran into his side. Jerry too was thrown, but was only bruised; nobody could tell how he escaped, he always said 'twas a miracle. When poor Captain was got up, he was found to be very much cut and knocked about, Jerry led him home gently, and a sad sight it was to see the blood soaking into his white coat, and dropping from his side and shoulder. The drayman was proved to be very drunk, and was fined, and the brewer had to pay damages to our master; but there was no one to pay damages to poor Captain.

The farrier and Jerry did the best they could to ease his pain, and make him comfortable. The fly had to be mended, and for several days I did not go out, and Jerry earned nothing. The first time we went to the stand after the accident, the Governor came up to hear how Captain was.

"He'll never get over it," said Jerry, "at least not for my work, so the farrier said this morning. He says he may do for carting, and that sort of work. It has put me out very much. Carting indeed! I've seen what horses come to at that work round London. I only wish all the drunkards could be put in a lunatic asylum, instead of being allowed to run foul of sober people. If they would break their *own* bones, and smash their *own* carts, and

---

1 Monument to the Great Fire of London, located in the City of London near the north side of London Bridge.

lame their *own* horses, that would be their own affair, and we might let them alone, but it seems to me that the innocent always suffer; and then they talk about compensation! You can't make compensation—there's all the trouble, and vexation, and loss of time, besides losing a good horse that's like an old friend—it's nonsense talking of compensation! If there's one devil, that I should like to see in the bottomless pit more than another, it's the drink devil.

"I say, Jerry," said the Governor, "you are treading pretty hard on my toes, you know; I'm not so good as you are, more shame for me, I wish I was."

"Well," said Jerry, "why don't you cut with it, Governor? you are too good a man to be the slave of such a thing."

"I'm a great fool, Jerry, but I tried once for two days, and I thought I should have died: how did you do?"

"I had hard work at it for several weeks; you see, I never did get drunk, but I found that I was not my own master, and that when the craving came on, it was hard work to say 'no.' I saw that one of us must knock under—the drink devil, or Jerry Barker, and I said that it should not be Jerry Barker, God helping me: but it was a struggle, and I wanted all the help I could get, for till I tried to break the habit, I did not know how strong it was; but then Polly took such pains that I should have good food, and when the craving came on, I used to get a cup of coffee, or some peppermint, or read a bit in my book, and that was a help to me: sometimes I had to say over and over to myself, 'Give up the drink or lose your soul? give up the drink or break Polly's heart?' But thanks be to God, and my dear wife, my chains were broken, and now for ten years I have not tasted a drop, and never wish for it."

"I've a great mind to try at it," said Grant, "for 'tis a poor thing not to be one's own master."

"Do Governor, do, you'll never repent it, and what a help it would be to some of the poor fellows in our rank if they saw you do without it. I know there's two or three would like to keep out of that tavern if they could."

At first Captain seemed to do well, but he was a very old horse, and it was only his wonderful constitution, and Jerry's care, that had kept him up at the cab-work so long; now he broke down very much. The farrier said he might mend up enough to sell for a few pounds, but Jerry said, no! a few pounds got by selling a good old servant into hard work and misery, would canker all the rest of his money, and he thought the kindest thing he could do for the fine old fellow, would be to put a sure bullet through his heart, and then he would never suffer more; for he did not know where to find a kind master for the rest of his days.

The day after this was decided, Harry took me to the forge for some new shoes; when I returned Captain was gone. I, and the family all felt it very much.

Jerry had now to look out for another horse, and he soon heard of one through an acquaintance who was under groom[1] in a nobleman's stables. He was a valuable young horse, but he had run away, smashed into another carriage, flung his lordship out, and so cut and blemished himself, that he was no longer fit for a gentleman's stables, and the coachman had orders to look round, and sell him as well as he could.

"I can do with high spirits," said Jerry, "if a horse is not vicious or hard-mouthed."

"There is not a bit of vice in him," said the man, "his mouth is very tender, and I think myself, that was the cause of the accident; you see he had just been clipped, and the weather was bad, and he had not had exercise enough, and when he did go out, he was as full of spring as a balloon. Our governor, (the coachman I mean), had him harnessed in as tight and strong as he could, with the martingale,[2] and the bearing rein, a very sharp curb,[3] and the reins put in at the bottom bar; it is my belief that it made the horse mad, being tender in the mouth and so full of spirit."

"Likely enough; I'll come and see him," said Jerry.

The next day, Hotspur[4]—that was his name, came home; he was a fine brown horse, without a white hair in him, as tall as Captain, with a very handsome head, and only five years old. I gave him a friendly greeting by way of good fellowship, but did not ask him any questions. The first night he was very restless;

---

1 Groom's helper, or stable boy.
2 A harness attachment that adds additional leverage to the reins via straps that run between the horse's legs and are attached to the girth.
3 A curb bit has a long shank and a curb chain that runs under the horse's jaw, magnifying the leverage. The combination here describes a very harsh, restrictive mode of harness (see illustrations in Appendix E4).
4 The nickname of Sir Henry Percy (1364–1403), a fiery, impetuous nobleman killed in a rebellion against Henry IV.

instead of lying down, he kept jerking his halter rope up and down through the ring, and knocking the block about against the manger till I could not sleep. However, the next day, after five or six hours in the cab, he came in quiet and sensible. Jerry patted and talked to him a good deal, and very soon they understood each other, and Jerry said that with an easy bit, and plenty of work, he would be as gentle as a lamb; and that it was an ill wind that blew nobody good, for if his lordship had lost a hundred-guinea favourite, the cabman had gained a good horse with all his strength in him.

Hotspur thought it a great come down to be a cab-horse, and was disgusted at standing in the rank, but he confessed to me at the end of the week, that an easy mouth, and a free head, made up for a great deal, and after all, the work was not so degrading as having one's head and tail fastened to each other at the saddle. In fact, he settled in well, and Jerry liked him very much.

CHAPTER FORTY FIVE

Christmas and the New Year are very merry times for some people; but for cabmen and cabmen's horses, it is no holiday, though it may be a harvest. There are so many parties, balls, and places of amusement open, that the work is hard and often late. Sometimes driver and horse have to wait for hours in the rain or frost, shivering with cold, whilst the merry people within are dancing away to the music. I wonder if the beautiful ladies ever think of the weary cabman waiting on his box, and his patient beast standing, till his legs get stiff with cold.

I had now most of the evening work, as I was well accustomed to standing, and Jerry was also more afraid of Hotspur taking cold. We had a great deal of late work in the Christmas week, and Jerry's cough was bad; but however late we were, Polly sat up for him, and came out with the lantern to meet him, looking anxious and troubled. On the evening of the New Year, we had to take two gentlemen to a house in one of the West End Squares; we set them down at nine o'clock and were told to come again at eleven, "But," said one of them, "as it is a card party, you may have to wait a few minutes, but don't be late."

As the clock struck eleven we were at the door, for Jerry was always punctual. The clock chimed the quarters—one, two, three, and then struck twelve, but the door did not open.

The wind had been very changeable, with squalls of rain during the day, but now it came on sharp driving sleet, which seemed to come all the way round; it was very cold, and there was no shelter. Jerry got off his box and came and pulled one of my cloths a little more over my neck; then he took a turn or two up and down, stamping his feet; then he began to beat his arms, but that set him off coughing; so he opened the cab door and sat at the bottom with his feet on the pavement, and was a little sheltered. Still the clock chimed the quarters, and no one came. At half-past twelve, he rang at the bell and asked the servant if he would be wanted that night.

"Oh! yes, you'll be wanted safe enough," said the man, "you must not go, it will soon be over," and again Jerry sat down, but his voice was so hoarse I could hardly hear him.

At a quarter past one the door opened, and the two gentlemen came out; they got into the cab without a word, and told Jerry where to drive, that was nearly two miles. My legs were numb with cold, and I thought I should have stumbled. When the men got out, they never said they were sorry to have kept us waiting so long, but were angry at the charge: however, as Jerry never charged more than was his due, so he never took less, and they had to pay for the two hours and quarter waiting; but it was hard-earned money to Jerry.

At last we got home; he could hardly speak, and his cough was dreadful. Polly asked no questions, but opened the door and held the lantern for him. "Can't I do something?" she said.

"Yes, get Jack something warm, and then boil me some gruel;" this was said in a hoarse whisper, he could hardly get his breath, but he gave me a rub down as usual, and even went up into the hayloft for an extra bundle of straw for my bed. Polly brought me a warm mash that made me comfortable, and then they locked the door.

It was late the next morning before anyone came, and then it was only Harry. He cleaned us and fed us, and swept out the stalls; then he put the straw back again as if it was Sunday. He was very still, and neither whistled nor sang. At noon he came again and gave us our food and water; this time Dolly came with him; she was crying, and I could gather from what they said, that Jerry was dangerously ill, and the doctor said it was a bad case. So two days passed, and there was great trouble indoors. We only saw Harry and sometimes Dolly. I think she came for company, for Polly was always with Jerry, and he had to be kept very quiet.

On the third day, whilst Harry was in the stable, a tap came at the door, and Governor Grant came in. "I wouldn't go to the house, my boy," he said, "but I want to know how your father is."

"He is very bad," said Harry, "he can't be much worse; they call it bronchitis; the doctor thinks it will turn one way or another to-night."

"That's bad, very bad," said Grant, shaking his head; "I know two men who died of that last week; it takes 'em off in no time; but whilst there's life there's hope, so you must keep up your spirits."

"Yes," said Harry quickly, "and the doctor said that father had a better chance than most men, because he didn't drink. He said yesterday the fever was so high, that if father had been a drinking man, it would have burnt him up like a piece of paper; but I believe he thinks he will get over it; don't you think he will, Mr. Grant?"

The Governor looked puzzled, "If there's any rule that good men should get over these things, I am sure he will, my boy; he's the best man I know—I'll look in early to-morrow."

Early next morning he was there. "Well?" said he.

"Father is better," said Harry, "mother hopes he will get over it."

"Thank God!" said the Governor, "and now you must keep him warm, and keep his mind easy, and that brings me to the horses; you see, Jack will be all the better for the rest of a week or two in a warm stable, and you can easily take him a turn up and down the street to stretch his legs; but this young one, if he does not get work, he will soon be all up on end as you may say, and will be rather too much for you; and when he does go out, there'll be an accident."

"It is like that now," said Harry, "I have kept him short of corn, but he is so full of spirit I don't know what to do with him."

"Just so," said Grant; "now look here, will you tell your mother that if she is agreeable, I will come for him every day till something is arranged, and take him for a good spell of work, and whatever he earns, I'll bring your mother half of it, and that will help with the horses' feed. Your father is in a good club,[1] I know, but that won't keep the horses, and they'll be eating their heads off all this time: I'll come at noon and hear what she says," and without waiting for Harry's thanks, he was gone.

At noon I think he went and saw Polly, for he and Harry came to the stable together, harnessed Hotspur, and took him out.

For a week or more he came for Hotspur, and when Harry thanked him or said anything about his kindness, he laughed it off, saying, it was all good luck for him, for his horses were wanting a little rest which they would not otherwise have had.

Jerry grew better steadily, but the doctor said that he must never go back to the cab-work again if he wished to be an old man. The children had many consultations together about what father and mother would do, and how they could help to earn money.

One afternoon, Hotspur was brought in very wet and dirty. "The streets are nothing but slush," said the Governor, "it will give you a good warming, my boy, to get him clean and dry."

---

1 Benefit clubs provided insurance against loss of income for members, who paid a small weekly or monthly premium that entitled them to a cash benefit in case of illness.

"All right, Governor," said Harry, "I shall not leave him till he is; you know I have been trained by my father."

"I wish all the boys had been trained like you," said the Governor.

While Harry was sponging off the mud from Hotspur's body and legs, Dolly came in, looking very full of something.

"Who lives at Fairstowe, Harry? Mother has got a letter from Fairstowe; she seemed so glad, and ran upstairs to father with it."

"Don't you know? Why it is the name of Mrs. Fowler's place—mother's old mistress, you know—the lady that father met last summer, who sent you and me five shillings each."

"Oh! Mrs. Fowler, of course I know all about her, I wonder what she is writing to mother about."

"Mother wrote to her last week," said Harry; "you know she told father if ever he gave up the cab-work, she would like to know. I wonder what she says; run in and see, Dolly."

Harry scrubbed away at Hotspur with a huish! huish! like any old ostler.

In a few minutes Dolly came dancing into the stable. "Oh! Harry! there never was anything so beautiful; Mrs. Fowler says, we are all to go and live near her; there is a cottage now empty that will just suit us, with a garden, and a hen house, and apple trees, and everything! and her coachman is going away in the spring, and then she will want father in his place; and there are good families round, where you can get a place in the garden, or the stable, or as a page boy; and there's a good school for me; and mother is laughing and crying by turns, and father does look so happy!"

"That's uncommon jolly," said Harry, "and just the right thing, I should say; it will suit father and mother both; but I don't intend to be a page boy with tight clothes and rows of buttons. I'll be a groom or a gardener."

It was quickly settled that as soon as Jerry was well enough, they should remove to the country, and that the cab and horses should be sold as soon as possible. This was heavy news for me, for I was not young now, and could not look for any improvement in my condition. Since I left Birtwick I had never been so happy as with my dear master Jerry; but three years of cab-work, even under the best conditions, will tell on one's strength, and I felt that I was not the horse that I had been.

Grant said at once that he would take Hotspur; and there were men on the stand who would have bought me; but Jerry said I should not go to cab-work again with just anybody, and the Governor promised to find a place for me where I should be comfortable.

The day came for going away. Jerry had not been allowed to go out yet, and I never saw him after that New Year's eve. Polly and the children came to bid me good-bye. "Poor old Jack! dear old Jack! I wish we could take you with us," she said, and then laying her hand on my mane, she put her face close to my neck and kissed me. Dolly was crying and kissed me too. Harry stroked me a great deal, but said nothing, only he seemed very sad, and so I was led away to my new place.

PART IV.

CHAPTER FORTY SIX
JAKES AND THE LADY

I was sold to a corn dealer and baker, whom Jerry knew, and with him he thought I should have good food and fair work. In the first he was quite right, and if my master had always been on the premises, I do not think I should have been over-loaded, but there was a foreman who was always hurrying and driving everyone, and frequently when I had quite a full load, he would order something else to be taken on. My carter, whose name was Jakes, often said it was more than I ought to take, but the other always overruled him, "'twas no use going twice when once would do, and he chose to get business forward." Jakes, like the other carters, always had the bearing rein up, which prevented me from drawing easily, and by the time I had been there three or four months, I found the work telling very much on my strength.

One day, I was loaded more than usual, and part of the road was a steep uphill: I used all my strength, but I could not get on, and was obliged continually to stop. This did not please my driver, and he laid his whip on badly, "Get on, you lazy fellow," he said, "or I'll make you." Again I started the heavy load, and struggled on a few yards; again the whip came down, and again I struggled forward. The pain of that great cart whip was sharp, but my mind was hurt quite as much as my poor sides. To be punished and abused when I was doing my very best was so hard, it took the heart out of me. A third time he was flogging me cruelly, when a lady stepped quickly up to him, and said in a sweet earnest voice,

"Oh! pray do not whip your good horse anymore; I am sure he is doing all he can, and the road is very steep, I am sure he is doing his best."

"If doing his best won't get this load up, he must do something more than his best, that's all I know, ma'am," said Jakes.

"But is it not a very heavy load?" she said.

"Yes, yes, too heavy," he said, "but that's not my fault, the foreman came just as we were starting, and would have three hundred-weight more put on to save him trouble, and I must get on with it as well as I can." He was raising the whip again, when the lady said,

"Pray stop, I think I can help you if you will let me."

The man laughed.

"You see," she said, "you do not give him a fair chance; he cannot use all his power with his head held back as it is with that bearing rein; if you would take it off, I am sure he would do better—*do* try it," she said persuasively, "I should be very glad if you would."

"Well, well," said Jakes, with a short laugh, "anything to please a lady of course. How far would you wish it down, ma'am?"

"Quite down, give him his head altogether."

The rein was taken off, and in a moment I put my head down to my very knees. What a comfort it was! Then I tossed it up and down several times to get the aching stiffness out of my neck.

"Poor fellow! that is what you wanted," said she, patting and stroking me with her gentle hand; "and now if you will speak kindly to him and lead him on, I believe he will be able to do better."

Jakes took the rein—"Come on, Blackie." I put down my head, and threw my whole weight against the collar; I spared no strength; the load moved on, and I pulled it steadily up the hill, and then stopped to take breath.

The lady had walked along the footpath, and now came across into the road. She stroked and patted my neck, as I had not been patted for many a long day. "You see he was quite willing when you gave him the chance; I am sure he is a fine-tempered creature, and I dare say has known better days; you won't put that rein on again, will you?" for he was just going to hitch it up on the old plan.

"Well, ma'am, I can't deny that having his head has helped him up the hill, and I'll remember it another time, and thank you, ma'am; but if he went without a bearing rein, I should be the laughing stock of all the carters; it is the fashion, you see."

"Is it not better," she said, "to lead a good fashion, than to follow a bad one? A great many gentlemen do not use bearing reins now; our carriage horses have not worn them for fifteen years, and work with much less fatigue than those who have them; besides," she added in a very serious voice, "we have no right to distress any of God's creatures without a very good reason; we call them dumb animals, and so they are, for they cannot tell us how they feel, but they do not suffer less because they have no words, but I must not detain you now; I thank you for trying my plan with your good horse, and I am sure you will find it far better than the whip. Good day," and with another soft pat on my neck she stepped lightly across to the path, and I saw her no more.

"That was a real lady, I'll be bound for it," said Jakes to himself, "she spoke just as polite as if I was a gentleman, and I'll try her plan, uphill, at any rate;" and I must do him the justice to say, that he let my rein out several holes, and going uphill after that, he always gave me my head; but the heavy loads went on. Good feed and fair rest will keep up one's strength under full work, but no horse can stand against over-loading; and I was getting so thoroughly pulled down from this cause, that a younger horse was bought in my place. I may as well mention here, what I suffered at this time from another cause. I had heard horses speak of it, but had never myself had experience of the evil; this was a badly-lighted stable; there was only one very small window at the end, and the consequence was, that the stalls were almost dark.

Besides the depressing effect this had on my spirits, it very much weakened my sight, and when I was suddenly brought out of the darkness into the glare of daylight, it was very painful to my eyes. Several times I stumbled over the threshold, and could scarcely see where I was going.

I believe, had I stayed there very long, I should have become purblind,[1] and that would have been a great misfortune, for I have heard men say, that a stone-blind horse was safer to drive, than one which had imperfect sight, as it generally makes them very timid. However, I escaped without any permanent injury to my sight, and was sold to a large cab owner.

---

1 Almost blind; having impaired vision.

I shall never forget my new master, he had black eyes and a hooked nose, his mouth was as full of teeth as a bull dog's, and his voice was as harsh as the grinding of cart wheels over gravel stones. His name was Nicholas Skinner, and I believe he was the same man that poor Seedy Sam drove for.

I have heard men say, that seeing is believing; but I should say that feeling is believing; for much as I had seen before, I never knew till now the utter misery of a cab-horse's life.

Skinner had a low set of cabs and a low set of drivers; he was hard on the men, and the men were hard on the horses. In this place we had no Sunday rest, and it was in the heat of summer.

Sometimes on a Sunday morning, a party of fast men would hire the cab for the day; four of them inside and another with the driver, and I had to take them 10 or 15 miles out into the country, and back again: never would any of them get down to walk up a hill, let it be ever so steep, or the day ever so hot—unless indeed, when the driver was afraid I should not manage it, and sometimes I was so fevered and worn that I could hardly touch my food. How I used to long for the nice bran mash with nitre[1] in it that Jerry used to give us on Saturday nights in hot weather, that used to cool us down and make us so comfortable; when we had two nights and a whole day for unbroken rest, and on Monday morning were as fresh as young horses again; but here, there was no rest, and my driver was just as hard as his master. He had a cruel whip with something so sharp at the end that it sometimes drew blood, and he would even whip me under the belly, and flip the lash out at my head. Indignities like these took the heart out of me terribly, but still I did my best and never hung back; for as poor Ginger said, it was no use; men are the strongest.

My life was now so utterly wretched, that I wished I might, like Ginger, drop down dead at my work, and be out of my misery; and one day my wish very nearly came to pass. I went on the stand at eight in the morning, and had done a good share of work, when we had to take a fare to the railway. A long train was just expected in, so my driver pulled up at the back of some

---

1 Nitre powder was used in the treatment of inflammation; Jerry likely administered nitre to help prevent serious inflammatory injury.

of the outside cabs, to take the chance of a return fare. It was a very heavy train, and as all the cabs were soon engaged, ours was called for. There was a party of four; a noisy blustering man with a lady, a little boy and a young girl and a great deal of luggage. The lady and the boy got into the cab, and while the man ordered about the luggage, the young girl came and looked at me.

"Papa," she said, "I am sure this poor horse cannot take us and all our luggage so far, he is so very weak and worn up; do look at him."

"Oh! he's all right, miss," said my driver, "he's strong enough."

The porter, who was pulling about some heavy boxes, suggested to the gentleman, as there was so much luggage, whether he would not take a second cab.

"Can your horse do it, or can't he?" said the blustering man.

"Oh! he can do it all right, sir; send up the boxes, porter: he could take more than that," and he helped to haul up a box so heavy, that I could feel the springs go down.

"Papa, papa, do take a second cab," said the young girl in a beseeching tone; "I am sure we are wrong, I am sure it is very cruel."

"Nonsense, Grace, get in at once and don't make all this fuss; a pretty thing it would be, if a man of business had to examine every cab-horse before he hired it—the man knows his own business of course: there, get in and hold your tongue!" My gentle friend had to obey; and box after box was dragged up and lodged on the top of the cab, or settled by the side of the driver. At last all was ready, and with his usual jerk at the rein, and slash of the whip, he drove out of the station.

The load was very heavy, and I had had neither food nor rest since the morning; but I did my best as I always had done, in spite of cruelty and injustice.

I got along fairly till we came to Ludgate Hill,[1] but there, the heavy load and my own exhaustion were too much. I was struggling to keep on, goaded by constant chucks of the rein and use of the whip, when—in a single moment—I cannot tell how, my feet slipped from under me, and I fell heavily

---

1 A steep, famously treacherous section of road in London, which heavily laden horses in harness had difficulty climbing in slippery weather.

to the ground on my side; the suddenness and the force with which I fell, seemed to beat all the breath out of my body. I lay perfectly still; indeed I had no power to move, and I thought now I was going to die. I heard a sort of confusion round me, loud angry voices, and the getting down of the luggage, but it was all like a dream. I thought I heard that sweet pitiful voice saying, "Oh! that poor horse! it is all our fault." Someone came and loosened the throat strap of my bridle, and undid the traces which kept the collar so tight upon me. Someone said, "He's dead, he'll never get up again." Then I could hear a policeman giving orders, but I did not even open my eyes; I could only draw a gasping breath now and then. Some cold water was thrown over my head, and some cordial[1] was poured into my mouth, and something was covered over me. I cannot tell how long I lay there, but I found my life coming back, and a kind-voiced man was patting me and encouraging me to rise. After some more cordial had been given me, and after one or two attempts, I staggered to my feet, and was gently led to some stables which were close by. Here I was put into a well-littered stall, and some warm gruel was brought to me, which I drank thankfully.

In the evening I was sufficiently recovered to be led back to Skinner's stables, where, I think they did the best for me that they could. In the morning Skinner came with a farrier to look at me. He examined me very closely, and said, "This is a case of overwork more than disease, and if you could give him a run off for six months, he would be able to work again; but now there is not an ounce of strength in him."

"Then he must just go to the dogs,"[2] said Skinner, "I have no meadows to nurse sick horses in—he might get well or he might not; that sort of thing don't suit my business, my plan is to work 'em as long as they'll go, and then sell 'em for what they'll fetch, at the knacker's or elsewhere."

"If he was broken-winded,"[3] said the farrier, "you had better have him killed out of hand, but he is not; there is a sale of horses coming off in about ten days; if you rest him and feed him up, he may pick up, and you may get more than his

---

1 Pleasant tasting medicine.
2 Be sold for meat.
3 A chronic respiratory condition in which the horse struggles to breathe or wheezes during exercise.

skin is worth at any rate." Upon this advice, Skinner rather unwillingly, I think, gave orders that I should be well fed and cared for, and the stable man, happily for me, carried out the orders with a much better will than his master had in giving them. Ten days of perfect rest, plenty of good oats, hay, bran mashes, with boiled linseed mixed in them, did more to get up my condition than anything else could have done; those linseed mashes were delicious, and I began to think after all, it might be better to live than go to the dogs. When the twelfth day after the accident came, I was taken to the sale, a few miles out of London. I felt that any change from my present place must be an improvement, so I held up my head, and hoped for the best.

At this sale, of course I found myself in company with the old broken-down horses—some lame, some broken-winded, some old, and some, that I am sure it would have been merciful to shoot. The buyers and the sellers too, many of them, looked not much better off than the poor beasts they were bargaining about. There were poor old men, trying to get a horse or a pony for a few pounds, that might drag about some little wood or coal cart. There were poor men trying to sell a worn-out beast for two or three pounds, rather than have the greater loss of killing him. Some of them looked as if poverty and hard times had hardened them all over; but there were others, that I would have willingly used the last of my strength in serving; poor and shabby, but kind and human, with voices that I could trust. There was one tottering old man that took a great fancy to me, and I to him, but I was not strong enough—it was an anxious time! Coming from the better part of the fair, I noticed a man who looked like a gentleman farmer, with a young boy by his side; he had a broad back and round shoulders, a kind, ruddy face, and he wore a broad-brimmed hat. When he came up to me and my companions, he stood still, and gave a pitiful look round upon us. I saw his eye rest on me; I had still a good mane and tail, which did something for my appearance. I pricked my ears and looked at him.

"There's a horse, Willie, that has known better days."

"Poor old fellow!" said the boy, "do you think, grandpapa, he was ever a carriage horse?"

"Oh yes! my boy," said the farmer, coming closer, "he might have been anything when he was young: look at his nostrils and his ears, the shape of his neck and shoulder; there's a deal of breeding about that horse." He put out his hand and gave me a kind pat on the neck: I put out my nose in answer to his kindness; the boy stroked my face.

"Poor old fellow! see, grandpapa, how well he understands kindness. Could not you buy him and make him young again as you did with Ladybird?"

"My dear boy, I can't make all old horses young; beside, Ladybird was not so very old, as she was run down and badly used."

"Well, grandpapa, I don't believe that this one is old; look at his mane and tail. I wish you would look into his mouth, and then you could tell; though he is so very thin, his eyes are not sunk like some old horses."

The old gentleman laughed, "Bless the boy! he is as horsey as his old grandfather."

"But do look at his mouth, grandpapa, and ask the price; I am sure he would grow young in our meadows."

The man who had brought me for sale now put in his word. "The young gentleman's a real knowing one, sir: now the fact is, this 'ere hoss is just pulled down with overwork in the cabs; he's not an old one and I heerd as how the vetenary[1] should say, that a six months run off would set him right up, being as how his wind was not broken. I've had the tending of him these ten days past, and a gratefuller, pleasanter animal I never met with, and 'twould be worth a gentleman's while to give a five-pound note for him, and let him have a chance. I'll be bound he'd be worth twenty pounds next spring."

The old gentleman laughed, the little boy looked up eagerly.

"Oh! grandpapa, did you not say, the colt sold for five pounds more than you expected? you would not be poorer if you did buy this one."

The farmer slowly felt my legs, which were much swelled and strained; then he looked at my mouth—"Thirteen or fourteen, I should say; just trot him out, will you?"

I arched my poor thin neck, raised my tail a little, and threw out my legs as well as I could, for they were very stiff.

"What is the lowest you will take for him?" said the farmer as I came back.

"Five pounds, sir; that was the lowest price my master set."

"'Tis a speculation," said the old gentleman, shaking his head, but at the same time slowly drawing out his purse—"quite a speculation! Have you any more business here?" he said, counting the sovereigns into his hand.

"No, sir, I can take him for you to the inn, if you please."

"Do so, I am now going there."

They walked forward and I was led behind. The boy could hardly control his delight, and the old gentleman seemed to enjoy his pleasure. I had a good feed at the inn, and was then gently ridden home by a servant of my new master's, and turned into a large meadow with a shed in one corner of it.

---

1 Veterinarian.

Mr. Thoroughgood, for that was the name of my benefactor, gave orders that I should have hay and oats every night and morning, and the run of the meadow during the day, and "you Willie," said he, "must take the oversight of him; I give him in charge to you." The boy was proud of his charge and undertook it in all seriousness. There was not a day when he did not pay me a visit; sometimes picking me out from amongst the other horses, and giving me a bit of carrot, or something good, or sometimes standing by me whilst I ate my oats. He always came with kind words and caresses, and of course I grew very fond of him. He called me Old Crony, as I used to come to him in the field and follow him about. Sometimes he brought his grandfather, who always looked closely at my legs—"This is our point, Willie," he would say; "but he is improving so steadily, that I think we shall see a change for the better in the spring."

The perfect rest, the good food, the soft turf and gentle exercise, soon began to tell on my condition and my spirits. I had a good constitution from my mother, and I was never strained when I was young, so that I had a better chance than many horses, who have been worked before they came to their full strength. During the winter my legs improved so much, that I began to feel quite young again. The spring came round, and one day in March, Mr. Thoroughgood determined that he would try me in the phaeton. I was well pleased, and he and Willie drove me a few miles. My legs were not stiff now, and I did the work with perfect ease.

"He's growing young, Willie; we must give him a little gentle work now, and by midsummer he will be as good as Ladybird: he has a beautiful mouth, and good paces, they can't be better."

"Oh! grandpapa, how glad I am you bought him!"

"So am I, my boy, but he has to thank you more than me; we must now be looking out for a quiet genteel place[1] for him, where he will be valued."

---

1 I.e., a private owner rather than a commercial situation.

CHAPTER FORTY NINE
My Last Home

One day during this summer, the groom cleaned and dressed me with such extraordinary care, that I thought some new change must be at hand; he trimmed my fetlocks and legs, passed the tarbrush over my hoofs, and even parted my forelock. I think the harness had an extra polish. Willie seemed half anxious, half merry, as he got into the chaise with his grandfather.

"If the ladies take to him," said the old gentleman, "they'll be suited, and he'll be suited: we can but try."

At the distance of a mile or two from the village, we came to a pretty low house, with a lawn and shrubbery at the front, and a drive up to the door. Willie rang the bell, and asked if Miss Blomefield, or Miss Ellen was at home. Yes, they were. So, whilst Willie stayed with me, Mr. Thoroughgood went into the house. In about ten minutes he returned, followed by three ladies; one tall pale lady wrapped in a white shawl, leaned on a younger lady, with dark eyes and a merry face; the other, a very stately-looking person, was Miss Blomefield. They all came and looked at me and asked questions. The younger lady—that was Miss Ellen, took to me very much; she said she was sure she should like me, I had such a good face. The tall pale lady said that she should always be nervous in riding behind a horse that had once been down, as I might come down again, and if I did, she should never get over the fright.

"You see, ladies," said Mr. Thoroughgood, "many first-rate horses have had their knees broken through the carelessness of their drivers, without any fault of their own, and from what I see of this horse, I should say, that is his case; but of course I do not wish to influence you. If you incline, you can have him on trial, and then your coachman will see what he thinks of him."

"You have always been such a good adviser to us about our horses," said the stately lady, "that your recommendation would go a long way with me, and if my sister Lavinia sees no objection, we will accept your offer of a trial, with thanks." It was then arranged that I should be sent for the next day.

In the morning a smart-looking young man came for me; at first, he looked pleased; but when he saw my knees, he said in a disappointed voice, "I didn't think, sir, you would have recommended my ladies a blemished horse like that."

"Handsome is—that handsome does," said my master; "you are only taking him on trial, and I am sure you will do fairly by him, young man, and if he is not as safe as any horse you ever drove, send him back."

I was led home, placed in a comfortable stable, fed, and left to myself. The next day, when my groom was cleaning my face, he said, "That is just like the star that Black Beauty had, he is much the same height too; I wonder where he is now." A little further on, he came to the place in my neck where I was bled, and where a little knot was left in the skin. He almost started, and began to look me over carefully, talking to himself: "White star in the forehead, one white foot on the off side, this little knot just in that place;" then looking at the middle of my back—"and as I am alive, there is that little patch of white hair that John used to call 'Beauty's threepenny bit,' it must be Black Beauty! Why Beauty! Beauty! do you know me? little Joe Green, that almost killed you?" And he began patting and patting me as if he was quite overjoyed.

I could not say that I remembered him, for now he was a fine grown young fellow, with black whiskers and a man's voice, but I was sure he knew me, and that he was Joe Green, and I was very glad. I put my nose up to him, and tried to say that we were friends. I never saw a man so pleased.

"Give you a fair trial! I should think so indeed! I wonder who the rascal was that broke your knees, my old Beauty! you must have been badly served out somewhere; well, well, it won't be my fault if you haven't good times of it now. I wish John Manly was here to see you."

In the afternoon I was put into a low Park chair and brought to the door. Miss Ellen was going to try me, and Green went with her. I soon found that she was a good driver, and she seemed pleased with my paces. I heard Joe telling her about me, and that he was sure I was Squire Gordon's old Black Beauty.

When we returned, the other sisters came out to hear how I had behaved myself. She told them what she had just heard, and said, "I shall certainly write to Mrs. Gordon, and tell her that her favourite horse has come to us. How pleased she will be!" After this I was driven every day for a week or so, and as I appeared to be quite safe, Miss Lavinia at last ventured out in the small close carriage. After this it was quite decided to keep me and to call me by my old name of "Black Beauty."

I have now lived in this happy place a whole year. Joe is the best and kindest of grooms. My work is easy and pleasant, and I feel my strength and spirits all coming back again. Mr. Thoroughgood said to Joe the other day, "In your place he will last till he is twenty years old—perhaps more." Willie always speaks to me when he can, and treats me as his special friend. My ladies have promised that I shall never be sold, and so I have nothing to fear; and here my story ends. My troubles are all over, and I am at home; and often before I am quite awake, I fancy I am still in the orchard at Birtwick, standing with my old friends under the apple trees.

★★★

If any readers of this Autobiography, wish to know more of the right treatment of horses, on the road, and in the stable, the Translator would recommend them to procure an admirable little book, price fourpence, entitled "The Horse Book."[1]

Its directions are short, clear, and full of common sense. It has been revised by no less an authority than Mr. Fleming, Royal Engineers, F.R.G.S., President of the Central Veterinary Medical Society; and Member of Council of the Royal College of Veterinary Surgeons. It has also been approved by other eminent Veterinarians.

It is published by the Royal Society for the Prevention of Cruelty to Animals, and can be obtained through any Bookseller.

---

1 *The Book of the Horse* by Samuel Sidney; see Appendix E3.

Appendix A: Biographical Context and Early Reception

1. From Mary Bayly, *The Life and Letters of Mrs. Sewell* (London: James Nisbet, 1890), 272, 276–78

[The earliest account of Anna Sewell's life was included as a chapter in Mary Bayly's biography of Sewell's mother, herself an accomplished author. Bayly was a family friend of the Sewells.]

Black Beauty was published near the end of the year 1877, and Anna lived just long enough to hear of its remarkable success. But can she ever know what a mighty power for good it has been, and is, in this country? We have frequent opportunities of conversing with the London City Missionaries to Cabmen. Their testimony is, that many agencies have been at work of late years which have greatly helped to ameliorate the condition both of the men and horses, such as Cabmen's shelters, systematic religious and temperance teaching, the watchful vigilance of the Society for Prevention of Cruelty to Animals, &c.; but they say nothing has told so strongly for good among the men themselves, or induced such humane treatment of horses, as the influence and teaching they have gained from *Black Beauty*. Both men and boys read it with the greatest avidity, and many declare it to be "the best book in the world." Many of our public organs, foremost among them the *Times,* have for some years past borne the strongest testimony to the remarkable improvement which has taken place in everything connected with Cabs and Cabmen. Perhaps few who chronicle these changes and improvements know how much of what they commend is due to the genius and prayers of one fragile woman....

The following letter from Mrs. Toynbee refers to Mr. Flower, the well-known friend of animals, who by his writings, his personal advocacy, indeed by every means in his power, has striven to ameliorate the sufferings of the brute creation—more especially of the horse. The letter is addressed to Mrs. Sewell:—

"*January* 29, 1878.

"Captain Toynbee and I went yesterday afternoon to see our friends the Flowers, in Hyde Park Gardens, and found Mr. Flower[1] in a complete state of enthusiasm over *Black Beauty.* 'It is written by a veterinary surgeon,' he exclaimed; 'by a coachman, by a groom; there is not a mistake in the whole of it; not one thing I wish altered, except that the cabman *should* have taken that half-crown. I shall show Mr. Bright that passage about horses in war. I *must* make the lady's acquaintance; she must come to London sometimes—she is my Araminta' (Do you remember Miss Edgeworth's 'Araminta, or the Unknown Friend'?).[2] He particularly wished me to say that he would like to write himself, but writing is troublesome to him, from the weakness of his hand. Are we right in supposing that the book is written (translated, by-the-bye) by your daughter? Is it being actively circulated? That was a point Mr. Flower was very anxious about ... Will you forgive so many questions, but Mr. Flower could talk of nothing else. Now and then, when the conversation strayed away to the war,[3] or anything else, he would exclaim 'How could a lady know so much about horses! I should like to have a talk with her; do persuade her to come to London.' I need not add anything—my *ignorant* admiration for *Black Beauty* would be so poor after Mr. Flower's thorough appreciation."

The following letter was written by Mrs. Sewell in reply to Mrs. Toynbee's :—

"I should have thanked you for your most welcome letter the day it came, but an infirm household and an invalid friend staying with us, obliged my pen to be quiet.

"Your letter was indeed a great encouragement both to me and Anna. It was the first of the kind that had come to

---

1 Edward Fordham Flower; see Appendix E4.
2 The reference is to a character in "Angelina, or the Unknown Friend," a short story published in *Moral Tales for Young People* (1801) by Maria Edgeworth (1768–1849). "Araminta" is the pen name of a character with whom the heroine carries on an idealized, sentimental correspondence.
3 The Russo-Turkish War of 1877–78.

hand, and was accordingly treasured. Many letters followed, but when I took yours to Anna, I said I was come to put her crown on. I assure you it was a triumphant moment. She had ventured to send a copy of her book to Mr. Flower, but had thought, if he noticed it at all, it would be chiefly to point out inaccuracies; but when his entire approbation came, it brought indeed a full measure of gladness and confidence. If he would add to his kindness by writing a few lines expressive of his commendation, he would be giving it a standing beyond what anyone else could do....

"We are expecting every day the proofs of the School Edition; we have both a great desire that it should become a reading-book in Boys' Schools. This also was the sanguine hope of the publisher, but his sudden death, just before its publication, has deprived it of his energetic aid.

"After all this about the book, I fancy you would be interested to know a little about the author. There is no doubt most persons will have imagined her a robust young woman, mostly in the saddle with the reins in her hand. Instead of this, for the last seven years she has been confined either to her bed or couch, and has not in all that time passed beyond the garden-gate. At the beginning of this time, the subject of the book took root in her mind and from time to time a few portions were dictated—reading or writing being equally impossible to her. Years went on, and no progress was made, except in her mind, where many pictures were clearly drawn and stored away in her memory.

"The year before last, she was so far improved in strength as to be able to write in pencil her clearly arranged thoughts, I immediately making a fair copy.[1] Her thoughts and pictures were the fruit of previous experience. When a child, she severely sprained both ankles, which ever after prevented her taking much walking exercise, and made riding and driving a necessity; and so it came to pass, between her and her own horse, and horses in general, a mutual confidence and friendship sprang up, and she learned all their secrets. She learned much through her ear, in this way quickly detecting if anything is wrong with a horse's foot, and through her eye she knows at once if anything annoys them."

---

1 A corrected, clean text of a manuscript, usually handwritten.

2. From George T. Angell, "Introductory Chapter" to the American Humane Education Society Edition of *Black Beauty* (New York: American Humane Education Society, 1890)

[American philanthropist George Angell (1823–1909) founded the Massachusetts Society for the Prevention of Cruelty to Animals in 1868 and the American Humane Education Society in 1889. Angell's decision to print and disseminate *Black Beauty* widely in the United States—and his characterization of it as "the *Uncle Tom's Cabin*" of the horse—marked a watershed moment in its reception.]

For more than twenty years *this thought* has been upon my mind.

Somebody must write a book which shall be as widely read as *Uncle Tom's Cabin*,[1] and *shall have as widespread and powerful influence in abolishing cruelty to horses, as* Uncle Tom's Cabin *had on the abolition of human slavery.*

Many times, by letter and word of mouth, I have called the attention of American writers to this matter and asked them to undertake it.

At last the book has come to me; not from America, but from England, where already over *ninety thousand copies have been sold.*

It was written by a woman, Anna Sewell.

It is the autobiography of an English horse, telling of kind masters and cruel, of happiness and of suffering. *I am glad to say that happiness predominates* and *finally triumphs.*

I have read each of its *two hundred and thirty eight beautifully printed pages from its cheerful beginning to its happy end,* and then called in the printers.

Through the kind gifts of friends I am enabled to pay *$265 for having it electrotyped,* and through the kindness of another friend am enabled to print a *first edition of ten thousand, at the marvellously low price of twelve cents each*—to which must be added, when sent by mail, *eight cents for postage,* etc.

As I have said, *over ninety thousand copies* have been already sold in England.

I want to print immediately *a hundred thousand copies.*

---

1 An extremely popular and widely read anti-slavery novel published in 1852 by American author Harriet Beecher Stowe (1811–96).

I want the power *to give away thousands of these to drivers of horses,* and in public schools, and elsewhere.

I want to send a copy postpaid to the editors of each of about *thirteen thousand* American newspapers and magazines.

I would be glad to have each reader of this paper, *who has ever loved or cared for a horse,* send me as large a check as he or she can afford, to be used in the distribution of this book.

Every such check will be acknowledged in "Our Dumb Animals,"[1] and at once passed into the treasury of our "American Humane Education Society," and be promptly used for the purpose for which it is sent.

I would be glad, if I had the means, to put a copy of it in *every home in America,* for I am sure there has never been a book printed in any language, the reading of which will be more likely to inspire love and kind care for these dumb servants and friends who toil and die in our service. I hope to live long enough to print and distribute *a million copies.*

The title of the book is Black Beauty, His Grooms and Companions.

3. Review of *Black Beauty, The Nonconformist* (9 January 1878)

[*Black Beauty* was not widely reviewed when it first appeared; the selection included here, from the weekly religious newspaper *The Nonconformist,* captures the tenor of early responses.]

If a good-tempered horse of varied experience, keen observation, and pretty long life could write, this is certainly the sort of book he would write. Miss Sewell has faithfully and lovingly studied the character, needs, and the treatment of this favourite friend and servant of man, in both good and bad incidents of his life, as well as the good and bad characters of his owners. She writes with some humour; with keenly sympathetic feeling, and with a strong and noble purpose that pervades every page. Her book is amusing, but we scarcely think of the amusement we have derived from it until we are finished, and we turn over some of

---

1   A periodical edited by Angell and published by the Massachusetts Society for the Prevention of Cruelty to Animals; it first appeared in 1868, the same year Angell founded the society.

the pages again. It is all effective, but the most effective portion is when Black Beauty becomes a London cab horse—and that portion everybody who employs a cab should read. Had the Society for the Prevention of Cruelty to Animals published this, we should say it had published its best, [sic] work. As it is, it would be difficult to conceive one more admirably suited to its purpose.

Appendix B: Victorian Science: Questions of Animal Emotion

[Prior to the publication of Darwin's *The Expression of the Emotions in Man and Animals* in 1872, scientific thinking had largely followed seventeenth-century French philosopher René Descartes's view of animals as automata whose responses were prompted by reflex rather than intellect or feeling. The emergence of evolutionary theories connecting human and non-human animals at mid-century prompted a new focus on animals' capacity to feel, think, and imagine. The following readings from late-century scientific texts are examples of early attempts to theorize animals' capacities for emotion.]

1. From Charles Darwin, *The Expression of the Emotions in Man and Animals* (London: John Murray, 1872), 12, 352, 361–62, 365–66, 367

[An English naturalist, Darwin (1809–82) published the groundbreaking *Origin of Species* in 1859, in which he outlined his theory of evolution. *The Expression of the Emotions* and *The Descent of Man,* both published in the 1870s, extend this earlier work.]

No doubt as long as man and all other animals are viewed as independent creations, an effectual stop is put to our natural desire to investigate as far as possible the causes of Expression. By this doctrine, anything and everything can be equally well explained; and it has proved as pernicious with respect to Expression as to every other branch of natural history. With mankind some expressions, such as the bristling of the hair under the influence of extreme terror, or the uncovering of the teeth under that of furious rage, can hardly be understood, except on the belief that man once existed in a much lower and animal-like condition. The community of certain expressions in distinct though allied species, as in the movements of the same facial muscles during laughter by man and by various monkeys, is rendered somewhat more intelligible, if we believe in their descent from a common progenitor. He who admits on general grounds that the structure and habits of all animals have been gradually evolved, will look at the whole subject of Expression in a new and interesting light.

... That the chief expressive actions, exhibited by man and by the lower animals, are now innate or inherited,—that is, have not been learnt by the individual,—is admitted by everyone. So little has learning or imitation to do with several of them that they are from the earliest days and throughout life quite beyond our control; for instance, the relaxation of the arteries of the skin in blushing, and the increased action of the heart in anger. We may see children, only two or three years old, and even those born blind, blushing from shame; and the naked scalp of a very young infant reddens from passion. Infants scream from pain directly after birth, and all their features then assume the same form as during subsequent years. These facts alone suffice to show that many of our most important expressions have not been learnt; but it is remarkable that some, which are certainly innate, require practice in the individual, before they are performed in a full and perfect manner; for instance, weeping and laughing. The inheritance of most of our expressive actions explains the fact that those born blind display them, as I hear from the Rev. R.H. Blair,[1] equally well with those gifted with eyesight. We can thus also understand the fact that the young and the old of widely different races, both with man and animals, express the same state of mind by the same movements.

... It is a curious, though perhaps an idle speculation, how early in the long line of our progenitors the various expressive movements, now exhibited by man, were successively acquired. The following remarks will at least serve to recall some of the chief points discussed in this volume. We may confidently believe that laughter, as a sign of pleasure or enjoyment, was practised by our progenitors long before they deserved to be called human; for very many kinds of monkeys, when pleased, utter a reiterated sound, clearly analogous to our laughter, often accompanied by vibratory movements of their jaws or lips, with the corners of the mouth drawn backwards and upwards, by the wrinkling of the cheeks, and even by the brightening of the eyes.

---

1 As Principal of Worcester Proprietary College for Blind Sons of Gentlemen, Blair advanced the cause of education for the blind in Victorian England.

We may likewise infer that fear was expressed from an extremely remote period, in almost the same manner as it now is by man; namely, by trembling, the erection of the hair, cold perspiration, pallor, widely opened eyes, the relaxation of most of the muscles, and by the whole body cowering downwards or held motionless.

... The movements of expression in the face and body, whatever their origin may have been, are in themselves of much importance for our welfare. They serve as the first means of communication between the mother and her infant; she smiles approval, and thus encourages her child on the right path, or frowns disapproval. We readily perceive sympathy in others by their expression; our sufferings are thus mitigated and our pleasures increased; and mutual good feeling is thus strengthened. The movements of expression give vividness and energy to our spoken words. They reveal the thoughts and intentions of others more truly than do words, which may be falsified. Whatever amount of truth the so-called science of physiognomy[1] may contain, appears to depend, as Haller[2] long ago remarked, on different persons bringing into frequent use different facial muscles, according to their dispositions; the development of these muscles being perhaps thus increased, and the lines or furrows on the face, due to their habitual contraction, being thus rendered deeper and more conspicuous. The free expression by outward signs of an emotion intensifies it. On the other hand, the repression, as far as this is possible, of all outward signs softens our emotions. He who gives way to violent gestures will increase his rage; he who does not control the signs of fear will experience fear in a greater degree; and he who remains passive when overwhelmed with grief loses his best chance of recovering elasticity of mind. These results follow partly from the intimate relation which exists between almost all the emotions and their outward manifestations; and partly from the direct influence of exertion on the heart, and consequently on the brain. Even the simulation of an emotion tends to arouse it in our minds....

We have seen that the study of the theory of expression

---

1 The study of character as a manifestation of physical characteristics, especially the face.
2 Albrecht von Haller (1708–77), Swiss scientist whose work posited the interrelationship between psychological and physical characteristics of the body.

confirms to a certain limited extent the conclusion that man is derived from some lower animal form, and supports the belief of the specific or sub-specific unity of the several races; but as far as my judgment serves, such confirmation was hardly needed. We have also seen that expression in itself, or the language of the emotions, as it has sometimes been called, is certainly of importance for the welfare of mankind. To understand, as far as possible, the source or origin of the various expressions which may be hourly seen on the faces of the men around us, not to mention our domesticated animals, ought to possess much interest for us. From these several causes, we may conclude that the philosophy of our subject has well deserved the attention which it has already received from several excellent observers, and that it deserves still further attention, especially from any able physiologist.

2. From Thomas Huxley, "On the Hypothesis that Animals Are Automata, and Its History," *Collected Essays I* (1874), 236–37

[Huxley (1825–95) was an English comparative anatomist and one of Darwin's most vocal public defenders. This essay, first presented as a public talk in Belfast in 1874, offers a reconsideration of Descartes's influential view that animals are machines without consciousness.]

But there remains a doctrine to which Descartes[1] attached great weight, so that full acceptance of it became a sort of note of a thoroughgoing Cartesian,[2] but which, nevertheless, is so opposed to ordinary prepossessions that it attained more general notoriety, and gave rise to more discussion, than almost any other Cartesian hypothesis. It is the doctrine that brute animals are mere machines or automata, devoid not only of reason, but of any kind of consciousness, which is stated briefly in the "Discours de

---

1 René Descartes (1596–1650), French philosopher and mathematician whose work proposed the dualism, or fundamental separation, of body (which he saw as a machine) and soul (or rational mind). In *Meditations* (1641) he argued that animals should be regarded as automata, or machines.

2 The view expounded by Descartes that the mind is entirely separate from the body.

la Méthode," and more fully in the "Réponses aux Quatrièmes Objections," and in the correspondence with Henry More....[1]

But though I do not think that Descartes' hypothesis can be positively refuted, I am not disposed to accept it. The doctrine of continuity is too well established for it to be permissible to me to suppose that any complex natural phenomenon comes into existence suddenly, and without being preceded by simpler modifications; and very strong arguments would be needed to prove that such complex phenomena as those of consciousness, first make their appearance in man. We know, that, in the individual man, consciousness grows from a dim glimmer to its full light, whether we consider the infant advancing in years, or the adult emerging from slumber and swoon. We know, further, that the lower animals possess, though less developed, that part of the brain which we have every reason to believe to be the organ of consciousness in man; and as, in other cases, function and organ are proportional, so we have a right to conclude it is with the brain; and that the brutes, though they may not possess our intensity of consciousness, and though, from the absence of language, they can have no trains of thoughts, but only trains of feelings, yet have a consciousness which, more or less distinctly, foreshadows our own.

I confess that, in view of the struggle for existence which goes on in the animal world, and of the frightful quantity of pain with which it must be accompanied, I should be glad if the probabilities were in favour of Descartes' hypothesis; but, on the other hand, considering the terrible practical consequences to domestic animals which might ensue from any error on our part, it is as well to err on the right side, if we err at all, and deal with them as weaker brethren, who are bound, like the rest of us, to pay their toll for living, and suffer what is needful for the general good. As Hartley[2] finely says, "We seem to be in the place of God to

---

1 English philosopher (1614–87) who attempted to apply Descartes's mechanistic philosophy to prove the existence of the soul. More wrote four letters to Descartes in 1648–49 and received two responses prior to Descartes's death in 1650. The two espoused very different views of the possibility of animal consciousness.

2 David Hartley (1705–57), British philosopher who argued both that there were continuities between humans and animals, and that insofar as animals experience emotions, humans are morally obligated to treat them with kindness.

them"; and we may justly follow the precedents He sets in nature in our dealings with them.

But though we may see reason to disagree with Descartes' hypothesis that brutes are unconscious machines, it does not follow that he was wrong in regarding them as automata. They may be more or less conscious, sensitive, automata; and the view that they are such conscious machines is that which is implicitly, or explicitly, adopted by most persons. When we speak of the actions of the lower animals being guided by instinct and not by reason, what we really mean is that, though they feel as we do, yet their actions are the results of their physical organisation. We believe, in short, that they are machines, one part of which (the nervous system) not only sets the rest in motion, and co-ordinates its movements in relation with changes in surrounding bodies, but is provided with special apparatus, the function of which is the calling into existence of those states of consciousness which are termed sensations, emotions, and ideas. I believe that this generally accepted view is the best expression of the facts at present known.

3. From George Romanes, *Animal Intelligence* (London: Kegan Paul, 1882), 8–9

[An English evolutionary biologist, Romanes (1848–94) was a friend and supporter of Darwin. Romanes defended and expanded on Darwin's theory of evolution in the two works included here, which represent contributions to the early study of animal behaviour.]

The terms sensation, perception, emotion, and volition need not here be considered. I shall use them in their ordinary psychological significations; and although I shall subsequently have to analyse each of the organic or mental states which they respectively denote, there will be no occasion in the present volume to enter upon this subject. I may, however, point out one general consideration to which I shall throughout adhere. Taking it for granted that the external indications of mental processes which we observe in animals are trustworthy, so that we are justified in inferring particular mental states from particular bodily actions, it follows that in consistency we must everywhere apply the same criteria.

For instance, if we find a dog or a monkey exhibiting marked expressions of affection, sympathy, jealousy, rage, &c, few persons are sceptical enough to doubt that the complete analogy which these expressions afford with those which are manifested by man, sufficiently prove the existence of mental states analogous to those in man of which these expressions are the outward and visible signs. But when we find an ant or a bee apparently exhibiting by its actions these same emotions, few persons are sufficiently non-sceptical not to doubt whether the outward and visible signs are here trustworthy as evidence of analogous or corresponding inward and mental states. The whole organisation of such a creature is so different from that of a man that it becomes questionable how far analogy drawn from the activities of the insect is a safe guide to the inferring of mental states—particularly in view of the fact that in many respects, such as in the great preponderance of "instinct" over "reason," the psychology of an insect is demonstrably a widely different thing from that of a man. Now it is, of course, perfectly true that the less the resemblance the less is the value of any analogy built upon the resemblance, and therefore that the inference of an ant or a bee feeling sympathy or rage is not so valid as is the similar inference in the case of a dog or a monkey. Still it *is* an inference, and, so far as it goes, a valid one—being, in fact, the only inference available. That is to say, if we observe an ant or a bee apparently exhibiting sympathy or rage, we must either conclude that some psychological state resembling that of sympathy or rage is present, or else refuse to think about the subject at all; from the observable facts there is no other inference open.

4. From George Romanes, *Mental Evolution in Animals* (New York: D. Appleton, 1884), 153–54

It will be remembered that the kind of Imagination which we have recently been considering belongs to what I consider a high level of development. That is to say, I consider the power of dreaming to occupy a place about one third of the distance between the first dawn of the imaginative faculty and its maximum development in a Shakespeare or a Faraday.[1] I so consider it because I believe that to pass through what I have called the first three stages, so as to arrive at the power of forming mental pictures independently of sensuous suggestions from without, the imaginative faculty has made so enormous a progress from its earliest beginnings, that the rest of its development along the same lines is really nothing more than a function of the faculty of Abstraction. Superimpose upon the psychology of a terrier which pines for its absent mistress an elaborate structure of abstract ideation, and the terrier's imaginative faculty would begin to rival that of man. Of course it will be said that abstraction presupposes imagination, and so undoubtedly it does; still the two are not identical, as is proved by the fact that for the building up of abstraction to any exalted height, language, or mental symbolism of some kind, is indispensable; and mental symbols are so many artifices for the saving of imagination.

Now if at first sight it seems absurd to accredit a mollusk with imagination, we must remember exactly what we mean by imagination in the lowest possible phase of its development. We mean merely the power of forming a definite mental picture, or of retaining a memory, no matter of how rudimentary a kind; provided that the memory implies some dim idea of an absent object or experience, and not, as in the case of an infant disliking the taste of strange milk, merely an immediate perception of contrast between an habitual and a present sensation. And that we find such a level of mental development as low down in the zoological scale as the Gasteropoda,[2] would seem to be proved by the fact already alluded to of limpets returning to their homes in the rocks after feeding. Of course the mental image which a limpet forms of its home in a rock cannot be supposed to be comparable in point of vividness or complexity with the mental image that a

---

1   Michael Faraday (1791–1867), English scientist who undertook groundbreaking work on electricity and magnetism. Faraday, who made many important scientific discoveries, believed in the role of intuition in scientific experimentation. In one of his lab journals he wrote "ALL THIS IS A DREAM. Still examine it by a few experiments. Nothing is too wonderful to be true, if it be consistent with the laws of nature; and in such things as these, experiment is the best test of such consistency" (*The Life and Letters of Faraday*, vol. 2, ed. Henry Bence Jones [Longman: London, 1870], 253).

2   Part of the mollusk family.

horse retains of its stall, or a dog of its kennel; still, such as it is, it is a mental image, and therefore betokens imagination. More vivid, and therefore more definite, is the mental image that a spider forms of her lair, who when dislodged and carried away to a short distance again returns to her old home. With a still further advance in the power of mental imagery we find supplied the psychological conditions for the ideation of cold-blooded Vertebrata, such as the determination displayed by migratory Fishes (notably the salmon) to visit particular localities in the spawning season. On the next level we reach the higher Crustacea, which, as we have already seen, are able to imagine in a high degree. Next we come to Reptiles, concerning which I may quote the following anecdote from Lord Monboddo:[1] "I am well informed of a tame serpent in the East Indies, which belonged to the late Dr. Vigot, once kept by him in the suburbs of Madras. This serpent was taken by the French, when they invested Madras, in the late war, and was carried to Pondicherry in a close carriage. But from thence he found his way back again to his old quarters, though Madras is over one hundred miles distant from Pondicherry." If we substitute yards for miles, similar cases are on record with regard to frogs and toads—which from being so numerous can scarcely all be false. And that some reptiles have an imagination passing into what I have called the third stage is proved by the case of the python mentioned in "Animal Intelligence," which, when sent to the Zoological Gardens, pined for its previous master and mistress. The Cephalopoda[2] and Hymenoptera[3] have already been alluded to. Lastly, on the next level we attain in Birds to imagination proved to be unquestionably of the third degree by the phenomenon of dreaming. Above this level it is not of so much interest to trace the improvement of the faculty. Such improvement throughout the subsequent levels till man,

---

1 James Burnett, Lord Monboddo (1714–99), Scottish philosopher and judge who contributed to early formulations of the concept of evolution.
2 Part of the mollusk family.
3 One of the largest orders of insects.

probably consists only in a progressive advance through imagination of the third degree—it being I think highly improbable, and certainly not betokened by any evidence, that imagination in any animal attains to what I have called the fourth degree, which I therefore consider distinctive of man.

Appendix C: Victorian Industry: Horse and Machine

[With the onset of widespread mechanization and industrialization in the nineteenth century, human notions of the machine began to reshape how horses were perceived and treated, particularly in urban environments. Not only was a machine's potential output expressed metaphorically (as horse power), but horses were increasingly treated as machines of conveyance. These selections illustrate both the emergence of this metaphorical equivalence, and the ways in which urban horses were treated as a result.]

1. From Fanny Kemble, *Record of a Girlhood* (1878), *The Longman Anthology of British Literature*, vol. 2B, 4th ed., ed. Heather Henderson and William Sharpe (Boston: Longman, 2010), 1092

[A well-known Victorian actress and popular author, Kemble (1809–93) wrote eleven volumes of memoirs.]

We were introduced to the little engine which was to drag us along the rails. She (for they make these curious little fire-horses all mares) consisted of a boiler, a stove, a small platform, a bench, and behind the bench a barrel containing enough water to prevent her being thirsty for fifteen miles,—the whole machine not bigger than a common fire-engine. She goes upon two wheels, which are her feet, and are moved by bright steel legs called pistons; these are propelled by steam, and in proportion as more steam is applied to the upper extremities (the hip-joints, I suppose) of these pistons, the faster they move the wheels; and when it is desirable to diminish the speed, the steam, which unless suffered to escape would burst the boiler, evaporates through a safety-valve into the air. The reins, bit, and bridle of this wonderful beast is a small steel handle, which applies or withdraws the steam from its legs or pistons, so that a child might manage it. The coals, which are its oats, were under the bench, and there was a small glass tube affixed to the boiler, with water in it, which indicates by its fullness or emptiness when the creature wants water, which is immediately conveyed to it from its reservoirs. There is a chimney to the stove, but as they burn coke there is none of the dreadful black smoke which accompanies the progress of a steam vessel. This snorting little animal, which I felt rather inclined to pat, was then harnessed to our carriage, and, Mr. Stephenson[1] having taken me on the bench of the engine with him, we started at about ten miles an hour. The steam-horse being ill adapted for going up and down hill, the road was kept at a certain level, and appeared sometimes to sink below the surface of the earth, and sometimes to rise above it. Almost at starting it was cut through the solid rock, which formed a wall on either side of it, about sixty feet high. You can't imagine how strange it seemed to be journeying on thus, without any visible cause of progress other than the magical machine, with its flying white breath and rhythmical, unvarying pace, between these rocky walls, which are already clothed with moss and ferns and grasses; and when I reflected that these great masses of stone had been cut asunder to allow our passage thus far below the surface of the earth, I felt as if no fairy tale was ever half so wonderful as what I saw.

2. From Philip Hamerton, *Chapters on Animals* (Boston: Roberts Brothers, 1874), 67

[Hamerton (1834–94) was an English art critic and prolific author.]

There does not exist in the minds of owners of horses generally that touch of romantic sentiment which translates itself in affectionate companionship and tender care. The horse is a valuable animal, and is, on the whole, looked after fairly well, his health is cared for, he is usually well fed, and horses used for private purposes are seldom overworked. But there is a remarkable absence of sentiment in all this, which is proved by the facility with which, in most European countries, men sell their horses, often for bodily infirmities or imperfections, in which there is no ques-

---

1 George Stephenson (1781–1848), a civil engineer known as the "Father of Railways," was responsible for building the first steam-powered railway line, the Liverpool and Manchester Railway. Kemble accompanied Stephenson on a test of the track prior to its official opening in 1830.

tion of temper, and especially by the custom of selling a horse which has done faithful service, merely because he is getting old and weaker than when in his prime. This last custom proves the absence of sentiment, the more completely that every one knows when selling an old horse that he is dooming him to harder work and worse keep, and that the certain fate of a horse which we part with because he is old, is a descent to harder and harder conditions, till finally he is worked to death in a cab, or in a cart belonging to some master little less miserable than himself.

3. From W.J. Gordon, *The Horse World of London* (London: The Religious Tract Society, 1893), 160–64

[An author and journalist, Gordon published books and tracts on a wide variety of subjects. The selection here belongs to a group that documented modern life at the end of the nineteenth century.]

This rest on the seventh day is far more important to a horse's well-being than many a hackney owner is disposed to admit. Burke,[1] in a letter to a member of the National Assembly of France, in 1794, attributed much of the evil of the Reign of Terror to the continuance of sittings without the intermission of the Day of Rest. "They who always labour," he said, "can have no clear judgment. You never give yourselves time to cool, and exhaust your brains like men who burn out their candles and are left in the dark." Wilberforce used to warn Pitt[2] that he would shorten his life if he worked without rest. Mr. Gladstone[3] ascribes much of his vigorous old age to his Sabbath rest. Apart from the religious view of the question, it is notable that even in Paris the desire for a day of rest is more and more increasing. A meeting was lately held there, in the hall of the Geographical Society, by

---

1 An Irish political theorist and philosopher, Edmund Burke (1729–97) wrote *Reflections on the Revolution in France* (1790), in which he opposed the shift from traditional models of society.
2 William Wilberforce (1759–1833) was an English politician who adamantly supported the abolition of slavery; William Pitt the Younger (1759–1806), who was twice prime minister of England, first encouraged Wilberforce to take up the abolitionist cause.
3 William Ewart Gladstone (1809–98), four-time prime minister of England, whose political career spanned the Victorian age.

an association called "The People's League for Sunday Rest." Churchmen and laymen, Protestants and Roman Catholics, and all classes were represented, the Abbé Garnier[1] closing with an eloquent address on the advantages to the State of a periodical respite from toil.

And necessary as it may be for man, it is at least as necessary for his horse. In the famous speech of Lord Erskine,[2] on introducing for the first time in the House of Peers a bill dealing with cruelty to animals, he spoke much about the "rights" of those over whom we have been given the mastery. "Man's dominion," he said, "over the lower animals is very large; and it is his not merely by superior knowledge and power, but also by Divine appointment. The dominion is not absolute, but is limited by the obligations of justice and mercy"—as declared in the Commandment, where the cattle are in this respect placed on the same footing as the children, the servants, and the stranger within the gates. The mercy of which injunction is manifest, even were its wisdom not one of the commonplaces of experience.

A most gratifying testimony to the soundness of this ancient law, even—to use his own words—"as a mere matter of business," was given by Bianconi[3] at an early meeting of the British Association for the Advancement of Science. Before the railroad found its way to Ireland, the whole of the mail traffic was there run on Bianconi's cars. He thus came to own more horses than any man of his time, and he averred that as the result of many years' trial he got far more work out of them when he ran them for only six days a week, and that for a long period he had made it a rule to give each of them a weekly day of rest.

"A merciful man is merciful to his beast," or, in Scriptural phrase, "A righteous man regardeth the life of his beast; but the

---

1 Theodore Garnier, a nineteenth-century Catholic clergyman and activist.

2 Thomas Erskine (1750–1823), who served as Lord Chancellor of England in the early nineteenth century, was actively involved in the cause of animal rights. In 1809 he introduced a Bill in the House of Lords for preventing malicious and wanton cruelty to animals.

3 Considered to be a founder of mass public transportation, Italian-born Carlo Bianconi (1786–1875) ran an extensive horse-drawn carriage service in Ireland in the early nineteenth century, prior to the coming of the railway.

tender mercies of the wicked are cruel" (Proverbs, xii, 10). If Justice requires that the rights of animals should be considered, much more does Mercy extend to their treatment. "There is implanted by Nature," says Lord Bacon,[1] "in the heart of man, a noble and excellent affection of mercy extending even to the brute animals, which by Divine appointment are subjected to this dominion." Dr. Chalmers,[2] in his eloquent sermon on Humanity to Animals, amplified and emphasised this. "It is," he said, "a virtue which oversteps as it were the limits of a species, and which prompts a descending movement on our part, of righteousness and mercy towards those who have an inferior place to ourselves in the scale of creation. It is not the circulation of benevolence within the limits of one species. It is the transmission of it from one species to another. The first is the charity of a world. The second is the charity of a universe. Had there been no such charity, no descending current of love and of compassion from species to species, what, I ask, would have become of ourselves? ... The distance upward between us and that mysterious Being who let Himself down from heaven's high concave upon our lowly platform, surpasses by infinity the distance downward between us and everything that breathes. And He bowed Himself thus far for the purpose of an example, as well as for the purpose of an expiation, that every Christian might extend his compassionate regards over the whole of sentient and suffering Nature." By Dr. Chalmers the duty of mercy to animals was thus lifted to the highest level of Christian ethics. In the same spirit are the words of that distinguished man of science and philanthropist, Dr. George Wilson:[3]—"There is an example as well as a lesson for us in the Saviour's compassion for men. Inasmuch as we partake with the lower animals of bodies exquisitely sensitive to pain, and often agonised by it, we should be slow to torture creatures who, though not sharers of our joys, or participators in our mental agonies, can equal us in bodily suffering. We stand, by Divine appointment, between God and his irresponsible subjects, and are as gods to them."

---

1 English philosopher, statesman, and scientist (1561–1626), Francis Bacon is considered to be the father of the modern scientific method grounded in empiricism.

2 Thomas Chalmers (1780–1847), a distinguished Scottish clergyman and moral philosopher.

3 Scottish professor of chemistry (1818–59) who also lectured at the Royal Veterinary College.

Descending from this high level of moral and religious duty, it may be remarked that absolute cruelty to horses is much on the decrease, owing chiefly to the activity of the police. But a growing proportion of horses of a certain class have their lives shortened and their value rapidly deteriorated by persistent overwork. Many of them, as Sir Benjamin Richardson[1] says, go from early life to premature death without the attention a steam-engine receives—the learned doctor being evidently aware that even a steam-engine has to be treated as daintily as a baby if it is to last long and work well—and the worst used of all our horses are the weary nags in traps and spring carts that crawl home so late on Sunday nights. In short, the hackney[2] is too useful a horse for his own good. Six days a week he works to earn money, and on the seventh he works to spend it. And so he is soon knocked up, and changes hands oftener than any horse in London.

1 Sir Benjamin Ward Richardson (1828–96), a physician who helped pioneer the use of anaesthesia for humans and researched humane methods for slaughtering animals.
2 A trotting horse used for routine driving and riding.

Appendix D: Animal Cruelty and Animal Rights

[Broad discussions about animal cruelty and animal rights were the focus of significant public debate in the final third of the nineteenth century. Intersecting in these debates were concerns about vivisection—the use of live animals for scientific experimentation—and religious, moral, and legal questions about man's responsibilities to other living beings. The selections included here illustrate the ways in which moral, religious, and legal discourse overlapped in public discussion about the treatment of animals.]

1. From Frances Power Cobbe, "The Rights of Man and the Claims of Brutes," *Studies New and Old of Ethical and Social Subjects* (London: Trübner, 1865), 226–30

[An Irish activist, Cobbe (1822–1904) was also a prolific author whose work explored the moral and ethical aspects of animal rights and women's suffrage.]

What then remains of the obligation to consider the pain and pleasure of the sentient but un-moral animals? Is there any space left for it in the crowd of human duties? Surely there is a little space. Claims which are subordinated to higher claims are not (as we have already said) therefore abolished. Here is an error common both to our views of the relative claims of different human beings, and of the relative claims of brutes and men. There is in both cases a point where the rights of the secondary claimant come into the field, else were there in morals the anomaly of moral obligations which should never oblige any one. Where is this point to be found?

We have already said that in regulating the precedency of human claims, the point is found where there ceases to be any kind of equality between the wants of the two claimants. Where the wants are equal (or anything like equal) the nearest comes first, the remoter afterwards. If a father need bread to save him from starvation, and a friend need it also for the same purpose, the father's claims must come first. But if the father need it only to amuse himself by throwing it to fowls on the river, and the friend need it to save him from death, then the father's claims go to the ground, and the friend's become paramount. This principle is continually neglected in human affairs, and the neglect causes great moral errors. The parent, husband, wife, or child whom affection and duty both direct to make their nearest and dearest the object of their "precedency of benevolence," continually fall under the temptation to make them their exclusive objects, and evade other obligations under the delusion that they are all merged in the one primary obligation. The same thing takes place in the case of animals. Men say, "Human obligations come before all obligations to the brutes. Let us wait till all human beings are virtuous and happy, and then it will be time to attend to the brutes." But we are no more morally justified in the one case than in the other, neither in merging all human duties in duties to one individual, nor in waiting to consider our obligations to the animals to those Greek kalends[1] when all human wants will be abundantly supplied.

The point where the inferior claim of the brute, as of the man, must come into the field, can only be in each case where there ceases to be any kind of equality between the superior and inferior claims. We must consider carefully what can constitute the relative claims of beings of such different rank. Passing below the last human claimant on our benevolence, we find a "great gulf fixed."[2] With the rationality and moral freedom of the agent, life itself has so far altered its value that we no longer recognize in it any of the sanctity which pertained to the life of a man; nor can the creature's comfort or enjoyment of any kind be put in the balance. We can in no case say that the claim of life for the brute is the same thing as the claim of life for a man; nay, even of security, or food, or comfort of any kind for the man. Everything which could be fairly interpreted to be a want for the man must

---

1   An expression indicating a time that is indefinitely remote, or does not exist; it alludes to the fact that the Greeks did not share the Roman division of time (kalends were the beginning of each new phase of the Roman calendar).

2   Luke 16:26: "And beside all this, between us and you there is a great gulf fixed: so that they which would pass from hence to you cannot; neither can they pass to us, that *would come* from thence."

have precedence over even the life of the animal. But here we must stop. Those cruel impulses of destruction, which we may call wantonness in a man, have no claims to be weighed against the brute's life and welfare. His gluttonous tastes, his caprices, his indolence, have no claims. Here the claims of the brute come on the field. Our obligations to consider its humble happiness must appear here or nowhere. They are postponed utterly to man's *wants*. They stand good against his *wantonness*. Practically, where does the principle lead us? Simply to this—that we may slay cattle for food, and take the fowls of the air and the fish of the sea to supply our table; but that we may not (for example) torture calves to produce white meat, nor slash living salmon to make them more delicate, nor nail fowls to the fireside to give them diseased livers. We may use horses and asses in our ploughs and our carriages, but we have no right to starve and torture our poor brute servants for our avarice or malignity. We may clear every inhabited country of wild beasts and noxious reptiles and insects whose existence would imperil our security or militate against our health or cleanliness, or who would devour our own proper food; but we have no right to go into untrodden deserts to take away the lives of creatures who there have their proper home, nor to kill in our own country harmless things like sea-gulls and frogs for the mere gratification of our destructive propensities.

And further. Besides these limits to the taking of life, there are limits to the infliction of pain. Here, again, if the pain be necessary, if the life demanded by human wants cannot be taken without the infliction of some degree of pain; or if (without killing a brute) we are obliged to put it to some suffering, to fetter it for our security, or for any similar reason, here, also, we may be justified. But though we may thus inflict pain for our want, we are no more justified in inflicting it than in taking life for our wantonness. If from the odious delight in witnessing suffering, or from furious tempers, or parsimony, or idle curiosity, we put an animal to needless torture, we stand condemned; we have offended against the law requiring us to refrain from inflicting pain on any being which, by its sentient nature, is sensible to pain.

These views are surely almost self-evident. To affirm the contrary and maintain that we have a right to take animal life in mere wantonness, or to inflict needless torture upon animals, is to deny that a sentient being has any claims whatever, or that his capacity for suffering pain and enjoying pleasure ought to determine in any way our conduct towards him. For if that capacity for enjoyment is not to protect his life (i.e., the whole sum of his pleasures) against our wanton destruction, nor his capacity for pain protect his nervous frame from our infliction of needless torture, there is nothing left to be imagined of occasion wherein his claims could be valid.

2. From John Duke Coleridge, *The Lord Chief Justice of England* [*Baron Coleridge*] *on Vivisection* (London: Victoria Street Society for the Protection of Animals from Vivisection, 1881), 3–4, 7–8

[John Duke, first Baron Coleridge (1820–94) was an English judge and politician. A great-nephew of the poet Samuel Taylor Coleridge (1772–1834), he held a number of distinguished posts including Attorney General for England and Wales and Lord Chief Justice of England. As Vice-President of the Victoria Street Society, the original name of the National Anti-Vivisection Society, Coleridge published this tract in the wake of public interest in the subject following the report of the Royal Commission (1875) and the Cruelty to Animals Act (1876).]

Is, then, the present law reasonable? It is the result of a most careful inquiry conducted by eminent men in 1875, men certainly neither weak sentimentalists nor ignorant and prejudiced humanitarians, men amongst whom are to be found Mr. Huxley and Mr. Erichsen, Mr. Hutton and Sir John Karslake.[1] These men unanimously recommended legislation, and legislation, in some important respects, more stringent than Parliament thought fit to pass. They recommended it on a body of evidence at once interesting and terrible. Interesting indeed it is from the frank apathy to the suffering of animals, however awful, avowed by some of the witnesses; for the noble humanity of some few; for the curious ingenuity with which others avoided the direct and verbal approval of horrible cruelties which yet they refused to condemn; and in some cases for the stern judgment passed

---

1 All were appointees to the 1875 Royal Commission of Inquiry on vivisection. Huxley (see Appendix B2) and John Eric Erichsen (1818–96) were scientists, Richard Holt Hutton (1826–97) was a journalist, and Sir John Karslake (1821–81) a lawyer.

upon men and practices, apparently now, after the lapse of six years, considered, worthy of more lenient language. Terrible the evidence is for the details of torture, of mutilation, of life slowly destroyed in torment, or skilfully preserved for the infliction of the same or diversified agonies, for days, for weeks, for months, in some cases for more than a year. I want not to be, if I can help it, what Mr. Simon[1] calls a "mere screamer;" nay, if possible, to avoid that yet more fatal imputation upon an Englishman which Dr. Wilks[2] brings against his opponents, that we "lack a sense of the ludicrous." I wish to use quiet language, but I must, nevertheless, at all hazards own that, sharing probably the lower and less sensitive organizations of the monkey, the cat, and the dog, I fail altogether to see the joke which he sees, in any attempt to stay these tortures; and further that to read of them, not in the language of "paid scribes and hired agitators," but in the language of these humane and tender men who first inflict them and then describe them, makes me sick. [...]

I deny altogether that it concludes the question to admit that vivisection enlarges knowledge. I do deny that the gaining knowledge justifies all means of gaining it. To begin with, proportion is forgotten. Suppose it capable of proof that by putting to death with hideous torment 3000 horses you could find out the real nature of some feverish symptom, I should say without the least hesitation that it would be unlawful to torture the 3000 horses. There is no proportion between the end and the means. Next, the moment you touch man, it is admitted that the formula breaks down; no one doubts that to cut up a hundred men and women would enlarge the bounds of knowledge as to the human frame more speedily and far more widely than to torture a thousand dogs or ten thousand cats. It is obvious; but it was admitted over and over again that experiments on animals were suggestive only, not conclusive, as to the human subject. Espe-

---

1   Sir John Simon (1816–1904), a Fellow of the Royal Society and highly regarded pathologist, gave evidence before the 1875 Royal Commission on Vivisection supporting the cause of scientific experimentation on animals.

2   Eminent Victorian physician Samuel Wilkes (1824–1911), a Fellow of the Royal Society and later President of the Royal College of Physicians, supported the use of vivisection in scientific experiments, contributing to a public discourse prompted by the Royal Commission.

cially is this the case with poisons, some of the deadliest of which do not appreciably affect some animals, and as to all of which it is admitted that it is not safe to argue from their effects on animals to their effects on man. As to man himself, it was not so long ago that medical men met with a passion of disavowal, what they regarded as an imputation, viz., the suggestion that experiments were tried on patients in hospitals. I assume the disavowal to be true; but why, if all pursuit of knowledge is lawful, should the imputation be resented? The moment you come to distinguish between animals and man, you consent to limit the pursuit of knowledge by considerations not scientific but moral; and it is bad logic and a mere *petitio principii*[1] to assume (which is the very point at issue) that these considerations avail for man but do not for animals. I hope that morals may always be too much for logic; it is permissible to express a fear that some day logic may be too much for morals.

3. From Henry Salt, *Animal Rights Considered in Relation to Social Progress* (New York: Macmillan, 1892), 11–17

[Salt (1851–1939) was a prolific English writer and social reformer, whose work examined humanitarian and animal-rights concerns. He was one of the first people to address the cause of animal rights, rather than the broader, more paternalistic cause of animal welfare.]

The fallacious idea that that the lives of animals have "no moral purpose" is at root connected with these religious and philosophical pretensions which Schopenhauer[2] so powerfully condemns. To live one's own life—to realize one's true self—is the highest moral purpose of man and animal alike; and that animals possess their due measure of this sense of individuality is scarcely open to doubt. "We have seen," says Darwin, "that the senses and intuitions, the various emotions and faculties, such as love, memory, attention, curiosity, imitation, reason, etc., of which man boasts, may be found in an incipient, or even sometimes in a well-developed condition, in the lower animals."

---

1 Latin term for circular reasoning.
2 Arthur Schopenhauer (1788–1860), German philosopher.

Not less emphatic is the testimony of the Rev. J.G. Wood,[1] who, speaking from a great experience, gives it as his opinion that "the manner in which we ignore individuality in the lower animals is simply astounding." He claims for them a future life, because he is "quite sure that most of the cruelties which are perpetrated on the animals are due to the habit of considering them as mere machines without susceptibilities, without reason, and without the capacity of a future."

This, then, is the position of those who assert that animals, like man, are necessarily possessed of certain limited rights, which cannot be withheld from them as they are now withheld without tyranny and injustice. They have individuality, character, reason; and to have those qualities is to have the right to exercise them, in so far as surrounding circumstances permit. "Freedom of choice and act," says Ouida,[2] "is the first condition of animal as of human happiness. How many animals in a million have even relative freedom in any moment of their lives? No choice is ever permitted to them; and all their most natural instincts are denied or made subject to authority." Yet no human being is justified in regarding any animal whatsoever as a meaningless automation, to be worked, or tortured, or eaten, as the case may be, for the mere object of satisfying the wants or whims of mankind. Together with the destinies and duties that are laid on them and fulfilled by them, animals have also the right to be treated with gentleness and consideration, and the man who does not so treat them, however great his learning or influence may be, is, in that respect, an ignorant and foolish man, devoid of the highest and noblest culture of which the human mind is capable.

Something must here be said on the important subject of nomenclature. It is to be feared that the ill-treatment of animals is largely due—or at any rate the difficulty of amending that treatment is largely increased—by the common use of such terms as "brute-beast," "live-stock," etc., which implicitly deny to the lower races that intelligent individuality which is most undoubt-

---

1 John George Wood (1827–89), British clergyman and author who helped popularize natural history. His *Animal Traits and Characteristics* was published in 1860.
2 Pen name of Marie Louise Ramé (1839–1908), British novelist and passionate animal advocate. Her novel *Puck* (1870) relates a dog's adventures and experiences in his own words.

edly possessed by them. It was long ago remarked by Bentham,[1] in his "Introduction to Principles of Morals and Legislation," that, whereas human beings are styled *persons,* "other animals, on account of their interests having been neglected by the insensibility of the ancient jurist, stand degraded into the class of *things*"; and Schopenhauer also has commented on the mischievous absurdity for the idiom which applies the neuter pronoun "it" to such highly organized primates as the dog and the ape.

A word of protest is needed also against such an expression as "dumb animals," which, though often cited as "an immense exhortation to pity," has in reality a tendency to influence ordinary people in quite the contrary direction, inasmuch as it fosters the idea of an impassable barrier between mankind and their dependents. It is convenient to us men to be deaf to the entreaties of the victims of our injustice; and, by sort of grim irony, we therefore assume that it is *they* who are afflicted by some organic incapacity—they are "dumb animals," forsooth! although a moment's consideration must prove that they have innumerable ways, often quite human in variety and suggestiveness, of uttering their thoughts and emotions.

Even the term "animals" as applied to the lower races, is incorrect, and not wholly unobjectionable, since it ignores the fact that *man* is an animal no less than they. My only excuse for using it in this volume is that there is absolutely no other brief term available.

So anomalous is the attitude of man towards the lower animals, that it is no marvel if many humane thinkers have wellnigh despaired over this question. "The whole subject of the brute creation," wrote Dr. Arnold,[2] "is to me one of such painful mystery, that I dare not approach it"; and this (to put the most charitable interpretation on their silence) appears to be the position of the majority of moralists and teachers at the present time. Yet there is urgent need of some key to the solution of the problem; and in no other way can this key be found than by the full inclusion of the lower races within the pale of human sympathy. All the promptings of our best and surest instincts point us

---

1 Jeremy Bentham (1748–1832), British utilitarian philosopher.
2 Thomas Arnold (1795–1842), headmaster of Rugby School from 1828 to 1841; a prominent figure in educational reform, he was also the author of widely read sermons.

in this direction. "It is abundantly evident," says Lecky,[1] "both from history and from present experience, that the instinctive shock, or natural feelings of disgust, caused by the sight of the sufferings of men, is not generically different from that which is caused by the sight of the suffering of animals."

If this be so—and the admission is a momentous one—can it be seriously contended that the same humanitarian tendency which has already emancipated the slave, will not ultimately benefit the lower races also? Here, again, the historian of "European Morals" has a significant remark: "At one time," he says, "the benevolent affections embrace merely the family, soon the circle expanding includes first a class, then a nation, then a coalition of nations, then all humanity; and finally its influence is felt in the dealings of man with the animal world. In each of these cases a standard is formed, different from that of the preceding stage, but in each case the same tendency is recognized as virtue."

But, it may be argued, vague sympathy with the lower animals is one thing, and a definite recognition of their "rights" is another; what reason is there to suppose that we shall advance from the former phase to the latter? Just this; that every great liberating movement has proceeded exactly on those lines. Oppression and cruelty are invariably founded on a lack of imaginative sympathy; the tyrant or tormentor can have no true sense of kinship with the victim of his injustice. When once the sense of affinity is awakened, the knell of tyranny is sounded, and the ultimate concession of "rights" is simply a matter of time. The present condition of the more highly organized domestic animals is in many ways very analogous to that of the negro slaves of a hundred years ago: look back, and you will find in their case precisely the same exclusion from the common pale of humanity; the same hypocritical fallacies, to justify that exclusion; and, as a consequence, the same deliberate stubborn denial of their social "rights." Look back—for it is well to do so—and then look forward, and the moral can hardly be mistaken.

---

1   Irish historian William Edward Hartpole Lecky (1838–1903). His major works include *A History of European Morals from Augustus to Charlemagne* (2 vols., 1869), alluded to in the following paragraph.

Appendix E: Bits, Bearing Reins, and Equine Management

[In the second half of the nineteenth century, specific discussion about cruelty to horses focused on a range of issues, including the treatment of cab, omnibus, and draft horses, and the fashion for using a bearing rein on harness horses that became popular among the wealthier classes. Sewell addresses these issues directly in *Black Beauty*.]

1. From Henry Curling, *A Lashing for the Lashers: Being an Exposition of the Cruelties Practised upon the Cab and Omnibus Horses of London* (London: Schulze, 1851), 10–13

[Henry Curling (1802–64) was a military officer, prolific novelist, and author of pamphlets such as the one extracted below.]

There is no question about the great accommodation afforded to the public by cabs and omnibuses—an accommodation so great that we could not possibly get on without it, and our readers will therefore hardly be pleased with our remarks. But to them we say, that the barbarities we have described are absolutely detrimental to that accommodation. A steady and even swift pace is better maintained through a long day's work, by a moderate use of the lash, than by its misusage. "To climb steep hills, requires slow pace at first," says Shakspere[1] [*sic*]; and if the cab-driver began his day's career with less rage and fury, instead of overdriving his horse the first fare he gets, the brute would be more able for his long day's work. But the horse is generally overdone ere five miles are whipped out of him, and the rest of his work is all labour and strain, a regular battle against weariness, illness, and incapacity.

Far be it from us to place a human being upon a par with a brute beast, or to suppose that a Christian man could by possibility be subjected to what a horse is put to endure, even for five minutes—the

---

1 In *Henry VIII* 1.1.

superiority of man over all other animals is allowed on all hands—nevertheless, if we might suggest a slight trial, in order to convince a cab-driver how greatly he acts against sense and humanity, and at the same time prove our case to him feelingly, we would merely ask any cab or omnibus-driver, given to misusage of the whip, to place himself in charge of a common truck, and drag it up Holborn Hill;[1] then, whilst he labours at the dead pull, let him imagine for a moment the effect upon himself of what he is so partial to; let him imagine a series of strong jerks, fretting his jaws, and a continued compliment of heavy lashes over his bare loins. He will then, perhaps, be able to appreciate the effects of his own system, and how at last it whips the spirit of a horse quite out of the animal.

There is little doubt, as before said, that in some instances the drivers may be exonerated from blame, and that a portion of the cruelties practised are the result of inconsiderate conduct in those who hire their services and even reward their brutality.

Indeed, from many conversations I have had with cab-drivers on the subject, and wherever the gross incivility of the man has not urged him to resent all question between himself and victim, I have invariably found the blame laid as much on others as himself. I could recount many dialogues I have had on the subject; the accompanying will perhaps suffice.

"What the h—ll would you have us do?" said a cabman one day, on my observing the distressed state of his horse, and that, although he whipped it frightfully, he could hardly get it along. "This here horse aren't got no go in him. Some chaps hired me to take 'em to Mitchem[2] yesterday, and made me gallop almost all the way there and back. His wery[3] heart's whip'd out on him. There was five on 'em, and they had drink at every public-house almost along the road. They all took a turn at driving, and regularly gruelled the horse; and now I must whip his heart out to make him go at all."

On another occasion, late one rainy night, I got into a cab, hoping to get quickly to my destination, but after a slow progress through half a dozen streets, the vehicle came to a dead stop, and the driver told me, with an oath, that his horse was done. Accordingly, on alighting, I found the animal had sunk down, and was dying. The sight was a sad one. The great lumbering cab looked a huge instru-

---

1 An area of central London.

2 Mitcham is a suburb in South London, about 7 miles from Charing Cross (London's centre).

3 Cockney slang for "very."

ment of torture. There lay the horse, chained to it in death; and, as the fellow was about to try and whip him up, I seized his whip. The weight of the instrument surprised me so much, that I was induced to examine it by the light of a gas-lamp. It was, I found, a sort of knout, the thong having large knobs of twisted leather at intervals. As I looked at the prostrate horse, I upbraided the driver for his cruelty. He excused himself by saying it was his night whip, an instrument he owned he dared not use in the day, but absolutely necessary to make use of against the horse in question.

"And is that my fault?" he urged. "Why, that 'ere 'oss has been ill a long time, but master would have money as long as I could whip it out on him; and if I had refused, there's plenty as would have done the job. You don't know what night work and night 'osses is, I see, or you wouldn't trouble yourself about such a paltry concern as this."

2. From Sir Arthur Helps, *Some Talk about Animals and Their Masters* (London: Strahan, 1873), 58, 80–81

[Sir Arthur Helps (1813–75) was an author and public servant whose work was concerned with social reform. As Clerk of the Privy Council, Helps was involved in administering the Cattle Disease Prevention Act (1866); his thoughts on livestock transport prompted by this experience led him to write *Some Talk about Animals*.]

I maintain that my dictum is substantially right, that you have only, by the aid of imagination, to enter fully into what we may reasonably conceive to be the feelings of animals, to be most tender and kind towards them. Even such talk as we have just had, which might not appear at first to bear upon the subject, is most useful. Only think of the ways, habits, and peculiarities of any creature, and you become tolerant towards it. I will exemplify what I mean. The horse is a most timid and nervous animal. By the way, I observed that not one of you was inclined, in your imaginary choice of animal life, to become a horse or any animal that has much to do with man. Well, the horse, as I said, is a most timid and nervous animal. The moment you have recognized this fact, you are able, by the aid of imagination, to enter, as it were, into its terrors, and you do not beat a creature merely because it is afraid. [...]

Postscript: I may mention that in the course of this conversation Mr. Milverton read the following letter, which he had found in an *Echo* newspaper of last July; the suggestion therein made was highly approved of by himself and the other Friends in Council.[1] I did not introduce it into the conversation on account of its length; but it appears to be well worth considering.

Breaks for Omnibuses.

To the Editor of the *Echo*.

Sir, Every afternoon, when I take a peep behind my winkers, I see you, and none but you, fluttering on the top of the lumbering caravan which Destiny has thought good to oblige me to lug along the slippery streets of London, and I often say to myself and to my partner in misery, "How is it that that 'ere light-weight, as is up to everything, don't pitch into them as is responsible for the needless labour inflicted on us poor horses through the want of drags to stop the 'bus?[2] Why, you must have seen, times and times, how the collar is pulled nearly over our heads every time we stop, to say nothing of our teeth being crushed, and our necks nearly wrung off (almost all my pals have toothache, but we don't let on that we have it, for it ain't pleasant to have melted lead poured into a tooth, as is how they stop our poor old grinders); and this pretty operation of stopping (I mean the 'bus, not the teeth) is performed a couple of hundred times every day of our lives.

Now, they tell me that there is a gentleman who has power to cause these drags to be put on omnibuses, under the driver's feet, as in Manchester, him, I mean, as had little flags stuck on the cabs a short time ago. Suppose he knew that he would be sticking a year or two on our lives by making a stopping drag a condition of a 'bus licence, don't you think he would do it? Yes, bless him; but though he is a kind-hearted gentleman, he don't ride on 'buses, and don't

---

1 Many of Helps's books feature the "Friends in Council," an imaginary group of associates. This literary conceit allowed Helps to develop dialogues on themes, so that multiple perspectives could be developed. It was inspired by his early association with the Cambridge Apostles, or Cambridge Conversazione Society, in which members met weekly to present and discuss set topics. In these dialogues, Milverton generally presents the perspective of Helps himself.

2 Black Beauty also remarks on the need for a drag to help horses descending hills; see p. 82, n. 1.

know what we have to suffer now. All the drivers know and would bless him if he did so, for I hear them say their arms is pulled off with the stopping (what must our poor mouths be?).

And another thing is, that, if we had drags, less of those stupid bipeds that are continually running before the 'bus, would be injured. I should be rather pleased than otherwise if we now and then ran over a 'bus proprietor; but it goes to my heart when an old person, or a little child toddles out into the roadway, and all the people cry out, 'Hoi!' and the driver nearly tugs our heads off, and, do all we can, we can't stop the 'bus in time: it pushes us on before it, and down goes the unfortunate human with a leg broken, or worse! Some of us horses have heard say that there is a society for preventing cruelty to animals (and our treatment is cruelty), but I don't believe it, leastways the society does, I suppose, ride on 'buses. Now, dear *Echo*, couldn't you row them up all round, and get us drags, and you shall have our blessing; but here comes Jem to harness me for my day's work, so no more at present from your humble and obedient old

'Bus Horse.

3. From Samuel Sidney, *The Book of the Horse* (1873; new ed., London: Cassell, 1892), 251–52, 313, 361

[Samuel Sidney was the pen name of Samuel Solomon (1830–83), who published extensively on agriculture and animal care in the Victorian era. In the first edition of *Black Beauty*, Sewell included a note directing readers interested in the proper treatment of horses to a revised edition of *The Book of the Horse*, which she references incorrectly as *The Horse Book* (see p. 193.)]

The brilliant idea occurred to Lord Cadogan,[1] a cavalry officer of the period, of reducing the tails of his dragoon horses to a short dock—whether this was with a view to saving his soldiers the trouble of cleaning those long tails, and avoiding the nuisance of the splashes uniforms and accoutrements must have received from such hair streamers, or whether the debased taste of the age made him really think the appearance of his regiment improved by bobtails,

---

1 William Cadogan, 1st Earl Cadogan (1675–1726), a senior cavalry officer under the Duke of Marlborough, instituted the persistent fashion for brutally docking tails through the bone when he required that all the horses in Queen Anne's regiment be docked.

history does not relate—the next step was to turn bobtails into plug tails, by cutting all the hair for the last two or three inches of the dock. Having thus succeeded in disfiguring the hind-quarters of dragoon horses to the utmost, some monster devised the additional barbarity of cropping their ears. The operation became fashionable, like many hideous and barbarous fashions which are supposed to improve and adorn the heads of women in 1873.

[...] The practice of cropping the ears has now entirely disappeared, although it was not uncommon to find even hunters thus tortured and disfigured as late as 1840; while to a much later date the stupid fashion of depriving cart-horses of their fly-flappers was usual in several counties. [...] In 1873 the tails are cut according to the character of the horse and the style of the carriage. Since that date the vile fashion of short docks has again come into fashion and in imitation of polo ponies, even well-bred full-sized horses are turned into caricatures by hogging[1] the flowing mane, one of the most picturesque points of a blood horse.[2]

[...] It cannot be too often repeated that good bitting gives control without pain. A bit that gives pain, or rather, that produces pain that the horse cannot cause to cease by dropping his head to the right position and yielding, is inexcusable. A tight curb-chain and powerful bit make the horse poke out his chin; and then an ignorant person pulls harder, tightens the curb, and resorts to a bit still more severe.

[...] The proper and only way in which the bearing-reins should be allowed is when two conditions are observed: first, the snaffle-bit, instead of being drawn up into the cheeks, wrinkling and almost tearing them, should hang full *a quarter of an inch from the corners of the mouth*, next, the bearing-rein should be of such a length that the moment the horse raises his head to move into a trot it should become amply slack.

[...] But this is not the sort of "fit" that satisfies your London coachman of the highest fashion. He begins by drawing up the gag-bit until he has enlarged the horse's mouth by at least a couple of inches. He then adds a curb-bit of an inch too wide and four inches too long, quite regardless of the size of the horse's mouth,

---

1 Shaving off the mane and forelock.
2 A reference to the Thoroughbred, a hot-blooded, pedigreed breed of horse originating in eighteenth-century England, or its progenitors from the Middle East and North Africa, often referred to collectively as Arabians.

and having curbed this up tight, takes up the reins, climbs on his box, and makes, whether moving or standing at a door, a display very satisfactory to the distinguished owners, who have not the least idea that their horses are enduring agonies for hours.

The result is shown by degrees in foaming, bleeding mouths, lolling tongues, roaring, spavins,[1] restiveness—results to which less attention is paid because the greater number of the finest carriage-horses are jobbed,[2] and job-masters are at the mercy of the "bad coachman."

4. From Edward Fordham Flower, *Bits and Bearing Reins* (London: Cassell, 1875), 16–20

[Flower (1805–83) was a wealthy English brewer who dedicated the later part of his life to the task of raising public awareness about cruelty to horses. A tireless author of pamphlets and letters to newspapers, he was widely known for his criticism of the use of harsh bits and bearing reins on harness horses.]

The evils of Bearing-reins, of which the sole use is to hold the horse's head at an unnatural and dangerous height, have been so frequently and so conclusively pointed out, that it might have been hoped they would have become as obsolete as cropping, docking, and nicking.[3]

So far from this being the case, the evil has been continued in an aggravated form by the introduction of the "Gag bearing-rein."[4]

The mouth of the horse is extremely sensitive. The most valuable qualification for a horseman is that he should possess what is termed "Hands." The rarity of this qualification arises from

---

1 A chronic, debilitative injury to the hock joint of the hind leg, characterized by swelling.

2 Hired out for use from other owners; see pp. 120 ff.

3 Practices that alter the look and function of the horse's ears and tail, largely for purposes of fashion. Cropping was the mutilation of the ears, and docking the amputation of part of the tail. Nicking was the practice of severing the muscles in the tail so it could be artificially set at a high angle. Sir Oliver discusses his experience of this practice, as well as the related fashion for cropping the ears and tails of dogs, in the novel, pp. 66–67.

4 Sewell represents the discomfort associated with this harsh bit from the horse's perspective several times in the novel; see, for example, pp. 60 and 105.

the fact that the hand of man is naturally far less sensitive than the mouth of the horse. Hence ladies have generally better hands than gentlemen, and gentlemen better hands than grooms.

A horse in harness, without a bearing-rein, has the free command of his limbs, under the direction and control of his driver, communicated to him by the ordinary bit. If the driver has good hands the horse yields a prompt and ready obedience, and the most perfect sympathy exists between him and his master. A slip or a stumble is not likely to occur, and should it happen, recovery is easy.

The first step in the wrong direction is the use of the old-fashioned or simple bearing-rein.

Plate I.

COMFORT.

Fig. 4: "Comfort," from Edward Fordham Flower, *Bits and Bearing Reins* (1875).

In this the bearing-rein is attached to the ring of the driving-bit at B; it passes through a loop attached to the bridle at C, and is fastened to a hook on the pad at A. The pad is prevented from moving forward by the crupper. Thus the head and tail of the horse are tied together, more or less tightly, according as the bearing-rein and crupper are respectively buckled.

This bearing-rein acts as a single or fixed pulley, in which A, the power, is equivalent to B, the weight. A is the groom's hand or the power, B the horse's mouth or the weight, and C the pulley.

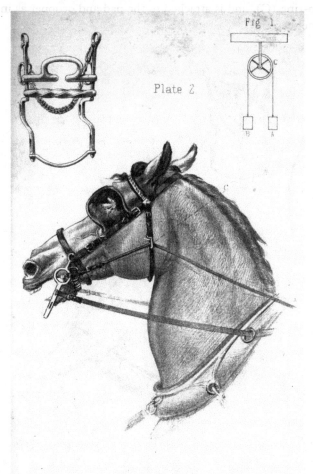

Fig. 5: "Discomfort," from Edward Fordham Flower, *Bits and Bearing Reins* (1875).

This bearing-rein may at any time be unhooked from the pad, and the horse thus released from its pressure; a great relief when kept standing for hours, and especially when going uphill.

Latterly a far more complicated and powerful instrument has come into fashion. This is the Bedouin, or Gag bearing-rein, which is attached to the top of the bridle (at E). It is then passed through a swivel attached to the separate bearing-rein bit, which has nothing to do with the driving. Thence it passes through the drop-ring (C), and is attached to the pad and crupper as in the former case.

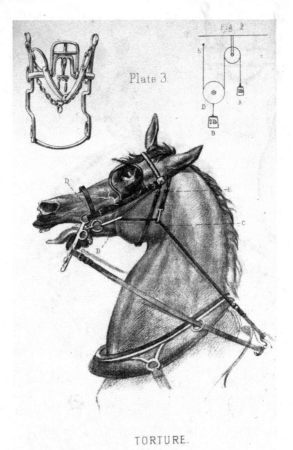

Fig. 6: "Torture," from Edward Fordham Flower, *Bits and Bearing Reins* (1875).

The effect of this is to double the power by which it can be tightened, for by mechanics we learn that 1 lb. applied at A is equivalent to 2 lbs. at B, a fact which everyone can prove for himself.

Thus it is evident what force is brought to bear on the horse's mouth, a sufficiently sensitive organ, even when unencumbered by another heavy bit, with cruel cutting power.

Severe as is the simple bearing-rein explained in Plate 2 [Fig. 5], its evil is doubled by the gag system, for its elevating power is, as we have shown, doubled, nor can the coachman relax this terrible and dangerous gag-bit, for separate as it is from the driving apparatus, it would fall out of the horse's mouth, and to put it in again would take time and persuasion, or rather force. The pain thus occasioned to the horse is intense. The action of every muscle is impeded. If a false step is taken, recovery is rendered difficult. Discomfort makes the poor animal restless. The impatient movements occasioned by his distress are not unfrequently visited by a cut from the whip of an ignorant coachman; the horse is called unruly and ill-tempered, when he is only miserable. Some new instrument of torture is forced into his mouth in the shape of a bit, devised for the very purpose of inflicting pain, until, with temper and mouth both ruined, he passes into the hands of a 'busdriver or cabman, when his bearing-rein is cast aside, and for the first time he is treated with common sense and humanity.

It is a severe penance to any man who loves a horse to walk along the fashionable streets or the Park, and to witness the sufferings of horses from this absurd and cruel practice.

Little does the benevolent dowager who sits absorbed in the pages of the last tract of the "Society for Prevention of Cruelty to Animals" know of the sufferings of the two noble animals by whom she is leisurely drawn along the "Lady's Mile."[1]

She probably fancies that the high prancing step, and the toss of the head which scatters flakes of foam at every step, are expressions of pride and satisfaction at their task, when in fact they are occasioned by pain, and a vain attempt to obtain a momentary relief from their suffering.

---

1 A carriage-drive along the northern bank of the Serpentine in Hyde Park, London, where fashionable Victorians showed off their horses, carriages, and fashionable clothes.

5. From Samuel Smiles, *Duty* (London: John Murray, 1880), 376–78

[Samuel Smiles (1812–1904) was a Scottish author, best known for the self-published *Self-Help* (1859), an enormously popular and influential book advocating self-education that drew heavily on anecdote to promote its aims. Smiles went on to publish a series of similar books in which he enshrined the middle-class values of thrift and self-control, including *Character* (1871), *Thrift* (1875), and *Duty* (1880).]

There is no slavery in England! But look at the 'bus and cab and cart horses, and you will find that slavery exists for horses. It was said by James Howell, Clerk of the Council,[1] as long ago as 1642, that England is called "The hell of horses, and not without cause." Cabs are driven by worn-out animals, and one or more of their feet are full of pain. You see how one of them gently lifts up its fore foot, and gently lets it down again. Perhaps the road along which it is driven is full of big stones, along which it has to crawl. Ask the cart-horse how it is treated. It is doomed through a long life of labour to be kicked and flogged, to strain and stagger under its burdens, to bear heat and cold and hunger without resistance. At last he is consigned to the knacker's yard.

To mitigate the torture of heavy laden horses, climbing and often slipping on the steep streets leading from the Thames near London Bridge, a kind lady came out daily with her servant, and strewed the roads with gravel. We have often seen her in the midst of the traffic, under the very noses of the horses, strewing gravel along the paths; she continued this work for many years. When she died, she did not forget the poor horses. She left a considerable sum in the hands of trustees, to be applied "for ever" to the distribution of gravel in steep and slippery London roadways. Her name should not be forgotten. She was Miss Lisetta Rest; and had filled the place of organist at the Church of Allhallows, Barking, Tower Street, for forty-three years.

Ask the carriage horse, galled with its detestable bearing rein, drawing the proud beauty along the Row, its mouth covered with foam and sometimes with blood; and what would it say? That

---

1 Crown-appointed senior position in the civil service dating back to 1540.

men and women were alike its merciless tyrants. And yet such ladies go to anti-vivisection meetings to protest against cruelty to animals![1]

Man has enslaved the horse, the ass, the camel, the reindeer, and other animals. They do his bidding; they bear his burdens; they lose a life of freedom in one of pain and labour. They groan and wince under the lash, the curb, and the chain. At one steeple-chase[2] at Liverpool no less than five horses had to be killed after the race. Three had their backs broken, and two had their legs snapped.

"I sometimes think," said Sir Arthur Helps, "that it was a misfortune for the world that the horse was ever subjugated. The horse is the animal that has been the worst treated by man; and his subjugation has not been altogether a gain to mankind. The oppressions he has aided in were, from the earliest ages, excessive. He it is to whom we owe much of the rapine of 'the dark ages.' And I have a great notion that he

---

1 [Smiles's note:] The following letter is from the *Times,* April 28, 1880:— "Sir—In the cause of helpless suffering I appeal to you for a little space in your columns to protest against the cruelty practised daily on carriage horses—generally those of the most valuable kind. Besides the tight bearing-rein, bits are now in use which cause positive torture. A well-appointed landau, drawn by a magnificent pair of grays, passed me yesterday in Bond Street; the bearing-rein was frightfully tightened, and the mouth of the 'off' horse was *foaming with blood.* Is it possible, I thought, that the young couple, the occupants of the carriage, can know of all this suffering? To those who, like myself, love horses and study their comfort, these sights are heartrending. We are close observers of horses, and can see at a glance if they are at ease. Alas! nothing escapes us, and the afternoon's drive is almost daily embittered by sights such as I have described—either the mouth full of blood, or the tongue swollen and nearly black from the pressure of the bit, the head braced up to an unnatural position, with other signs of distress. I would ask, is all this miserable suffering inflicted by ignorance, or heedlessness, or merciless cruelty? Let me entreat those who are the owners of horses to have mercy on them; they are among the noblest of God's creatures, and the most devoted and faithful servants of man." [Bond Street, from the eighteenth century onward, was a fashionable shopping street connecting Oxford Street and Piccadilly in the West End of London.]

2 A race over distance in which horses must jump obstacles such as hedges, ditches, and barred gates at a full gallop.

has been the main instrument of the bloodiest warfare. I wish men had their own cannon to drag up-hill. I doubt whether they would not rebel at that. And a commander obliged to be on foot throughout the campaign would very soon get tired of war."

Works Cited and Select Bibliography

Bayly, Mary. *The Life and Letters of Mrs. Sewell.* London: Nisbet, 1889.

Bending, Lucy. *The Representation of Bodily Pain in Late Nineteenth-century English Culture.* Oxford: Clarendon, 2000.

Chitty, Susan. *The Woman Who Wrote* Black Beauty: *A Life of Anna Sewell.* London: Hodder and Stoughton, 1971.

Cosslett, Tess. *Talking Animals in British Children's Fiction, 1786-1914.* Aldershot, Hampshire: Ashgate, 2006.

Davis, Philip. "Victorian Realist Prose and Sentimentality." *Rereading Victorian Fiction.* Ed. Alice Jenkins and Juliet John. Houndsmills, Basingstoke: Macmillan, 2000. 13–28.

Dingley, Robert. "A Horse of a Different Color: *Black Beauty* and the Pressures of Indebtedness." *Victorian Literature and Culture* 25.2 (1997): 241–51.

Dorré, Gina. *Victorian Fiction and the Cult of the Horse.* Aldershot, Hampshire: Ashgate, 2006.

Ferguson, Moira. *Animal Advocacy and Englishwomen, 1780–1900: Patriots, Nation, and Empire.* Ann Arbor: U of Michigan P, 1998.

Gavin, Adrienne E. *Dark Horse: A Life of Anna Sewell.* Stroud, Gloucestershire: Sutton, 2004.

Greene, Anne Norton. *Horses at Work: Harnessing Power in Industrial America.* Cambridge, MA: Harvard UP, 2008.

Guest, Kristen. "*Black Beauty,* Masculinity, and the Market for Horseflesh." *Victorians Institute Journal* 38 (2010): 9–22.

Helps, Sir Arthur. *Some Talk about Animals and Their Masters.* London: Strahan, 1873.

Kaplan, Fred. *Sacred Tears: Sentimentality in Victorian Fiction.* Princeton, NJ: Princeton UP, 1987.

Kean, Hilda. *Animal Rights: Political and Social Change in Britain since 1800.* London: Reaktion, 1998.

Lansbury, Coral. *The Old Brown Dog: Women, Workers, and Vivisection in Edwardian England.* Madison: U of Wisconsin P, 1985.

Mangum, Teresa. "Animal Angst: Victorians Memorialize Their Pets." *Victorian Animal Dreams: Representations of Animals in Victorian Literature and Culture.* Ed. Deborah

Dennenholtz Morse and Martin A. Danahay. Aldershot, Hampshire: Ashgate, 2007. 15–34.

Mason, Jennifer. *Civilized Creatures: Urban Animals, Sentimental Culture and American Literature 1850–1900*. Baltimore: Johns Hopkins UP, 2005.

McShane, Clay, and Joel A. Tarr. *The Horse in the City: Living Machines in the Nineteenth Century*. Baltimore: Johns Hopkins UP, 2007.

Miele, Kathryn. "Horse-Sense: Understanding the Working Horse in Victorian London." *Victorian Literature and Culture* 37.1 (2009): 129–40.

Morse, Deborah Denenholtz. "'The Mark of the Beast': Animals as Sites of Imperial Encounter from *Wuthering Heights* to *Green Mansions*." *Victorian Animal Dreams: Representations of Animals in Victorian Literature and Culture*. Ed. Deborah Dennenholtz Morse and Martin A. Danahay. Aldershot, Hampshire: Ashgate, 2007. 181–200.

Oswald, Lori Jo. "Heroes and Victims: The Stereotyping of Animal Characters in Children's Realistic Animal Fiction." *Children's Literature in Education* 26.2 (1995): 135–49.

Padel, Ruth. "Saddled with Ginger: Women, Men, and Horses." *Encounter* 55.5 (1980): 47–54.

Ritvo, Harriet. *The Animal Estate: The English and Other Creatures in the Victorian Age*. Cambridge, MA: Harvard UP, 1987.

Stibbs, Andrew. "*Black Beauty*: Tales My Mother Told Me." *Children's Literature in Education* 22.3 (1976): 128–34.

Stoneley, Peter. "Sentimental Emasculations: *Uncle Tom's Cabin* and *Black Beauty*." *Nineteenth-Century Literature* 54.1 (1999): 53–72.

Velten, Hannah. *Beastly London: A History of Animals in the City*. London: Reaktion, 2013.

From the Publisher

A name never says it all, but the word "Broadview" expresses a good deal of the philosophy behind our company. We are open to a broad range of academic approaches and political viewpoints. We pay attention to the broad impact book publishing and book printing has in the wider world; for some years now we have used 100% recycled paper for most titles. Our publishing program is internationally oriented and broad-ranging. Our individual titles often appeal to a broad reader-ship too; many are of interest as much to general readers as to academics and students.

Founded in 1985, Broadview remains a fully independent company owned by its shareholders—not an imprint or subsidiary of a larger multinational.

For the most accurate information on our books (including information on pricing, editions, and formats) please visit our website at www.broadviewpress.com. Our print books and ebooks are also available for sale on our site.

broadview press
www.broadviewpress.com